JOURNEY
TO THE
Highlands

ROBBIE & CARALYN

KEIRA MONTCLAIR

Cover Design and Interior format by The Killion Group
http://thekilliongroupinc.com

OTHER NOVELS BY KEIRA MONTCLAIR

THE BAND OF COUSINS
HIGHLAND VENGEANCE
HIGHLAND ABDUCTION
HIGHLAND RETRIBUTION
HIGHLAND LIES

THE CLAN GRANT SERIES
#1- RESCUED BY A HIGHLANDER-Alex and Maddie
#2- HEALING A HIGHLANDER'S HEART-
Brenna and Quade
#3- LOVE LETTERS FROM LARGS-Brodie and Celestina
#4-JOURNEY TO THE HIGHLANDS-Robbie and Caralyn
#5-HIGHLAND SPARKS-Logan and Gwyneth
#6-MY DESPERATE HIGHLANDER-Micheil and Diana
#7-THE BRIGHTEST STAR IN THE HIGHLANDS-
Jennie and Aedan
#8- HIGHLAND HARMONY-Avelina and Drew

THE HIGHLAND CLAN
LOKI-Book One
TORRIAN-Book Two
LILY-Book Three
JAKE-Book Four
ASHLYN-Book Five
MOLLY-Book Six

JAMIE AND GRACIE- Book Seven
SORCHA-Book Eight
KYLA-Book Nine
BETHIA-Book Ten
LOKI'S CHRISTMAS STORY-Book Eleven

THE SOULMATE CHRONICLES
#1 TRUSTING A HIGHLANDER

**THE SUMMERHILL SERIES-
CONTEMPORARY ROMANCE**
#1-ONE SUMMERHILL DAY
#2-A FRESH START FOR TWO
#3-THREE REASONS TO LOVE

STAND-ALONE NOVEL
FALLING FOR THE CHIEFTAIN-3rd in Enchanted Falls

CHAPTER ONE

1263, Autumn
Ayrshire, Scotland

Caralyn of the Crauford House stilled, shushing her lass of eight summers to silence with a swish of her hand. Laughter echoed across the land—not the happy sound so loved by her clan, but the ribald guffaws of invaders hell-bent on doing their worst. That sound inched up the back of her neck, raising the hairs there.

Norsemen. Rumors of the pillaging already done by the men on those Norse galley ships had spread through the small coastal villages of Scotland like wildfire, but she had hoped they would somehow miss her small fishing village, tucked away at the edge of her clan. Caralyn peeked out through the fur coverings across her window and saw her worst nightmare—men with torches running up the paths between cottages, hollering in a foreign tongue.

Caralyn whirled to face her daughter and whispered, "Ashlyn, get your sister."

They tore through the two room cottage for the wee lassie, her beloved wean. "Gracie? Gracie, where are you?" As they stepped into the bed chamber, her blonde haired, blue-eyed daughter waddled toward her, her arms raised in the usual manner to entice her mama to lift her up. At just over two summers, she spoke little, but understood everything.

Caralyn picked Gracie up and moved toward the back door. "Get the sack, Ashlyn."

They had been warned the Norse could come. King Haakon

of Norway, furious at the actions of the Scottish King Alexander III, had sailed up the Firth of Clyde. Rumor had said the enemies were headed to the royal burgh at Ayr, but given the number of longboats and galleys anchored off Arran, they could stop anywhere along the way. Men at war could be ruthless; that much she knew, especially after the tales she had heard about their plundering in other seaside villages. The raven banners of Haakon's fleet had already been seen off Kintyre, where his men had ravaged the mainland.

Why had Malcolm taken her guards with him the other day? Now they were completely without protection. Caralyn had done what she could to prepare, forcing her daughters to practice hiding over and over. Simply put, the Norsemen would have to kill her first before they touched her lassies.

Ashlyn appeared around the corner, tying the small sack to her waist. "Mama, come with us?"

Caralyn put her fingers to her daughter's lips. "Shush, love. I will follow as soon as I can. Now do as we practiced. Take your sister and run until you find the rocks, then hide. Do not come out for any reason. I will find you."

The look of terror in her daughter's eyes wrenched her gut. Someday, she vowed she would eliminate the fear in Ashlyn's eyes, but today, she had no choice but to send them ahead without her. She knew what she had to do to protect her bairns. If she were to go with the girls, the Norseman would follow them. Caralyn would draw the attackers away and distract them; she knew what they wanted.

Caralyn knelt and kissed both girls. "Promise mama. Do you hear me, Ashlyn? Mama could not bear to have anything happen to her sweet lassies." She pushed them out the back door and followed behind them. "Go."

As soon as she stepped outdoors, her ears rang from a sharp war whoop. She turned to see a large man with a flaming torch race for her cottage. Only a few had made it this far, but her home could be brought down with a single torch. He touched the edge to the corner of the roof and the thatch roared to life, burning and smoking in a fury.

The man's gaze caught hers and he grinned before he yelled in exultation, throwing his torch in the dirt and beating his chest as if she were a glorious prize. Aye, she knew what he wanted. She yelled, "Run, Ashlyn. Run!"

Caralyn took off in the opposite direction, hoping she'd caught his attention enough for him to leave the girls and follow her. Out of the corner of her eye, she noticed Ashlyn running toward the beach as they had planned. Caralyn fingered her dagger in the folds of the pocket she had sewn into her skirts. A last resort. *Lord, help me be strong, I will fight. I will fight for my girls. Please help me.*

Her boots carried her down the path toward the center of the village where the fishermen kept their boats. Was anyone around to help? She glanced over her shoulder and noticed the Norseman had fallen for her plan and chased after her, his long strides bringing him closer every instant. Peeking to her right, she thanked God that her girls could no longer be seen and she prayed they were safe. Ashlyn was a strong lass, as she had been forced to be. The Lord would keep them in his hands.

A large paw grabbed her hair and wrenched her backward. She landed with a grunt and her assailant chuckled. The raw odor of filthy flesh assaulted her nostrils as she glanced up to see the smile on his dirt-encrusted face. She recognized that look. It was an expression of sheer, perverse desire; this man hadn't been with a woman for so long that sexual need fueled his every move. He craved her body for what it was, a means to an end, with flagrant disregard for her soul and her emotions. Licking the side of her face, he palmed her breast through her wool gown. He was no different than any other man. He wouldn't stop until he raped her.

So be it. He could do as he wished with her as long as he stayed away from her lassies. She would do anything to guarantee their safety. Rape her, beat her, she could handle anything as long as he didn't touch her daughters.

One meaty hand clutched a death grip on her arm, and he pulled her up and turned to the side of the path as if looking for a spot to bed her. But he stilled, listening to his surroundings, glancing all around. She guessed he looked for his comrades, but none were visible.

As if having made a decision, he yanked her arm and tugged her behind him toward the coastline. She struggled to keep up as he took an alternate route through a thick group of trees. What in hell was he planning? Caralyn had been able to calm herself when she'd expected to be thrown into the bushes and forced to submit to him. She dreaded his touch, but she understood such a fate. She could handle it. Now she swallowed in an attempt to slow her pounding heart because she had no idea where they were going. The unknown frightened her and she knew not what he was about. His demeanor had transformed, subtly, but enough for her to know his goal had changed. As soon as they broke through the trees onto the vast shoreline, he yelled down the beach to his friends. Caralyn stumbled along beside him, but froze when her gaze settled on their destination, realization smacking her hard between the eyes.

A longboat. He was dragging her to his ship. He wanted to take her on his galley to service all his comrades, too. Not another female was in sight, though she saw one unmoving clump of wool not far away. A shock of hair stuck out from the pile. Who was it, someone she knew? Was she already dead? *Calm yourself, Caralyn, you can beat them, but only if you are in control.* She forced several deep breaths into her lungs, willing herself to relax.

But she couldn't. A longboat, he was taking her to the longboat, and he would tear her away from her girls. And what would become of her once she stepped onto that ship? They would use her as they saw fit, then toss her overboard. She could swim, but not from the center of the firth.

Never. Never would he get her onto that ship. She had to think and act quickly. She thought of her girls, of Gracie's big blue eyes staring at her. Who would care for them if something happened to her? They were her life, quite simply. The only thing she valued in this entire world sat hidden between rocks down the beach. Even though she hadn't been able to provide the best of lives for them, she was determined to change that if she survived this ordeal.

Unleashing the pent up anger for all the injustices she had been dealt, she corralled that fury, directing it toward this one man in front of her. The foreigners could beat her, have their way with her, but she was not leaving her daughters, not now, not ever. They were still quite a distance from the ship, enough for her to fight and get away. And fight she would.

Caralyn screamed and grabbed her dagger from her hidden pocket, sinking it into the brute's thigh. He bellowed and let go of her arm for an instant, just enough time for her to dart away. She scurried back toward the path, but didn't make it far before he grabbed her plaited hair, swung her around, and slapped her.

Cheers went up from the galley ship, but no one came to the man's aid, thankfully. This would be a performance for his shipmates to watch. The lass against the Norseman, and she would fight with everything she had.

"You vile brute, leave me be!" She screamed and clawed, spit and bit. He hit her in the belly, but the pain didn't sway her. When he looked away from her for a moment to remove the dagger from his thigh, she kicked him in the groin and he crumpled to the ground, losing the knife in the sand. Hoots from the galleys continued. Pivoting, she tried to run, but he grabbed her ankle and she toppled face down into the gravel. He pulled her back slowly toward him, running his hand over her bare leg under her skirts. She flipped onto her back and kicked him in the jaw with her other foot.

He cursed and released her.

Caralyn searched for her dagger in the sand, but didn't see it. The lout managed to get to his feet and swayed over her. Pushing herself upright, she grabbed the biggest rock she could find and swung it straight at his head. When she connected with his temple and a resounding thud rang out in the air, she hoped he would fall, but instead he stared at her, a low growl tearing through his throat and settling into a furious expression. He picked her up by both arms and tossed her in the air. Unable to catch her fall, she hit the ground at an odd angle, twisting her ankle under her. She screamed in pain as she landed in the dirt. He jumped on top of her, pulled his fist back, set to demolish her face, and the last thing she recalled before darkness enveloped her was Gracie's sad eyes.

CHAPTER TWO

Captain Robbie Grant led his group of warriors down the coastal path, through small villages and cottages. Naught. Alexander of Dundonald, King Alexander III's steward, had sent them south of Ayr in case King Haakon of Norway's galleys were coming ashore to pillage and steal. Desperate to establish his sovereignty over the Western Isles, the Norwegian ruler had sent multiple ships and many men to Scotland. Now they were anchored off Arran, waiting for instructions. It would be easy for him to send a few over to the coastal villages to wreak havoc and commandeer for food and supplies.

He split his men and sent half down a different path while he headed straight for one of the fishing villages speckled along the beautiful coastal waters. Before he saw anything, his nose warned him of impending trouble—smoke, billowing toward them from the south. Spurring his horse, he led his men in a charge, hoping to discover the source of the pungent odor. As they neared the village, they passed a few huts already in flames.

He yelled to his best friend, Tomas. "I don't like the looks of this."

"Aye, could be bad." Tomas nodded, his gaze raking the area for foreigners.

Robbie pointed toward the flaming huts and nodded to a group of warriors. "Check for survivors. We'll continue on." Driven by an unknown force, he headed to the coastline. He yelled to Tomas as his friend rode back to join him. "Do you see any Norse yet?"

Tomas, who had led some of Robbie's men on a wide route

of the small village and through the forests, shook his head.

That was when Robbie heard it—the keening sound of a lass in pain.

He glanced at Tomas. "Saints above, they're attacking ahead of us."

Bringing his horse to a full gallop, he followed the lass's screeches to the beach. In a moment, he assessed the situation. One galley ship full of invaders sat on the distant edge of the shoreline, yelling and hooting about something on the beach. A few seconds later, he understood. A lone Norseman was battering a Scottish woman nearby to the cheers of his comrades. Robbie sent several warriors down the beach toward the boat with orders to use their bows to take the invaders out.

The dark-haired lass on the beach fought the lout with all she had, pummeling and kicking him in every place she could reach. Robbie unsheathed his sword and headed straight at the fool, the girl's screams fueling his fury. Not noticing Robbie, the brute pulled his fist back and punched her square in the face, knocking her out before turning to his companions with his fist in the air and shouting his satisfaction at his achievement.

Robbie headed straight toward the fool, hoping to take advantage of his momentary distraction. Even though his friends yelled at the lone man to try to warn him, he ignored them, too busy celebrating his victory over the wee lass. When the lout turned back around, he was just in time to watch Robbie's sword skewer him straight through his belly, the shock in his face visible before he crumpled to the ground.

The rest of the surviving Norsemen scrambled onto the galley as soon as they saw the Scottish warriors headed their way along with multiple arrows in flight. They shoved off, not willing to risk an attempt to retrieve their comrade's dead body from the beach. Robbie jumped off his horse and knelt down next to the lass, praying he wasn't too late. The woman's eyes were closed, but her comeliness did not escape him. She had dark brown hair, blowing in the wind around her like billowing silk. Only a few strands were still held back—a testament to how hard she had fought. Her face had a haunting beauty beneath the bruising and the pale coloring. He settled both hands on the stone and sand next to her, then bent down to see if he could hear her breathing. A slight sigh escaped her lips and he sat back on his haunches, grateful she still lived.

His warriors, who had sent the Norse rowing furiously from shore, returned to assist him. He waved his men on, giving instructions to check down the shoreline for more galleys while he tended the wounded woman.

How he wished his sister Brenna, the healer, was at his side. She would know exactly how to help the woman. He surveyed the girl as she lay on the beach, wondering if she had any broken bones. Her left ankle was swollen, but it didn't appear broken. Multiple open wounds were spread across her skin as if she had been towed across the stone. Grit and dirt sullied most of them. The lass had clearly been dragged from one of the nearby cottages, and the brute who'd taken her had been intent on hauling her onto the retreating galley.

The saints above must have been watching over the young lady, and it was a good thing Robbie and his men had arrived when they did. He cringed at the thought of the treatment she would have received at the hands of a galley full of lonely, battle-crazed shipmates. Had she not screamed and fought with such bravery and persistence, she'd be on that ship.

Tomas came by to report to him. "We have found no more Norseman ashore, Grant," he said from atop his horse. "There are no galleys south, and no evidence of any more pillaging. The only cottages in flames are those near here and they are contained. Too far gone to stop. Many of the other cottages are empty."

"Get me a skein of water, Tomas. I want to see what I can do for the lass before the others find their way back to report to me."

"She's still alive?" Tomas asked.

"Aye, she lives, but I don't know for how long."

"He did a fine job battering the beauty, aye?" Tomas grabbed the skein from his horse before joining Robbie on the seashore.

"Aye, she will be one sore lass when she awakens." He couldn't help but sigh. "*If* she awakens."

Tomas handed his skein of water to Robbie. "She isn't alert

enough to drink."

"Och, I know. Can you not see all the crystals of gravel and pebbles in her torn skin? My sister is mad about cleaning wounds." Robbie said. "Hold her leg up for me so I can rinse the grit off as much as possible. Better to do it now while she is unconscious."

Tomas did as he was ordered and then let a slow whistle out as soon as he spied the long legs beneath her skirts. "A magnificent one, aye? 'Tis sad to see her so mistreated."

"Keep your eyes off her legs, Tomas," Robbie barked.

"Och, so you are taken with her, old friend? Haven't seen that in a while." Tomas's grin stretched across his face.

"How in hellfire can I be taken with one I haven't spoken to? You are a loggerheaded dimwit sometimes." Robbie tore a piece of cloth from her skirt to scrub the dirt away as much as possible.

"'Twould be good for you to find a lass to relieve your stress. You spend too much time forcing yourself to work harder."

"Aye, but 'tis the only time I have been offered the chance to prove myself. You know how often I have been left at the keep to protect the clan while my brothers are out battling." Robbie switched to clean her other leg.

"'Tis no easy job protecting a clan the size of the Grants."

"Och, aye, but there has never been a need to use my battle skills since we have never been attacked."

"And 'tis a good thing, too." Tomas smiled at his friend.

"Aye, but this is my chance to prove my mettle. And I won't allow a lass to distract me from my purpose. I fight for the Scots and I lead the Grant warriors. I can't lose my focus."

"We shall see, my friend. What will you do with her?" Tomas quirked his brow at him.

"Send a couple of men to the few occupied cottages and see if she has family nearby. If not, we head back to the camp at the royal burgh. She'll travel with me."

Tomas's eyes widened. "Travel with you?"

"I can't leave her here, now, can I? Where in hell did you leave your brain, Tomas?" Robbie shook his head in frustration.

Tomas chuckled, his eyes twinkling. "Och, can't wait to witness this. 'Twill be entertaining, for sure. I hope to be by your side when you ride up to the Dundonald with a lass across your lap."

CHAPTER THREE

When Caralyn opened her eyes, she stared straight up at a coarse tent over her head. The sun was just coming up, but she had no idea where she was or whose tent she was in. Her face ached something fierce, and she gingerly ran her fingers across her features, detecting crusted blood, swelling around her eye and cheekbone, and a cut lip. What had happened? Her breath hitched at the shooting pain whenever she touched the swollen areas. Oh, dear God, what had happened and where were her bairns?

She moved her legs, but groaned as pain shot from her ankle up to her hip. Her eyes fluttered shut, longing for a return to the blissful darkness, but something prompted her to stay alert. Turning on her side, she moaned at the soft fur beneath her. She was alone in the tent, which was larger than any she had ever seen. Tears threatened to spill down her cheeks, but she controlled them, pulling strength from her gut. Her skin was flayed in multiple places, and memories surfaced of the churlish Norseman who had dragged her toward the seashore.

She managed to get herself to a sitting position and muttered, "Nay! My lassies…" She had sent them to their hiding spot in the rocks. They must still be there. She pushed against the ground and tried to raise herself to a standing position in the tent, clutching a plaid that had been her blanket to cover her, but not caring what she had on underneath or who saw her bare skin. Her daughters. She had to find them. A keening whimper reached her ears and she realized it came from her own lips. She finally stood and made her way to the flap in the tent, limping in pain, but vowing not to stop for anyone or anything. Stepping outside on one foot, she accidentally dropped the plaid to the ground and gripped her shift as she peered at her surroundings, only to find a sea of male faces staring back at her. Confusion clouded her mind. Where was she? Who were these men?

The reception from this group of men confused her. They didn't make any insulting remarks about her lack of clothing and none of them tried to grab at her; they just stared at her in concern. She pushed through the crowd, ignoring the pain in her ankle as she moved forward, trying to find someone, anyone, who could help her find her lassies.

"Please, someone help me," she shouted to the sky, not caring who responded to her urgent plea.

"Lass, doesn't look like you should be up and about."

"The Captain won't be happy to see you out of his tent."

At first, she halted as their comments registered in her mind. She must be a sore sight to receive such a response. But there was naught they could say that would sway her from her purpose. Continuing, she stared at the men as she passed, hoping for someone to step forward and help her.

"My daughters? Does anyone know where my daughters are?"

Naught. The men stared at each other in confusion. She had to stay focused.

A whistle stopped all the men in their tracks and eerie silence descended on the group of warriors dressed in red plaid. Caralyn didn't stop; she couldn't stop. She had only one goal, to find her bairns. A large man wrapped in the same red plaid surged through the group, bellowing at everyone to stand back. "Leave her be, I said. Finish your duties."

The apparent leader of the warriors stood in front of her with his hands on his hips, his gaze sending the men scurrying in various directions. When his eyes settled on her, her breath hitched in response to his good looks. It had been a long time since she had seen a man this handsome. He didn't speak, but reached his arm out in an attempt to usher her back into the tent.

Caralyn would not have it.

"Nay, do not push me inside. I need to leave." She shoved

against his rock hard chest and swatted his hands, grappling with anything she perceived as a possible threat. Glancing around at the strange surroundings, she paused to ask, "Where exactly am I?"

"Lass, you are in the Clan Grant warriors' camp. My name is Captain Robbie Grant and I am in charge of these men. We are awaiting orders from our king about the war with Norway."

"Where are my lassies? Take me to them. You have them, don't you? You found them?" She raked her hand through her tangled locks, frantic to make sense of everything, especially when he shook his head in response. *Nay, nay, nay.* "Why did you bring me here? I need to find my daughters. Tell me you didn't leave them alone in the cold night?"

"What daughters? I found you on the beach south of Ayr. You were attacked by a lone Norseman. He was dragging you to his galley when I saw him punch you in the face. He knocked you senseless, lass." The pity in his eyes told her how bad the situation had been.

Panic rushed through Caralyn's body as she locked eyes with him. Sweat dripped from her palms so she fisted her hands in her shift. She would do anything to make the reality of the situation change, but there was no avoiding the fact that her girls were missing.

Captain Grant held his hand out toward the tent. "Please, I will explain everything that I know."

Caralyn had no choice. She moved toward the tent and allowed him to hold the flap back for her. Her shoulders slumped as the truth came down hard on her. She was entirely dependent on this one man right now.

Reining in her anxiety, she reached for the strength she needed to listen and plan.

"There were no young ones around you," Captain Grant said once the tent was closed behind them. "You didn't leave them behind in the cottage, did you?" His gray eyes bore through her, giving her something unexpected—a strange sense of support.

She shook her head. "Nay, I sent them to their hiding spot."

"Where? I saw no one."

"There is a group of craggy boulders not far from shore. I

trained them to hide there in case of an attack so they couldn't be seen by anyone." Tears formed on her lashes. "I must go. They must still be there."

"What's your name?" He reached down to pick up a plaid— probably the one she'd dropped on her way out of the tent— and tossed it over her shoulders. She cringed in response. The warrior held his hands up. "Lass, you have my word as a Grant Highlander, I won't hurt you."

"What makes you any different? All men hurt me." She chewed on her thumbnail, eyeing him carefully.

"Nay, I won't. As I told you, I am a Grant, and my sire taught me different. I'll ne'er raise a hand to a woman. You can trust me. Now, tell me your name and I'll do what I can to help you."

She flicked her gaze to the big Highlander before returning her attention to her thumbnail. Was it true? Could she trust him? He had kind eyes, gray flecked with silver. It couldn't hurt to give him her name, she decided. "Caralyn. Caralyn of the Craufords."

"And you have two daughters?"

"Aye." She stepped on her left ankle and flinched when she remembered she couldn't put all her weight on it, but he caught her before she tumbled. Captain Robbie Grant was massive and broad-shouldered, with bronzed skin from the sun and light brown hair. His upper arms looked like tree trunks from the rippling muscles visible through his tunic. But for some strange reason, she trusted him, and not because of his appearance. No, there was something different about his camp, his warriors. They didn't seem to be the typical roughshod warriors. They had almost treated her with respect. Was that it?

He held his arm out to help her balance. "What do they go by?"

"Gracie is just over two summers and Ashlyn is eight." Her decision made, her voice dropped to a whisper. "Will you help me? Please? I have to find my bairns."

CHAPTER FOUR

Riding his horse down to South Ayr for a second time, Robbie thought he would lose his mind for sure. He could not believe how his day had gone. After striding toward his tent at dawn to find the gorgeous lass, dressed in naught but a shift, standing amongst his warriors, what else could he do but go daft? Fortunately, his men understood he wouldn't tolerate any misuse of a woman, but still, they were only human and Caralyn Crauford, if that was her real name, had the most glorious breasts he had ever seen. And it was undeniable that the sight of her had commanded his attention, too. The fact that she was so worried about her daughters made him feel guilty for appreciating her body, but saints above, the lass had the most beautiful form he had ever seen. And those nipples? They had to be the deepest shade of peach, and he yearned to see them bared. Glory, what he wouldn't give to suckle her until she cried out his name.

Fortunately, his sense of duty overtook his loins, and he had brought her into his tent to find out what he could do for her. The only thing she had told him was her name and that she had two missing daughters. Since he had a younger sister, Jennie, as well as three nephews and three nieces, he had made the only decision possible. There were two young lassies on their own in South Ayr, so he was heading back to the area where he'd first found her. His commander, Alexander of Dundonald, would not be pleased with the delay, but knowing first-hand what the Norse were capable of, he could do naught but follow his gut. If the Norsemen had managed to find her wee lassies, all he could do was shake his head at the thought of what might have befallen them.

Being in charge of the largest group of Highland warriors, at last count around three hundred and fifty, was a major undertaking. Widespread war was imminent, Robbie could feel it, which was also the reason his commanding officer would be unhappy with his decision. He had left another warrior in charge before heading out with Tomas to try and find the girls. They had to act fast in case the Grant warriors were called into battle. Robbie was determined to be there when he was needed. He would make his clan proud, even if he lost his life in the endeavor.

Caralyn had begged to come along, but they'd convinced her that her injury would only slow them down.

Robbie came down the path and slowed to a canter, shouting at Tomas. "Check the cottages and make sure there is no evidence of any bodies."

Glancing at the burned cottages, he hoped the wee lassies had known enough to stay away from the embers. When he found the area of large rocks near the beach, he stopped. This had to be the place Caralyn had described. "Gracie? Ashlyn?"

Silence.

Tomas rejoined him. "No bodies that I could find. Looks as though everyone got out in time in the two cottages I checked."

He and Tomas dismounted before wandering through the area, and searched in between the rocks, but there was no sign of the little girls. Hellfire, he had to find them. "Head down the beach, Tomas. I'll go this way. The thought of two lassies out here alone churns my belly. Where could they be?"

Robbie pictured what Caralyn Crauford's face would look like if he was forced to inform her that he had been unable to locate her daughters. He couldn't allow that to happen. He suddenly understood why his brother Alex had been so driven to help his now-wife Maddie when they first met. His devotion to her and his determination to save her from abuse had made him a new man.

Just as Robbie was about to head in a different direction, he heard a sound to his left in a group of trees. Jerking his head in that direction, he froze. A wee lass about the age of his niece, Lily, stood just behind the front row of trees. She made no sound, just peered at him, curiosity apparently winning over the need to hide.

"Gracie?" Robbie took a few more steps toward the lass, but then he stopped in his tracks, not wanting to scare her away.

"Gracie," he squatted down not far from the bairn. "Your mama is with me at my camp. She sent me to rescue you and bring you and your sister back to her. Where is Ashlyn?" No answer. She stared at him with the biggest pair of blue eyes he had ever seen. She did not smile or cry, just stared. He stood and moved a few steps closer.

A voice broke through the trees. "Gracie doesn't like men."

"Ashlyn? My name is Captain Robbie Grant. I have come to help you. Your mama sent me. Are you both unhurt?"

Ashlyn popped out from behind a large tree trunk. "You aren't the man who dragged her to the beach." She pointed to Tomas coming toward them. "Who is that?"

"Nay, I'm not the one who hurt your mama. I would never hurt a woman or a child. You can trust me, lass. And you can trust my friend."

Her unwavering gaze caught his. "You're the man who took her away on your horse. But you killed the bad man first. You ran him through with your sword after he punched our mama in the face."

She stood straight and proud, just as her mother did. Unfortunately, that told him quite a bit about her past. They hadn't lived an easy life. This lass of eight summers had protected her sister and kept them both alive overnight, a stark tribute to her character.

"Aye, lass, 'twas me. I'm sorry you had to see that." Robbie nodded to Tomas, who had made a slow approach and was now standing next to him. "This is my friend, Tomas."

She moved to her sister's side and grasped the wee lass's hand. "I didn't let Gracie watch, just me. I had to see where Mama was. But you took her and I didn't know where she had gone. I searched for her last night. Is Mama safe?"

"Aye, your mama hurt her leg, and she has some bruises, but she'll be fine in a few days. She is verra worried about you. You and Gracie are good?"

"We aren't hurt, just hungry. We ran out of oatcakes. Gracie is verra hungry."

Robbie held his hand out to the young girl. "Come with me. I have a couple of oatcakes in the satchel on my horse."

"Please give them to Gracie. She needs to eat more than I do." Ashlyn leaned down to her sister and whispered in her ear. "Come, Gracie. This man has an oatcake for you."

Gracie peered up at her sister and nodded. Robbie waited, expecting to see a smile cross the wean's face at the mention of food, but her expression never changed. Tomas followed them over to the horses.

Guessing at his thoughts, Ashlyn said, "She never smiles, Captain Grant, nor does she talk."

"She doesn't need to talk or smile, as long as she eats." He led the two waifs over to his horse and dug in his bag until he produced two oatcakes. "Do you have anything you wish to bring with you, lass?"

"Aye, my sack is behind the tree. Gracie, stay with Captain Grant for a moment while I get our things." She let go of Gracie's hand and ran back into the trees.

Robbie held the oatcake out for Gracie. She grabbed it from his hand and sat on the ground. She devoured the food, but never took her wide eyes off him. When Ashlyn returned, he offered her an oatcake, too, but she handed it over to Gracie, who finished it in seconds. He handed Ashlyn his skein of water.

"Ashlyn, you need to keep your strength up. You must eat as well. Tomas, do you have another oatcake with you?"

"Gracie needs it more. I am fine." She leaned over her sister and brushed the crumbs from her mouth and skirts before helping Gracie drink from the skein. "Thank you for saving our mama." She handed the water back to Robbie.

Tomas handed an oatcake to Ashlyn. "Here, lass, this is for you."

Ashlyn paused for a moment before she took it, stuffing it into the folds of her skirt. "My thanks. I will eat it later. Can we go see her now?"

"Aye, you may ride with Tomas and Gracie can ride with me. Tomas will tie your things to his saddle." He handed the sack to his friend.

"But Gracie won't go with you. It's as I said, she doesn't like men."

"Even her da?"

"She doesn't know her da, and my da died several years ago."

Gracie eyed both men warily. She stood up and walked over to her sister, clasping Ashlyn's hand. "She will probably have to ride with me."

Robbie wasn't about to argue. "Fine. I'll hand the girls up to you after you mount, Tomas." Once Tomas was in his saddle, Robbie settled Ashlyn in front of him. When Robbie reached for Gracie, she held her arms up to him, but when he lifted her toward Tomas, she shook her head vehemently.

Ashlyn whispered, "I told you there would be trouble with her. Gracie has only known mean men."

Robbie peered into the wee one's eyes. He didn't relish the idea of finding out about the mean men in her life or why she never smiled. After a short pause, Gracie's hand popped up and pointed directly at Robbie's horse. Ashlyn sucked in a breath in apparent surprise.

Robbie didn't wait to see if the girl would change her mind. He didn't have time. He mounted with the lass under his arm, then settled her in front of him. Rather than complaining or crying, she clung to his forearm.

"Captain Grant, you must be special." Ashlyn smiled from Tomas's horse.

Robbie started his horse at a slow trot, but Gracie never flinched, just continued to hang on tight to his arm. She was a sweet wee thing, but sad she never smiled. When he increased to a gallop, Tomas following behind him, he checked on the lass again, but she seemed fine. Less than half a mile later, Gracie leaned back and fell asleep in his lap, her thumb propped in her mouth.

CHAPTER FIVE

Caralyn paced back and forth not far from the path, making her way over every once in a while to see who was headed toward camp. She had tried to convince Captain Grant to take her with him, but to no avail.

Her concern was that he didn't understand her lassies. Given her daughters' experience with men, there was a chance they'd refuse to come back with the Highlanders, even if they managed to locate them. Thanks to Malcolm and his nasty friends, Gracie distrusted all men. When she mentioned this to Captain Grant, he had laughed and said, "How old is she? I think we can find a way to bring her back."

So now she paced with worry. Even though her ankle pained her, she couldn't stop her frenzied gait. One of the warriors had fashioned a large branch to help bear her weight, but she was too frantic with apprehension to slow down enough to use it. What would she do if he came back without her girls, what would she do next? What could she do?

This was all her fault. She did her best to be a good mother. Unfortunately, in order to take care of her daughters, she had been forced to make some difficult decisions. She had done some things she wasn't exactly proud of, but her girls were doing well. They always had food in their bellies, and she had been able to keep up the small cottage they lived in until the Norse came along.

Her parents had died long ago, and her husband, Ashlyn's sire, had been dead for several years, too. She had been on her own for a while. Life hadn't been easy, but she did what she had to in order to survive. A cloud of dust stirred in the distance. Not moving from her spot by the path, she kept her eyes fixed on the movement until the horses came into her line of sight. As soon as she could tell Robbie Grant was in the lead, she held her breath, squinting in the sun to see if one or both of her girls was with him.

When she finally determined Gracie was in front of him, she jumped up and down, ignoring the pain in her ankle. Tomas was riding hard behind him, so Ashlyn had to be on the other horse. She hobbled down the lane, unable to contain her excitement. Tears of relief spilled down her cheeks as Robbie stopped his horse and handed Gracie down to her.

Caralyn sobbed. "Gracie, oh my wee Gracie." She held her daughter to her chest, then tilted her head back so the wee one's face was in front of her. "You are unhurt, my sweet?"

Gracie nodded, patted her mother's cheek, and returned her thumb to her mouth. Ashlyn jumped down from Tomas's horse and ran over to her mother. Caralyn clung to her eldest. "Lass, I am so proud of you. Thank you for taking care of your sister."

After kissing her lasses several times, she made her way to Robbie Grant, who had tied up his horse and was already striding back to his officer's tent. She grabbed his plaid from behind. "Captain Grant, please."

Robbie stopped and spun around. "Caralyn, my apologies, I didn't wish to interfere with your homecoming. I need to check on my men, then I'll help you decide what your next step is from here."

"Thank you, Captain Grant. From the bottom of my heart, I thank you for saving my bairns."

Robbie smiled. "You raised them well, Caralyn. They managed to survive out there on their own." Ashlyn had followed her, and he stopped speaking for long enough to pat the girl's shoulder. "Your daughter did a fine job."

Caralyn stared into Robbie's gray eyes, struck again by his good looks. His brown hair was almost blonde, and he had a warmth in his eyes she was not used to seeing in men. His raw appeal caught her off-guard this time. Aye, there was something very different about Robbie Grant, though he would want nothing to do with her once he found out what she was.

**

Dundonald was displeased with Robbie's plan, but ultimately he agreed to it.

The Highland warriors' camp was presently northeast of Kilmarnock, and after discussing the matter with Caralyn, Robbie decided the best and safest place for her and the lassies was Glasgow. Dundonald had suggested a priory near the city. A known healer there could help Caralyn with her wounds.

Dundonald didn't want to send Robbie with the warriors escorting the lass and her bairns. The high steward wanted him to be available to lead his men the instant fighting began. They received word there had been little movement by the Norsemen, however, so Dundonald allowed him to go. Robbie could ensure their safe travel to Glasgow, spend one night there, then return to camp within a day.

Robbie had to admit to himself that he wasn't just leading the expedition because he could do it best. Having missed out on many of his brothers' escapades, he now understood why saving someone held such meaning. He felt an unexpected and powerful need to protect Caralyn, Gracie, and Ashlyn. The feeling consumed him.

Ashlyn rode in front of Caralyn, and he noticed she kept an eye on everything Robbie did. Gracie had insisted in riding with him again, which had shocked Caralyn. The wee lass was asleep again on his lap, not the least bit concerned about where they were headed. After a time, Caralyn rode up next to him to check on her daughter, while Ashlyn made a point to peer at Gracie, too.

"Captain Grant," she said. "If Gracie bothers you, please say so, and I will move her onto my horse."

Robbie shook his head. How could such a wee thing bother him? "Och, she is no trouble, lass." He suspected he knew Caralyn's true motivation for making the offer. "You can trust me. I would hope you would know that by now. I have several nieces and nephews."

She stared straight ahead, as regal as any queen. Her brown hair was neatly plaited, revealing a face exquisite enough to transfix a man, but her green eyes were keen and watchful for her girls. She didn't allow the bruises to affect her countenance, though many of them must still pain her. She reminded him of a wild cat when it came to her daughters. How had she survived these hard times without anyone to protect her?

She heaved a sigh. "Aye, you have done much for me and my daughters. I just have trouble trusting men sometimes."

"Understood, especially after your most recent experience, but I suspect 'tis more than that. Anything you would like to share?" he asked, though he didn't expect an answer.

"Nay, there is naught to tell." Strands of hair escaped her plait and danced around her face. Saints above, she was a beauty. She seemed oblivious to her looks, or perhaps she just didn't care. She wasn't the type to search out a man's attention.

"You have no family in the area? What happened to your parents?"

"They died a long time ago. I do really miss them, especially my mama. It saddens me that my girls have never known their grandparents. How my mama would have cherished her granddaughters. She was the sweetest woman."

"Gracie's sire? Is he the reason she fears men?" He watched her reaction to his question, and it was quick, too quick.

"What would you know about Gracie's father?" The fury in her eyes let him know the lass had a temper. It also told him much about what she thought of the lass' sire.

"Naught. I just noticed he isn't around."

"I can take care of myself and my girls. At least, before the Norsemen came."

"You have done a fine job of raising your girls alone." Robbie dropped the subject, not wanting to fire her temper in front of Ashlyn.

Aye, he was certain Caralyn had been misused in the past, and that thought sparked even more feelings in his gut. He understood his desire to protect her and the wee lasses, but this was more than that... more than he wanted to admit. He had men to lead into battle. This was no time for him to get turned around over a lass. But he had vowed to help her and he wouldn't back down now.

In spite of the terrible timing, he felt the need to know her better. It wasn't just about her appearance—though she had a face and body to die for—he had to applaud and admire a lass who was a fighter, one who did all she could for her family. She'd survived unspeakable adversity and come out stronger.

Darkness had descended about an hour past when they finally located the priory where Dundonald had sent them. Robbie stood at the gate and explained their purpose, Gracie sound asleep over his shoulder, before the guard opened the gates and allowed them in.

As they pushed open the gates, a nun came along and issued clear instructions. "Your men sleep in the stables, my lord. We will find you a chamber and arrange for some food for your men. We do not have much, but we will share."

Robbie nodded his thanks and sent his men off in the direction of the stables. After helping Caralyn and Ashlyn to dismount, he handed Gracie over to her mother. He glanced at the surrounding area to see if all looked safe. Two or three guards were visible, but no one else stood out except a few nuns roaming the grounds.

The group followed the old woman inside the priory and down a drafty passageway, sparsely lit with dancing torches. Ashlyn moved closer to her mother and clutched her hand. Gracie continued to sleep.

The woman ushered them into a small hall and they settled at a table while the nun left to summon the prioress, promising to bring back some food for Robbie. He smiled at Caralyn and she glanced away, running her fingers through Ashlyn's hair.

"Mama, I am hungry." Ashlyn slumped next to her mother on the bench.

"Hush, love. We will eat with the sisters in a few moments, I am sure. Captain Grant will eat alone after we are taken to our chamber for the night." Caralyn glanced at Robbie. "I thank you for escorting us here, my lord."

"Robbie, please. I am no lord, I am from the Highlands."

"As you wish, Captain. You seem like nobility to me." She looked up into his eyes as she said it.

"Caralyn, I must admit, I wish circumstances were different so we could get to know each other better." He stared into her green eyes, hoping to see more than just appreciation for his role in saving her and her daughters.

"Captain Grant, I would like that as well, but you are from

the Highlands, and I am from the Lowlands. You won't be here long."

He thought he caught a flicker of longing in her eyes, but it disappeared before it could take life. "I would love to show you the Highlands. Have you ever been?"

"Nay, but I hear it is lovely." A hesitant smile crossed her face.

He reached over and brushed the back of his fingers across her bruised cheek. "I wish I had been there sooner."

"You have already done more for us than anyone has." She reached up and covered his hand with hers, closing her eyes as she leaned into his caress.

Robbie, totally puzzled, said, "How could that be? A lovely lass with two beautiful daughters? Ashlyn said your husband died a while ago. What happened?"

She shook her head, "A fishing accident."

The door opened and the prioress strode in, followed by several nuns. A tall woman with a kind yet serious face, Robbie guessed one did not argue with her much. The nuns behind her stood quietly, awaiting her instructions. She bowed to Robbie. "Good evening, my lord. Sisters, please help with the bairns." She stood back and waved her arms to hasten her assistants.

Robbie and Caralyn both stood. Caralyn gripped Ashlyn's hand. "Nay, please. I would like to keep my bairns with me."

The look of panic on Caralyn's face made the prioress pause. She came closer, searching Caralyn's face. "Did you say your bairns, my lady? Not you and your husband's bairns?"

Caralyn shook her head and laughed nervously. "Nay, this man isn't my husband. These are my daughters, Gracie and Ashlyn."

The prioress clasped her hands in front of her. "Pardon me, your spirits are similar. I thought you a couple." Her hand reached over and gently lifted Caralyn's chin, turning her face so she could view her in the light of the nearby torch. "He is not the man who made these bruises, I hope?"

Caralyn blushed. "Nay, Your Grace, he saved me from the man who hit me. Our cottage has been burned to the ground and we have nowhere else to go."

Robbie added, "I am Captain Robbie Grant of the Grant Highlanders. We came from the coastline. The Norse are in the firth waiting to land with thousands of men. Caralyn is a victim of one of King Haakon's galley ships that came ashore south of Ayr. The safest place for her family right now is inland."

The prioress's voice softened. "And I see the young lady needs a healer right now. And there are many here to help you with the bairns while you heal." The prioress clasped one of Caralyn's hands in hers.

"Your Grace," Robbie said, "I would be much obliged if you would take them in for now until she decides what to do next. I would also like to make a donation for your hospitality before I leave at daybreak."

"Of course, lad." She smiled and patted Gracie's back before she lifted the bairn from Caralyn's arms. "Please have a seat and I will return after I settle the lasses." She turned to exit but stepped aside in order to allow entry to the original nun, who was returning with a steaming bowl of soup and a chunk of dark bread for him.

The steam from the soup warmed his chin as he gazed after Caralyn. Since he hadn't eaten a warm meal in a long time, his sole interest should have been in the food, but he couldn't take his eyes off the departing shapes of the comely mother and her two girls. At the doorway, Caralyn twirled back and whispered, "Thank you, Robbie."

And with that, they were gone. Would he ever see her again?

CHAPTER SIX

Caralyn had settled both girls in a soft bed together. Full from a nourishing supper, they'd fallen asleep as soon as their heads hit the pillows. She had dozed for awhile, too, but now she was restless. The moonlight through the small window showed Gracie had her thumb in her mouth. How she loved her girls. Her eyes misted at the thought of what had almost befallen them. She had to do better. She had to make sure something like this would never happen again. How frightened the lasses must have been after hiding in the rocks for so long. They had been forced to sleep one night outside without her.

She closed her eyes against the onslaught of guilt, which tormented her even though she was fully aware the situation had been completely out of her control. After running her fingers through Gracie's golden locks, she climbed out of bed, searching for something to wear on her feet. There was something she had to do. She just had to.

After one last check on her slumbering lassies, Caralyn stepped into the cool passageway and closed the door behind her. Her girls were used to her leaving in the middle of the night. If they awakened, and she doubted they would, they wouldn't wander about. Thank goodness they had each other.

She tiptoed down the maze of corridors, rationalizing her actions as she searched for Robbie Grant's chamber. He was her savior. If he hadn't come upon her when he had, she would have been passed from man to man on a Norse ship, bound for who knows where. Had he not been willing to help her, how could she have found her girls with a sprained ankle? She limped down the passageway, intent on her mission. All she had been able to do was to give him her thanks. Words were not enough. Much as she loved her mother, she knew her mother would disagree with her choice, but her decision was made.

She knew what men wanted, and she intended to give it to him. She told herself it was only because she was grateful and not due to the blossoming in her heart, though she knew that to be a lie. Robbie had touched something inside her, something she didn't quite understand, but couldn't deny. The strength of this feeling left only one course of action: to act on it, even though she knew she risked severe punishment if she were caught.

When she found the right chamber, she opened the door, crept in, and closed it silently behind her. She waited until her eyes adjusted to the moonlight, watching the man slumbering in the small pallet, oblivious to the world around him. She was as certain as she had ever been about anything, that he would never hit her, that she would always be safe in Robbie Grant's hands. How she wished circumstances could be different and they could truly be a couple. But she knew it could never be.

Once she could see properly, she removed her shift and lifted the cool sheet from the bed and climbed in next to him. His eyes flew open and he reached for his dagger, but she stilled his hand. "'Tis naught for concern, Robbie. 'Tis only me."

Confusion crossed his features. He licked his lips and stared at her. Without saying another word, she cupped his face and kissed him. She kissed him with every ounce of her being, something completely out of character for her, but she so wanted to do it. This was different; Robbie Grant was different. She teased him with her tongue and he suddenly sprang to life, wrapping his arms around her and pulling her close. He wasn't wearing a stitch of clothing and his heat enveloped her. Basking in his masculine warmth drove an arrow of heat right to her core. His penis grew and pressed hard against her belly. She touched him, lightly at first—just on the tip—and then wrapped her hand around him.

Robbie groaned and crushed her in his embrace, kissing her passionately, angling his mouth so he could tease her with his tongue. She wanted more and encouraged him by rocking her pelvis toward him, rubbing his cock against her slick entrance, and pressing her full breasts against the coarse hairs of his chest. His hand cupped her breast, teasing her nipple with his thumb until it peaked. She moaned into his mouth, and ran her hand on his hip around to his bottom so she could pull him flush against her.

He let go of her mouth and stroked her nipple with his tongue, then suckled her until she cried out. His hand stroked the underside of her breast, a soft, tantalizing caress as he laved her nipple until she wanted to scream with pleasure, finally scraping his teeth over the fine sensitive tip. She grabbed his biceps just because she needed something to hold on to. She knew she couldn't keep him, but she didn't want to lose him yet—her body was screaming for satisfaction from so many places, and he hadn't tended them all. Her legs spread wide, parted by an unknown force, a pressure that had built up from the center of her being, fighting to get out and bring him to her, inside of her, everywhere. She wanted him everywhere.

His hand slid down her hip as he kissed her again, invading her mouth, ravishing her. He reached down until his fingers found her slick folds and parted them easily, sliding inside of her wet sheath until she groaned. She moved her body so his fingers mimicked what his staff would do to her soon. A fierce need raged through her body that she was powerless to stop.

"Now, please, Robbie. I need you now."

He pulled back and gazed at her. "Lass, we are in an abbey. Are you sure?"

"Aye, don't stop. I need you inside me." She reached for his shaft and teased her entrance with it, hoping it would send him over the edge. She guided him inside, moving on him in a slow tease as he slickened her juices even more.

And she knew he was lost. He groaned and thrust fast inside her. She sighed in sheer bliss as he filled her, caressed her insides with his hardness. She grabbed his hips and forced him to speed up, hitting her hard, stroking her passage until she wanted to scream. Her body thrummed in response, forcing a frenzy in her that was totally out of her control. She clung to him with a desire and a hunger even she didn't understand, a need so deep that it possessed her soul, every nerve in her body ready to explode. Her nails dug into his biceps when he reached down to touch her nub. She almost screamed but he brought his lips down on hers again, swallowing her moans of pleasure as she shattered and convulsed under him, her muscles contracting on him until he spilled his seed inside her, moaning her name as if she were the only person on the earth.

He kissed her brow and then both cheeks before finally settling on her lips. "Cara, that was amazing." He kissed her tenderly and she wallowed in his gentleness, his hand gliding over her skin, caressing her, almost treasuring her.

She gazed into his gray eyes, wondering what was different about this man. He had catered to her needs, as if she mattered, worrying about her pleasure before his own. When had that happened to her before? He'd caressed her nub at exactly the right time, shattering her into a thousand pieces, bringing her release the likes of which she'd never experienced before. Oh, she had gone over the edge before, but not like this. She'd never experienced such sensuality combined with safety and intimacy. This was lovemaking, not sex. It was an experience to treasure in her heart and relive again and again.

They held each other for a few moments until his soft touch set off another thrum in her body, a delicious blooming of sensitivity that she was incapable of shutting down. She closed her eyes to enjoy the decadent feeling, something only Robbie Grant could conjure up.

Her mother's voice seemed to whisper in her ear. *My dear, this is wrong. You know I love you, but this is wrong. Remember what I have taught you. Please. He is a good man, but do not sully yourself.*

There was no guilt, no reckoning, and no regret. Much as she loved her, she wouldn't allow her mother to tarnish this experience.

Mother, stay away. You will not make me feel guilty about this. She trusted Robbie Grant, believed in him, would let him control her body for the short time they would have together.

She pushed against his shoulders and he rolled onto his back, taking her with him. She sat up, running her hands over his body in a slow caress. His body tensed each time she touched him. Glancing into his eyes, she smiled. In them she saw something different, more than just lust. Massaging each muscle in his arm, she reveled in his strength and his response to each squeeze of his hardness. Her hands trembled as she probed and pushed every inch of his upper body, gliding her fingers across his chest.

She leaned down and flicked her tongue over his nipple, then nuzzled and licked her way over to his other nipple. His cock came back to life underneath her slit. She could slide him inside her with just a touch, but she wanted to tease him a bit more. Her lips found their way over his taut abdomen until she was a breath away from his thick erection. Robbie shuddered underneath her as she continued her lascivious assault on his senses. This was an experience she would prolong to the greatest possible extent—because she could *feel* this time. This time she could take glory in every touch, every movement, every tingling they shared together.

Mama, you will not make me feel guilty about this. He saved your granddaughters. There is naught bad about this man. Nay, this one is good.

Moving down his body, she fluttered her tongue against the turgid tip of his manhood, tasting the salty drop of fluid there, before she took him full in her mouth. Robbie groaned and fisted his hands in her hair. His arousal inflamed her, goaded her to want more. She sucked him until he bucked against her, then his hands grabbed her under her arms, pulling her upright until his hard flesh sat directly underneath her pulsating mound.

Splaying her hands across his chest, she rocked and teased him a bit before impaling herself on him. His hands reached for her breasts, caressing them until she wanted to scream in delight. When he fondled her nipples, she rode him hard, taking him in as far as she could, her panting unwavering, relentless, forcing her to increase the pressure, the prodding, then ramming herself over his shaft until she convulsed, wave after wave of ecstasy shattering her core in delicious surrender. She could feel the moment he shot his seed into her, trying to stifle the roar in his throat as his hands grabbed her hips in a vise that didn't let go until he finished.

Her senses reeled until she settled back and the truth interrupted their serendipity.

Child, this is not how we raised you. Be a good girl. Stop.

Much as she tried, her mother wouldn't go away this time. Guilt crept back into the corners of her mind and she stilled, pushing against his chest. "Stop," she whispered. "Stop now. I am sorry, Robbie. I must go."

She hopped out of the bed, ignoring the expression on his shocked face. She closed her eyes in the hopes of willing away what she had just done. Turning her back, she tugged on her shift and made her way out of the chamber.

It needed to be the last time she ever saw him.

CHAPTER SEVEN

Robbie stood waiting at the gate the next morning. He had requested a meeting with the prioress before he and his warriors departed. He had tried to locate Caralyn all morning, but she was nowhere to be found. After awakening, he had spent several moments reliving the special night they'd spent together, but he couldn't come up with any explanation for her brusque departure. He had to find out what had caused her sudden change in attitude. Much as Tomas had tried to convince him otherwise, he would not leave without seeing her first. Hopefully, the prioress would help.

The prioress strode toward him, her hands clasped in front of her and a small smile on her face. "Yes, Captain Grant? You wished to see me?"

Robbie flashed his best smile before he cleared his throat, trying to win control over the desperation clawing at his belly. "Good morn to you, Your Grace. I have a donation for you before I leave." He handed her the coins and she nodded her thanks. *Go ahead and ask her. You can't leave without seeing Caralyn again.* "I would like to speak to the young woman and her family before I go. I am concerned about them. Would you please allow me a last visit? I won't take more than a few minutes."

The abbess stared at her hands before returning her gaze to his. "Unfortunately, Captain Grant, the lady does not wish to see you again."

Robbie forced his practiced smile. "Your Grace, I am sure the lady would be happy to see me for a moment. Are you sure? I rescued her from the hands of a vile brute. I just wish to

set my mind at ease and see they are whole and well." This
could not be happening to him. First she made wild love to
him, then ran out of his chamber without explanation, and now
she wouldn't even speak to him? What had he done?

"Captain, I am sure your winsome smile works on many
lassies, but not me. The lady is traumatized and will be for
quite some time. She needs to rest. I suspect there is more in
her past than what you witnessed."

"Excuse me?" His winsome smile? He didn't know how to
respond. He forced himself to focus on Caralyn. Aye, she did
need to rest in order to heal from the Norseman's attack, but
what did the prioress mean by traumatized? Caralyn had been
capable of functioning yesterday. "I don't understand."

"I would guess this isn't the first time she has been battered,
whether physically or emotionally. We have yet to determine
all her damages, but we'll help her heal. The Lord will watch
over her here."

Robbie stared at the prioress. He had guessed as much about
Caralyn's past. But what did that have to do with him?
Yesterday, she had appeared happy to be in his presence. Last
night, she had come to him. Was it because of her past that she
had fled after their lovemaking?

The way she had left had totally unnerved him. At one
point, she had grabbed onto him as if she hoped never to let go.
Then, suddenly, she hadn't wanted anything to do with him.
Why had she gone from one extreme to the other? He didn't
understand the workings of the female mind.

Well, if Caralyn didn't want his touch, she had a different
way of showing it. Totally lost, all he could think about was
seeing her again, talking to her. He wouldn't just walk away.
He couldn't.

The abbess cleared her throat. "Mayhap you can return at a
later date. She may be ready to see you then. Good day and
may the Lord be with you and your men during this trying
time." She nodded and headed back down the well-worn path.

Robbie's gut clenched in response to his cold rejection. A
hand grasped his shoulder from behind, and he jerked his head
around to see Tomas standing there.

"Och, the lass was living alone for some time. 'Tis very

unusual, especially at the outskirts of her clan. There weren't many in the village since the Crauford House is a distance away. Who knows what lies in her background? We have orders from Dundonald to return to camp because the Norse could be at our doorstep at any moment. Consider your priorities, Grant. We must go."

Robbie nodded, knowing that everything Tomas said was true, but his gut argued with him. True, in the Lowlands, the clans were often referred to as houses, but he expected Scottish honor still directed them to protect their members. Someone had failed Caralyn.

He pivoted and followed Tomas to their horses, lost in his thoughts, but the feeling of being watched crept up his neck. Glancing back at the abbey, he saw a wee lass with yellow curls and a very serious face standing at a distant wrought iron gate, her hands grasping the cold metal. As soon as he looked at her, a tiny hand came up by her face and waved. No smile, but Gracie had at least said goodbye in her own way. He smiled and blew her a kiss.

***

Caralyn stood by the window, peeking through the fur and watching as Gracie tried to chase Robbie down the walkway. One of the sisters latched onto the wee lass and pulled her back. Why was Gracie trying to follow him? She hated Malcolm and any man he brought along.

Captain Robbie Grant was special, even for her daughter. Slow moving tears slid down her cheeks as she stared out at the lush grounds of the priory. The sister carried Gracie down a separate path before setting her onto the soft grass next to her sister, Ashlyn. As soon as the nun's hands released her, Gracie darted toward a small side gate, peeking out at the group of warriors and their horses.

Caralyn could hear the woman talking to her daughter not far from the window. "Cluck, cluck, my wee one. Those horsies are too big for you. Why, they would trample you in an instant." The sister raced after Gracie, but stopped to let her stare at the horses. "Can't hurt to let you watch them, now, can it?" The nun stood with her arms crossed as Gracie clung to the wrought iron bars of the gate, staring at the group of Grant warriors and their prancing destriers.

Caralyn had started crying as she watched Robbie Grant speak with the prioress. He had done his best to convince the good lady to let him in, but she had done as Caralyn had requested and denied him. She swiped at the tears running down her face, blurring her vision. She would never forget him—his kind eyes, his touch, his way with her daughters. He had done more for her in two days time than anyone had ever done for her. In return, she had done something she would live to regret. She had gone and lost her heart to him in a day. How did one fall in love so fast? Was it even possible?

Her body struggling with sobs that wrenched her very core, she couldn't pull herself away from the window. Robbie's shoulders visibly slumped as he moved toward his horse. An unknown force seemed to tug at him and he stopped, glancing over his shoulder in time to see Gracie lift her hand and wave at him from behind the gate. He smiled and blew her a kiss. Watching them, Caralyn placed her hands on either side of her head and bawled like she had never done before. Gracie trusted the Highlander and accepted him. Sobs erupted from Caralyn's gut because she knew her daughter had been able to do something she could not.

When Robbie disappeared into the distance, Caralyn sat down at the table in her room, rested her head on her arms and continued to cry, wailing so hard her body trembled.

She had let him walk out of her life.

A gentle hand rested on her shoulder. Caralyn started and lifted her gaze to see the prioress standing behind her.

"Child, if you wanted him to stay, I could have allowed it. He could have at least come inside to say goodbye to you and your children." She tipped her head toward the window. "Even your wean has developed a fondness for the lad."

"Nay, Your Grace, I couldn't," Caralyn sniffled.

"Lass, he seems like an honorable man. Why not? I know you are in pain from your injuries, but perhaps he could have helped you pass the time."

Caralyn stood, her breath hitching while she struggled to calm herself. When her breathing slowed, she lifted herself up and stepped to the side of the prioress. Turning to face the woman, she clasped her hands together and knelt on the floor. Looking up into the prioress's eyes, she grabbed the older woman's skirts and sobbed uncontrollably, burying her face in the folds of the black robe. "Forgive me, Mother, for I have sinned. Please bless my soul and those of my daughters."

The prioress rested the palms of her hands on top of Caralyn's head and sighed before beginning a litany of prayer. After a few moments, she said, "Child, what could one so young have done to cause such guilt, such regret?"

Caralyn lifted her gaze and began her confession.

The abbess tipped Caralyn's head back down so she could bow in prayer, but not before Caralyn caught the look of shock on the woman's face when she began her list of transgressions.

CHAPTER EIGHT

A huge storm blew in that night, but Robbie's crew managed to make it back to camp. When they arrived, Dundonald was there waiting for him, but the fighting hadn't started yet. They spent most of the day strategizing and sending scouts out, even in the blustery autumn gales.

The following day, tensions were up. More rumors abounded, and his men were ready for battle. The storm had slowed, so the mood in the camp improved. Several scouts left in early light and were back by midday.

Tomas and Angus barged into the captain's tent without announcing themselves. Robbie and Dundonald stared at the two Highlanders, knowing they brought important news.

"Their ships," Tomas panted. "Several ships have run aground and there are Norsemen running all over the coastline and the beach. They are trying to salvage what they can from the damaged longboats, but many are battling with the local Scots in the area. Word has it Haakon is coming ashore with more men."

"Anything you wish to add, Angus?" Robbie asked.

"Aye, get our arses down there before they take over."

Dundonald nodded and looked at Robbie. "Take half your force and I will send other clans as well. Leave half here in case of an attack from another direction. If you need them, send Tomas back."

This was it. Robbie couldn't believe it. The Scots were actually going to fight the Norse. He strode out of the tent and whistled for his men. They planned their attack and he mounted with two flank horsemen each carrying the Clan

Grant banner.

He had spoken with his brother, Brodie, a couple of hours ago, but he had headed off in search of a traitor. He said a brief prayer to protect all of his clan in this endeavor, as well as for guidance and wisdom to do what was best.

As soon as they neared the coastline, yelling and screaming rent the air, telling him the battle had already begun. He led his men into the melee, giving direction to his archers and his foot soldiers before he drove his men on horseback forward. He couldn't believe the number of Norsemen running in the area. The multiple ships run aground were a sight to see, with more Norse boats coming up the firth. He knew the Scots had to drive them back before all their other reinforcements arrived.

There were two main Norse forces, one on the mound not far from the beach and another group on the beach. He directed his warriors to attack the group on the mound, intent on driving them back to their ships.

They fought for hours without gaining much ground. Robbie had sent Tomas back to gather more of his men. He searched for Brodie or Alex in the battle, but there were so many different plaids, he couldn't find either of them. Finally getting the sense they were making headway, he heard shouts from behind him. He turned around in time to see Alex, a golden helm on his head and atop a mail-clad destrier, join the Scots with another hundred men on horseback, swinging their sword arms with a fury that the Norse were powerless to stop.

He bellowed the Grant war whoop when he noticed some of the Norse retreating to the beach. Alex was too far away to draw his attention, but at least Robbie could tell if he was hurt or not. Robbie continued, driven even more by the sight of his brother fighting down the beach from him. They had to drive the Norse back on their ships.

He swung his sword until he thought his arm would detach from its socket, but he never quit. Closer to nightfall, the Norse finally ran back aboard their ships and sailed away. The ground was littered with the dead, but the fighting was over.

At least for now.

***

The next morning, Robbie noticed the sense of relief

permeating the group gathered together after the Battle of Largs had ended, but no more than he after the fierce fighting he had participated in, an experience he would never forget. All the blood and gore, death, the constant worry of whether your comrades survived had framed one of the most difficult days of his life.

The worst of the fight for the Western Isles was over, or so everyone in attendance hoped. Robbie, Tomas, The Boyd, The Mure, and The Campbell all stood inside Alexander of Dundonald's tent. The Norwegians had been forced back onto their ships at Largs, though not without a long day's battle and many casualties on both sides.

Dundonald smiled as he recreated part of the fierce battle, his chest puffing out as he spoke. "Grant, your brother on his mailed destrier was pivotal in turning this battle's favor in our direction. What a sight he was to see with his golden helm. He fought like a crazed warrior, taking down everyone within twenty feet of him."

The men's hearty laughter at their commander's focal point joined the men in a different type of camaraderie, evidence of the amount of stress that needed to be relieved over the prior day's confrontations.

Robbie agreed with him. "Aye, Alex was impressive, but so were all our warriors. They fought and pressed together as one unit, forcing the Norse off the mound and to the beach, running tail and cowering back to their galley ships, a sight I won't soon forget." He slapped Tomas on the shoulder as they chuckled.

Robbie and his men had been fighting down the beach at the time, but had still been able to see Alex when he arrived, his horse Midnight prancing and rearing on his hind legs in excitement. Robbie had hoped to see his other brother, Brodie, nearby, but had never found him amongst the hundreds of Scots that had descended over the coastal battlefield.

"Och, aye, of course you are correct. Our lads were too much for the Norse. But 'twas the first time I have ever seen mail-clad horses." Dundonald shook his head as he stared at the dirt floor. "They were a sight to see."

The Mure spoke up. "Report on casualties? How many have

we lost?"

"I have my men searching the battleground as we speak. We'll bury our dead on the morrow after we get a count and a listing of their names." Dundonald's demeanor changed to a more serious nature.

"And my brother, Alex? Has anyone seen him after the battle?" Robbie held his breath without realizing it.

"Aye," Dundonald clasped his shoulder. "He survived. Last I saw him he was at the healer's tent. Your other brother took a leg wound. He was arranging for him to be brought home to your healer."

"Brodie was hurt?"

"Aye, not a fatal wound, but the healer on the field wanted to amputate. The Grant wouldn't allow it. Ordered a couple of warriors to escort him to your sister, Brenna. Did she truly save a laird's leg that had been hanging by a thread?"

Robbie nodded. "Aye, 'twas more than a thread, but she sewed him up."

"And she saved your niece and nephew from sure death?"

"Aye, 'tis true. Brenna is a great healer because she uses her own mind and the beliefs of my mother and grandsire."

Dundonald shook his head before continuing. "Good to know should I ever become gravely ill. I also told the Grant I was sending you south again, just until we are sure the Norwegians have retreated."

"'Tis likely we sent the Norsemen running all the way back to Arran." The Boyd had a grin of victory on his face.

"Aye, they collected their dead, unloaded what they could from their ships run aground and headed back down the firth. Hopefully, they head right past Arran and back to Norway."

A commotion interrupted their meeting. Two guards stood at the entrance to the tent and were detaining someone that was not happy.

As the voices grew, Dundonald pulled the flap aside. "Problem, lads?"

"Aye, this man, who claims to be a local merchant, is asking for Captain Grant."

Robbie's ears perked up as Dundonald continued. "State your purpose."

"I'm looking for my wife."

Robbie glanced at Tomas. What would he know of anyone's wife?

Dundonald looked back over his shoulder at Robbie. "Do you mind talking to the man?"

"Of course not. I'll help if I am able." Robbie, Tomas, and Dundonald stepped outside the flap.

A tall dark-haired man stood outside the tent, hands on his hips. He traveled on horseback along with a couple of his own guards. Robbie could tell with just a glance that he was the type not to soil his hands. He said with a smile, "Glad to assist if I may."

The stranger introduced himself. "Malcolm Murray. I'm here for my wife. Word has it she was at your camp not too long ago."

Robbie assessed him carefully. "Your wife? I haven't had anyone's wife in my camp."

Murray had a way about him that didn't strike true, not wanting to maintain eye contact. His eyes darted unnaturally, and he held an air of superiority Robbie didn't like.

"Listen, Captain. My wife's house is naught but stone and ashes. We lived in South Ayrshire and the local people tell me the Norse came, burned the houses to the ground and tried to kidnap some women, but Scots warriors carrying the Grant banner chased the Norse back onto their galleys. I want to know where my wife is."

As Murray spoke, his guards came up on either side of him, whether to protect him or threaten them, Robbie wasn't sure, but he managed to contain his desire to laugh. Who were the two brutes going to attack in a camp full of Highlanders?

Dundonald said, "Grant, are you sure you didn't see any women?"

His commander knew Robbie had gone to Glasgow with a woman, but Robbie sent him a pointed look, hoping he picked up on Murray's character and wouldn't give him away. Aye, he had taken Caralyn to Glasgow, but she wasn't married to his knowledge, and there had been no mention of children. He should be concerned about his daughters, too, wouldn't he?

Robbie stared straight ahead at Malcolm Murray, dressed in

his finery and his gloves. "Aye, I am certain. I didn't see any wife of yours. What's her name?"

"Catriona Crauford. She would have had two girls with her."

"And their names?"

The man's face turned dark in an instant. Aye, he must have been looking for Caralyn, but he didn't know the names of his daughters? Something was not right.

Murray's dark expression changed to a smug smile. "I think I know my daughters' names. Now, have you seen them or not? Where did you take them?"

Robbie's hands settled on his hips. "Sorry, I can't help you."

Murray stepped forward until he was a short distance from Robbie's face. "Can't help or won't?"

Robbie stepped closer. "Both. Be on your way."

Murray spun on his heel and mounted his horse. He used his crop on his horse's flank and took off, intentionally stirring a cloud of dust behind him.

As soon as the man's guards departed, Dundonald glanced at him before returning to the inside of the tent. "I don't understand your reasoning, but I won't interfere with the Captain of the warriors that just sent the Norse home."

Tomas's censure was clear. "I know their first names were different, but you lied about a man's wife?"

"His wife? Did you not notice how he said my wife's house instead of our house? Or that he didn't know the names of his own daughters?"

"Mayhap they aren't his daughters. Mayhap only Gracie is his."

Robbie's gaze narrowed. "Did you notice his wife's name is Crauford and his is Murray? Och, Tomas. You weren't paying attention."

"Still. Their house burned down, the last name is the same and she had two girls. It has to be her." Tomas's looked at him as if he was daft.

"I think if it were true, he would have asked about his two daughters straight on instead of last thing. I also recall that Ashlyn told me her father was dead and that Gracie had never known her father."

Tomas shrugged his shoulders and threw his arms up in the air. "So what are you saying?"

"I'm saying that something about this husband wasn't right. I don't know his purpose, but I will find out."

He hoped he would find out the truth, and that the truth he discovered would not be that Caralyn was lying about everything.

CHAPTER NINE

She collapsed into Robbie Grant's arms in relief. How she loved him, and he had finally come back for her. The heat from his touch warmed her body, her desire for him raced through her veins. She wanted more, so much more from him.

His hand caressed her skin, trailing a path across her belly and down her hips. The touch of his tongue ignited a fire in her that she reveled in, bringing her to the edge of the cliff where she waited for more from him so she could plummet into whorls of ecstasy and pleasure.

Robbie, I love you. Only you, no one else. He shook her arm and she wondered what he was doing.

Her eyes flew open, immediately recognizing the same dream she had experienced every night in the priory since Robbie had left, except tonight there was one difference.

A hand was splayed between her legs, teasing her, taunting her, while his other hand shook her arm. She knew who it was by his smell.

He snickered in the darkness. "You thought you could get away from me? But look at how wet you are for me, for my touch. Much as you wish to deny me, you can't, can you?"

Caralyn locked her legs together and pushed herself away from him. She wanted to scream and run at the same time. He had found her again.

Malcolm grabbed her leg and stilled her. "Do not move, my pretty one. Gus and Sorley are with your wee lasses as we speak and we had to knock out a few guards to get here. You cause so much trouble. Do as I say or you know what will happen...unless you need a reminder?"

Caralyn stared into the cruel gaze of the man who had controlled her life shortly after her husband's death. All her hope fluttered away. How could she have thought being in a priory would protect her? What could a group of nuns do to send Malcolm away?

His black hair was slicked straight back, as always, and his brown eyes appeared black as coal in the darkness of the night. While some thought him attractive, his nature ruined his good looks. He had naught in common with Captain Grant, even his hands were cold and hard, much like his soul. She had so hoped to protect her girls from him this time. "Please don't hurt my lassies. Please, Malcolm."

He leaned over and pressed his face between her legs, teasing her nub with his tongue. "Come for me and I will leave your girls alone." He continued his ministrations until she convulsed beneath him.

Tears rolled down her cheeks, anger at this man and at herself. She had been betrayed by her own body again. *You must learn to be strong for your daughters. Fight him!* She dug her fingernails into the tender skin of her opposite wrist, delighting in the pain. She deserved it. How could she find pleasure, even if it was against her will, when her sweet lassies were being held by two brutes?

He jerked her out of bed. "Come, do you remember who controls you now?"

She hung her head, unable to speak.

"I didn't hear you." His grip tightened on her arm.

"Aye," she whispered, frustration, despair and guilt weaving a familiar thread through her.

"You thought you could get away from me but never. I will never part with you, my Cat." He licked the side of her cheek and chuckled.

She cringed at the use of the name with which he'd christened her. Catriona. How she hated it. She hated the way it rolled off his tongue in the bedroom. She hated *him*.

"Come along. You are coming with me to Glasgow. That little cottage I found for you before no longer stands. We'll find another that is closer to the firth in Glasgow, where I spend most of my time. I need more of you."

"Anything, just promise not to hurt my daughters, Malcolm."

"As long as you are agreeable, the girls will be fine. Otherwise, I am sure we can find a switch somewhere along the road. But you know I mean what I say, don't you? Here," he tossed her gown to her. "Get dressed so we can leave now, princess." A few minutes later, he yanked her out the door.

There weren't many nuns around in the middle of the night. One man at the end of the passageway lay in a heap, though he still breathed. Gus and Sorley were already in the passageway, each holding one of her daughters. Caralyn's heart wrenched when she saw the fear in their eyes. How could she have thought an escape possible? The prioress had promised they could stay even after Caralyn had shared her fears. The kind nun had promised they would protect her. But there was no protecting her.

As they exited through one of the side gates, she noticed two of the guards were sprawled on the ground. Muttering a silent thanks that they were alive, she closed her eyes to block out the cold reality of her situation, even for an instant.

Malcolm was back. Again. And she would never, ever be free of him.

***

The Norse were gone, all their galleys headed back down the Firth of Clyde, and Robbie hoped they would never return again. Tomas and Robbie had just come from the Grant camp and were leaving the royal castle in Ayr, Tomas aiming directly for the nearest pub. Dundonald had advised Robbie to keep a few guards on hand for at least a sennight, so he ordered around fifty to stay at camp with Angus in charge, though they were allowed to travel to the royal burgh in Ayr. He had sent the rest of the Grant clan warriors back to the Highlands with news. There was to be a celebration the next day in Glasgow, but he had convinced Tomas that he needed to do one thing before he could celebrate with the rest.

"Please don't tell me you are daft enough to go chasing after the married woman." Tomas hopped off his horse and handed the reins to the stable lads near the local inn, where he intended to stay the night. "Finally, I get to sleep in a real bed and you wish to drag me back to the priory near Glasgow?"

Robbie remained on his horse as he spoke to his friend. "Just because you received some compensation from the king doesn't mean you have to spend it now. Besides, I tell you she isn't married."

"Only in your foolish mind is she not married. You looked her husband in the eye. And I need a restful sleep for a change. Mayhap I can find a sweet lass in the local pub to ease my aching bones."

"Then go find her. I'll go to the priory on my own. I'll be back in plenty of time for the celebration tomorrow." Robbie spurred his horse and headed down the village path, not wanting to bother his friend anymore. He could do this on his own. He just knew he wouldn't be able to sleep at night until he was certain the lass and her daughters were safe. He didn't trust Malcolm Murray and his louts. Not one bit.

Robbie smiled to himself when he heard a horse following him on the path out of town. Tomas. "And what are you planning to do when you arrive there?" his friend bellowed at him from his place on the path. "What is your ultimate plan?"

"I am going to make sure she is safe there and the fool didn't abduct her or something worse. 'Twill not take long to talk to a lass for a few moments. And if you don't wish to sleep under the stars again, I am sure the abbess will put the two of us up for one night."

He couldn't stop thinking about how the prioress had advised him to come back after a while to try and see Caralyn again. Slud, but every night he woke up with a stiff shaft thinking about the lass. Add to that the guilt he felt about leaving little Gracie to the potential torment of three brutes, and he wasn't sleeping at all. Still, he wasn't about to admit any of it to Tomas.

"Och, aye," Tomas growled, sending his horse into a full gallop.

After a mostly silent ride, the pair arrived at the abbey around dusk. Robbie dismounted and strode up to the gate. The guard asked him his business, then left to speak to the prioress. When he returned, he ushered the two inside and they waited in the same hall where Robbie had sat with Caralyn. Robbie paced the chamber while Tomas sat in a chair, crossed his arms, and stared at his friend. "Say what you need to say, Tomas. Get it out so you can put away that wicked grin you're always wearing."

Tomas crossed his arms and pushed back in the chair so it balanced on two legs only. "You're besotted. You won't listen to reason about this lass. Can you not get it through your thick skull that you made a mistake? I can't wait for the lass to walk in the room with a smile on her face so we can take our leave."

After several minutes, the prioress entered, a serious expression on her face.

"Good evening, Captain Grant. Please sit." She motioned him over to the table where Tomas was sitting. "How may I assist you?"

Robbie didn't like the look on her face. "Your Grace, I came to check on the young woman I brought here a fortnight ago, the one with two daughters. She had been beaten and had a swollen ankle, do you remember her?"

"Aye, of course I do. She was a lovely young lady, as were her daughters."

"Was?" Robbie's gut clenched as he held his breath, awaiting her response.

"Aye, I am afraid the man she lived with before the attack by the Norse came and stole her away in the middle of the night."

"Her husband?" Robbie's worst fear had come true. Malcolm Murray had abducted her.

"Och, I don't think they were married, but she did fear him. She had shared with me some of the problems she was having in Ayr. He was not the father of her daughters. He came in the middle of the night and knocked our guards out before going into her room and taking her with them."

"And the lassies?"

"Aye, they were taken, too. Though the guards swear he said he was her husband. They didn't give in, but that's what he claimed."

"Any idea where he may have taken them?" Even though she was a member of the church, Robbie wanted to reach over and shake the woman. What kind of protection had she offered the three lasses?

"Nay, I have no idea. I am sorry, Captain. I know you are fond of the lass."

Robbie jumped out of his chair and paced, but not before giving Tomas a glare. "Thank you, Your Grace. I know you did the best you could." Robbie walked out the door and headed down the passageway. The clicking of Tomas's boots on the stone let him know his friend wasn't far behind.

"Grant, we'll find them. They must be in Glasgow and it isn't that big a town. It only has four main roads in it. She's here somewhere." Tomas shouted, "Grant, wait."

Robbie ignored him and continued. He was almost to the end of the passageway, when he heard the prioress's footsteps behind them.

"Captain Grant?"

"Aye, Your Grace?" Robbie stopped and waited for the abbess to catch up with him.

"I know you are interested in her. I feel I need to say something."

"Aye, Abbess. Please speak your mind."

"I told you before I didn't know all the demons and the wounds she had suffered."

"Aye." Robbie had no idea what she was about to tell him.

"Now I do. After a long discussion with Caralyn, I wish to tell you that she is indeed a lovely young lady, but she will need a patient man at her side."

Robbie nodded, unsure of what to say.

She continued. "But you will have no regrets if you pursue her. She is special and has a warm heart. You are just what she needs, a kind and patient man. I think God wouldn't want you to give up on your quest for the lass. Something is indeed amiss."

"Thank you, Your Grace." Robbie cleared his throat and went back in the direction he'd come from. He didn't know what to say to that statement either. He glanced over at Tomas, whose smug look had been scrubbed off his face.

At the present, all he wanted to do was to locate Caralyn and her lassies. But he had absolutely no idea where to start.

CHAPTER TEN

Robbie Grant's eyes roved the great hall, hopeful to find Caralyn here. He and Tomas had scoured the entire town of Glasgow without finding one sign of the lass. He was counting on the fact that Malcolm Murray, a man who put on airs, would consider himself important enough to show up at the castle for the victory celebration.

Tomas interrupted his thoughts. "Good fortune for you that King Alexander decided to celebrate here in Glasgow instead of the royal burgh, aye?"

Too busy searching the area for Caralyn, Robbie did not even glance at his friend. "Och, but we should have found her by now. How does a lass just disappear?"

"Glasgow is much bigger with packhorses heading to ships in the firth."

"Don't even mention that possibility that they have left. She's in Glasgow. I can feel it."

"I hope you're correct. We need to find her so we can get her out of your mind and return to the Highlands where we belong."

Dundonald approached them, two strangers on his heels. "Gentlemen," he stepped back to allow his companions to stand at his side. "I would like to introduce you to Captain Grant, and his comrade, Tomas More of Drumiston. The Grant Clan, under their direction, was instrumental in garnering our win against the Norse at the Battle of Largs. Lord Montgomery and Baron Strathman would like to offer their thanks for your assistance in the name of the Scottish Crown."

Lord Montgomery spoke first. "My thanks for sending the

Norse running. Why, I hear they ran from the mound to the beach as soon as they saw you Highlanders heading their way."

Baron Strathman chuckled. "Captain Grant, were you the one with the golden helm? We heard many tales of a golden-helmed warrior's prowess in battle."

"Nay, 'twas my brother, Laird Alexander Grant, in the golden helm and on the mail-clad destrier. He is a fierce fighter."

"Our thanks for a quick end to the battle. We feared for our own vessels on the Firth of Clyde," Montgomery said.

"You are both merchants living in Glasgow?" Robbie sipped his ale, his heartbeat increasing while he struggled to maintain a calm exterior.

The two men nodded while Dundonald offered a quick bow and stepped away. Now was his chance. Perhaps they knew something of the blackguard who'd kidnapped Caralyn. "What do you know of a merchant named Malcolm Murray?"

Tomas gave him a pointed look before turning his attention back to their companions.

Robbie carefully assessed both men for any reaction to the name. Both of them looked uncertain at first, but recognition soon dawned on the baron's face. "Murray, you say? I think I have heard of the name. Why...Och, nay." He and Lord Montgomery exchanged a knowing look.

Robbie had to know more, as much as they could tell him. "Gentlemen? I'm asking a favor. Please tell me what you know. He is nae friend of mine. I am seeking information only."

Lord Montgomery nodded. "Malcolm Murray does claim to be a merchant and he is a wealthy man, but—" he cleared his throat before continuing, "—his business is questionable. That's all I can offer."

"Does he reside in Glasgow?"

"Aye, at a small keep at the edge of town."

Robbie nodded. "My thanks."

"Och, the pleasure has been ours, lads. We appreciate all you did to put an end to this nonsense with King Haakon of Norway. Time to return to normal business. Captain." Lord Montgomery clasped Robbie's shoulder before moving on to another group of men.

Robbie turned to Tomas. "There you have it. We need to find his keep, then I will have the answer to my questions."

"Aye," Tomas said. "Let's just hope he doesn't maintain many guards around his keep."

The festivities picked up as more Scots continued to file into the great hall. Minstrels wandered about, making their way through the mass and entertaining guests at will. Lasses serving food from small trays made their way around the periphery of the large chamber. Robbie grabbed a chunk of brown bread from a tray and started chewing.

"Tomas, there must be many men here who know Glasgow well. We just need to find the right ones and question them." He paused for a swig of ale.

"You may not need to do that," Tomas said.

"What?" Robbie froze as a strange feeling crept up his neck. Tomas nodded his head to their left.

Robbie turned his head, and there he was. Malcolm Murray strutted like a peacock, his arm gripping someone behind him. Robbie couldn't see her face yet, but he knew who it was—Caralyn. He recognized those silky threads of dark hair, those luscious curves. He would know her anywhere.

She turned and caught his gaze, blushing instantly and turning her head as fast as she could. Why? What had he done to make her deny him?

He didn't have to wait long for his answer. As soon as Murray spotted him, he made his way through the crowd and headed straight for him. He tugged Caralyn in front of him, one hand grasping her wrist, the other on her waist.

"Captain Grant, I would like you to meet my wife, Catriona."

Robbie could do naught but nod. "My lady." He wanted her to look at him, but she refused, keeping her eyes determinedly cast downward. Murray squeezed her waist. "Speak to the captain, love."

Caralyn kept her eyes down, but whispered, "Greetings, Captain."

Robbie didn't hesitate. "Greetings, Catriona." He dragged out her name as if to remind her of her lie. In the space of a few seconds, memories of their night together filled his senses, the feel of her body against his, of her soft skin beneath his caress. Her light scent teased him. Her passion had known no bounds, but now she couldn't even bring herself to look at him. Somehow, the name Caralyn fit her much better than Catriona. Glancing at Murray again, he said, "And how are your two daughters? What did you say their names were again?"

"I didn't. They're fine."

Robbie persisted. "Aline, Alison, Ashley..."

"Ashlyn." Caralyn blurted out her daughter's name, but then blushed and a queer expression crossed her face.

Fear. Robbie had seen it. She was afraid of her husband. He stared at her, willing her to lift her gaze, but she wouldn't. Darkness crept across her face, the most beautiful face he had ever seen, and he suddenly realized what had caused the change. Her husband had a tight grip on her thumb and was bending it backwards. Robbie grabbed hold of his arm and twisted. "Do you always treat your wife with such care, Murray? Release her."

Murray gritted his teeth. "I don't know what your game is, Captain, but she is my wife. I will do as I please with her. Do not ever look at her again if you value your life." He spun on his heel and tugged Caralyn behind him.

She turned her head back to Robbie and mouthed the words, "Help me."

They disappeared out the door.

Robbie headed for the door instantly, beckoning to Tomas. "Now. We're following, and if we get the chance, I'll steal her away tonight."

Tomas caught up with him by the stables. As soon as they caught sight of Murray, the two of them held back.

"Slud, he has five men with him," Tomas said. "You'll never get her tonight. That's six to two." He mounted his horse, but pranced in a circle rather than moving forward.

Robbie mounted his own horse. "Aye, there are too many around because of the festivities," he said. "But we can still discover where she lives."

CHAPTER ELEVEN

"Now do you wish to tell me the truth about Captain Grant, my love?" Malcolm Murray had brought her back to his keep.

She knew he was angry, but she was unsure of why. He knew nothing.

"Why does he know you? Why does he ask about you?" He grasped her and tightened his grip, his fingers biting into the tender flesh of her underarm.

They stood in his chamber, the door latched. She hated when he was angry. He didn't know how to control his temper and he usually took it out on her.

"Tell me!" He jerked her closer until she was a mere inch from his face.

"He's the one," she whispered. Oh, how she wished he could be the only male in her life. He was the only one to have treated her with any kindness, the only one who seemed to care about her at all.

"What?"

"The one who saved me from the Norseman. I told you about the man who punched me and tried to put me onto his galley." Tears misted in her eyes, but she tried not to lose control. "Captain Grant stopped him."

"So you were *with* him?" A familiar fury filled Malcolm's gaze.

"Nay, not like that. The Norseman knocked me out. When I awoke, I was in a tent in a camp full of Highland warriors."

"And?"

"And he went back to find my daughters and then took me to the priory."

"Did you have relations with him? Did you give my goods away for free? Or did you charge him?"

"Nay, I didn't."

He dropped her arm and slapped her cheek. Her hand came up to defend herself from his brutality.

"Men do not follow a woman around like that unless they have tasted her. Did you let him taste you? Did you?"

"Nay! I didn't do anything. My ankle was swollen; my face was all bruised and cut. I had open wounds all over my body from being dragged across the stones. You saw my wounds. I was in too much pain to even think about such a thing."

"You lie." He tossed her onto the bed. "You lie and you will pay for this. Never." He bent down and put his finger in her face. "Never let another man touch you unless I tell you to."

He grabbed his mantle and headed for the door.

Caralyn jumped out of the bed. "Where are you going? Please, my girls. Don't hurt them. This had naught to do with them." She rubbed her palm across her sore cheek.

He stopped at the door and turned, his hand still on the latch. "You will pay for this. You thought I would let you see them in a sennight? Absolutely not. You will not see your daughters until the next moon. Try and cuckold me again." Malcolm stalked out and slammed the door. "And don't leave this chamber!" he bellowed as he ran down the staircase.

Caralyn threw herself back on the bed. "Nay, nay, nay! My lassies. Please, nay. I have to see them." Sobs wrenched from her gut. How she hoped Robbie had heard her plea. Would he help her? Could he? She couldn't bear to be separated from her girls.

Why had this happened to her? She had finally convinced Malcolm to let them live alone in the cottage, with open visitations, of course, but now everything was ruined. Aye, he had left guards while he was away, and she had still been forced to do things she didn't want to do, but at least her daughters had been at her side. Just when she'd thought her life couldn't get any worse, Malcolm had found a new way to torture her.

Why had the Norse come along and ruined her life?

***

Two nights later, Caralyn rested on her side on the bed. Malcolm had just left after taking her body. She hated sex with him but she knew she had no choice. He owned her. He had her daughters. She had only seen them once since they left the priory. Ashlyn and Gracie's faces had told her everything; they were unhappy. Ashlyn had told her the place they were being kept was dirty, but they were unhurt.

Gracie had just stared at her with the same haunted look in her eyes, the look Caralyn had hoped to banish from the wee lass's gaze forever. She failed her daughters again. Now, she would do whatever Malcolm wanted just so she could see them again.

A slight rustling outside the window caught her attention. She lifted her head, listening, trying to determine the source of the low scratching. Pushing her covers back, she sat up and hung her legs over the side of the bed, shuffling her feet around to find her shoes. Tiptoeing over to the window, she tugged the fur back far enough to peek over the ledge.

A man had scaled her wall, using a rope secured on the rooftop apparently. For some reason, she didn't scream. Peering at the top of his head, she recognized the light brown hair, the broad shoulders, the strong hands. He paused for a moment, as if he could sense her presence at the window. Grasping the rope with one hand, he lifted his gaze to hers, and brought a finger to his lips, urging her to keep silent. Robbie Grant. She noticed his friend at the base of the rope.

Her heart soared at the sight of him. How she wished Robbie Grant could be by her side for the rest of her life. He would make the best father in the world. As his hand reached for the ledge, she pulled the fur back allowing him entrance to her chamber.

He stepped on the sill and brought himself up to full height, breaking out in a smile that showed his glorious white teeth. Winking at her, he hopped down next to her. "Greetings, lass."

"Robbie Grant, you must be daft. If Malcolm finds you here, he'll kill you."

Robbie winked at her. "Och, lass, do you really think Malcolm could do much damage to me on his own? He is naught without his big louts."

She couldn't help but smile. "I didn't think you would come."

His hand cupped her chin, his thumb caressing the line of her jaw for a brief moment. "Did you not ask me to help you? Do you think I could walk away from a lass in need? Och, I am a Grant warrior, love. I could never leave you in the hands of that monster."

Robbie bent down and brushed her lips with his, a tentative kiss, but one that made her want more. She parted her lips for him and he tasted her with his tongue, a sweet caress that caused her to lose her senses and lean into his embrace.

When he finished the kiss, she sighed in satisfaction, hoping there would be more kisses from this man who had stolen her heart. A mischievous grin crossed his features, melting her heart a bit more.

The expression on his face switched from winsome to serious in the matter of a few seconds. "Lass, we need to talk. Please tell me what goes on here. Is Malcolm your true husband?"

Caralyn's gaze dropped to the floor. "Nay." She plopped down onto the bed. "He is not my husband. I would never have agreed to wed him. He chose me when we lived in South Ayrshire. 'Twas after I lost my parents and my husband. My village had been a part of the Crauford house by the coastline, but we lost so many to sickness that few of us remained. I had nowhere else to go. He uses my lassies to blackmail me."

"Where are they now?" Robbie brushed the silky strands of her hair off her face in a soft caress.

Tears spilled down her cheeks. "I don't know. He was never this cruel in Ayrshire. Now he has hidden them from me, and if I don't do exactly as he commands, he says he won't allow any visits."

"When was the last time you saw them?"

"A few days ago," she blurted, her sobs causing her breath to hitch. "They are kept in a shabby room I know not where. Ashlyn says they stay with two men. Malcolm said I could see them once a sennight, but after seeing you, he said I couldn't see them for a whole moon."

"Och, Cara, I am sorry." He pulled her to her feet and

wrapped her in his warm embrace.

Why could they not be together? Robbie was everything she had ever wanted in a partner: warm, tender, loving, honorable, and safe. More than anything, she wanted to be safe, and she wanted her daughters to be safe, too. Why could they not live together as a family?

"Caralyn, why does he call you Catriona?"

"Och, I hate it. He says it's his name for me, and that I am never to be called Caralyn again. But the name my mama and papa gave me is Caralyn."

"What kind of business is Malcolm involved in?"

"I'm not sure. I think he deals in whisky and spices from the East, but I can't say for sure. Recently, he spoke of Irish bills. Sometimes he's gone for a long time. 'Tis why we lived in the cottage south of Ayr. He wanted me available whenever he came in on his ship. The vessel would sail to the pier in South Ayrshire, then move on toward Glasgow. He would get off and spend a few days with me, then move on. 'Twas never as bad as this, but it has never been happy. Robbie, what can I do? I hate him. Please help me."

"'Tis why I am here. Come with me now and I will help you find your girls."

"Nay!" She shoved his chest.

"Shush, lass. Do you want to be heard by the staff?" Robbie whispered.

Her hands came up to cradle her face as she shook her head hopelessly. "Nay, but I can't risk it. What if we couldn't locate my daughters? I could lose them forever. He would kill them if I wasn't here. He hates children."

"Lass, listen to me. We'll find them first." He took her hand in his, tugging it away from her face.

A small flame of hope burned inside her at the thought of being rescued and protected by Robbie. "Aye, that could work."

"But the lassies may not be willing to come with me."

"Gracie loves you. You're the only man she has ever willingly allowed near her. She will go with you. I know it in my heart. Please, Robbie. Find them first, then come for me."

Robbie tucked her in close, apparently weighing the

information she had given him. She couldn't lose her girls, but if Robbie managed to find them, they might have a chance at happiness together.

He reached down and cupped her face, kissing her tenderly, the kind of kiss that she would dream of and hold close to her heart in the days to come. He kissed her as if he had strong feelings for her, as if there was more to her than pleasing a man with her favors.

"Fine, lass, we'll try it that way. If you're in trouble, send a message to the priory. I will stop there occasionally to check. He does allow you to leave the house for worship?"

"Aye, with an escort, but I do go to the priory where you brought me."

"Then send a message through the nuns or the guards, and I will find you."

One more chaste kiss on the lips and he was gone. She licked her lips, wanting to savor the taste of the one man in her life she trusted and loved. Sneaking over to the window, her gaze followed the Highlander as he slid down the stone wall, landing as quietly as he had climbed. At the bottom, he glanced up and flashed her a quick smile before he disappeared into the night. Aye, she was desperately in love with Robbie Grant. But naught could come of it, she was sure.

CHAPTER TWELVE

Robbie and Tomas stood in front of the priory. Robbie had just finished a conversation with the guards and the prioress, explaining the situation and how to reach him if necessary. A messenger approached him astride his horse as they stood talking.

"Captain Grant?" The messenger awaited Robbie's answer.

"Aye. I'm Captain Robert Grant."

The lad leaned over his horse to hand him the parchment he was holding. "Message for you from Dundonald."

Robbie thanked him and took the letter, checking the seal before breaking the wax. After a quick read, he sighed and stared at his friend. "We have another mission."

"What now? I thought we could finally return to Clan Grant. We only have a few warriors left in the area. We can't do much with such a reduced force."

"I don't know, but Dundonald is asking for us to return to the royal burgh for instructions."

"'Tis all he states? No more information than that? Not how long a journey, or in what direction?"

"Och, he only says that we will be in Ayr for a short time before returning to Glasgow. But there is no mention of the mission. He can't be sending us to rebuild any of the cottages destroyed by the Norse, though. He promised he wouldn't use us for that."

Tomas's face fell. "The rescue of the lassies will have to wait, aye?" Apparently, his friend was drawn to the wee lassies, as he was.

"I hate to leave without finding Caralyn's daughters first.

My gut tells me Murray is not to be trusted and will keep moving. Who knows what he will do next? Bairns will get in his way and he may get rid of them without telling Caralyn, especially wee little Gracie."

"Mayhap we can find more out about Murray in the royal burgh. She was living just south of there not too long ago."

Robbie's expression was glum as he climbed back on his horse. "Good suggestion. We will see what we can discover about Malcolm Murray and his business. I hope we can return quickly. 'Twill not be easy locating two weans in this large city."

***

Dusk descended as Tomas and Robbie rode into Ayr. Robbie handed the reins of his horse to the stable lad and headed up toward the great hall, his boots clicking on the cobblestone. The town of Ayr seemed to be coming back to life after the threat of Haakon's men had passed. Though the Norsemen had not reached Ayr, the general feel of the townspeople had been poisoned by the possibility. Now there was a jovial attitude in the local pubs, no more drawn faces and fearful glances.

Whatever his assignment was, it had to be accomplished in as short a time as possible. His brothers had both been blindsided by lasses—Alex by Maddie, Brodie by Celestina—and he had sworn it would never happen to him. Now he knew differently. Before he had experienced great pride each time he strode inside the gates of the royal castle, but now, he just wished to finish his task and head back to Glasgow. He wanted to be near her.

The steward ushered Robbie into one of the king's many small solars. He hadn't seen the king's main solar since the day he and Brodie had been summoned to Ayr over the summer. As soon as he settled into a chair, Dundonald shoved the door open and spoke with a boom, his voice bouncing off the stones in the room. "Captain Grant, how nice to see you again. I appreciate your haste in attending my summons. Where is your guard, Tomas of Drumiston?"

Robbie bounded out of his chair to greet his superior officer. "Drumiston is outside tending our horses. I will convey the necessary information to him."

A knock sounded at the door, and the steward let Tomas in.

"Och, no need. Here he is now." Dundonald offered them both an ale before speaking. "Lads, I need you to handle a verra sensitive issue."

Robbie glanced at Tomas. "Aye, we are trustworthy, Chief."

"That I know, my son. Here is the information and I will send you on your way. You may want another one or two warriors with you on this mission." He circled the desk in the corner of the room and sat in the chair behind it with his hands folded in his lap.

"You are aware the Norsemen assaulted many of our people when they pillaged the areas in South Ayrshire and up to Loch Lomond, aye?"

Robbie and Tomas both nodded. "Aye, we were in South Ayrshire when one of their galleys unloaded men who set fire to a gathering of cottages."

Dundonald nodded. "Well, this won't be a complete surprise if you have already witnessed the Norsemen's brutality. As they headed south on the Firth of Clyde, one of the Norsemen's longboats came upon a lone Scottish merchant ship heading south. Some fools didn't listen to us when we advised our local merchants to postpone all journeys and keep all ships out of the Firth. The Norsemen overtook the ship, did what they needed to, then left the galley afloat in the waters of Arran. The ship has finally come ashore a bit south of here and I would like you to assist some of our men with the cargo. And since you have just come from there, I would like the cargo to be brought to the priory near Glasgow.

Robbie and Tomas exchanged perplexed glances. Robbie said, "Excuse me, what cargo are we dealing with that must be brought to Glasgow by land? I don't understand, Chief. Why not send it to Glasgow by ship as was intended?"

Dundonald's voice dropped to barely above a whisper. "Because the ship was loaded with women. No merchant has come forward to claim the ship. Our guess is that the women were headed for a life of slavery in the East."

"A ship full of women to be sold as slaves?" Tomas asked, incredulous at the implications of what Dundonald had said.

Robbie could only shake his head at the thought of what they might find. He had seen what one Norseman had done to one lass. The Norse would not have been pleased to be chasing their tails down the firth. How it must have delighted to come upon a ship full of inadequately protected women. "It makes one wonder, which fate would have been worse for them? The East or the Norse?"

Dundonald snorted. "I wish the bastard who owned the ship would claim his cargo so I could publicly cut his bollocks off for all to see. You'll need a strong stomach for this journey. What the Norsemen did to them isn't pleasant. I want the women brought to the priory to heal, you are to take care that no one sees them while you travel."

Robbie and Tomas left the solar and made their way out of the royal castle. As they strolled down the cobblestone courtyard inside the keep walls, a yell from outside the keep caught Robbie's ears.

"Grant, would you make haste? I need to speak to you."

The speaker stood just outside the castle gate, clearly unable to pass since he was not connected with the king. Robbie squinted, hoping to unmask the stranger.

"Will you stop your staring? Can you not recognize one of your sister's family members?"

Robbie peered at the man before breaking out into a broad smile. "Logan? Logan Ramsay? What in hellfire brings you here, you hedge-born halfwit?" He hurried out of the gate with Tomas fast behind him.

Logan grasped Robbie by both shoulders once they met on the cobblestones. "Half-wit, is it? We'll see what your brothers call you when you get home. They're vexed over your disappearance and sent me to find you."

Robbie cocked his head at his friend. "Somehow, I doubt my brothers sent you to find me." Logan's smirk told him he was correct in his assessment of the situation. "You couldn't stay in one place, so you came here on your own. Dundonald informed my brother of what I was doing, and I already sent one group of warriors home. My brothers couldn't have been overly concerned about my welfare. "

Logan chuckled. "Middling bastard. Does it make a

difference? Mayhap not your brothers, but the women are all worried about you, thinking you'll never return. You broke too many hearts in the Grant clan."

Robbie chuckled. "Now can we hear the truth? You just wanted to be in the thick of things again, Ramsay. You just can't settle for long."

Logan laughed. "Och, aye, that, too. Enough about my reasons for coming, though. What are you still doing at the king's castle, and where are you headed?"

Robbie thought for a moment. Dundonald had mentioned he might need more men. Riding a cart full of women wouldn't be easy, especially with the renegades outside of Glasgow. "You're here at just the right time. I need a couple more warriors for my next assignment. Will you join me?"

"Of course, 'twas my intention all along. Lead the way."

CHAPTER THIRTEEN

A couple of hours later, they neared the Kirk south of the royal burgh. Robbie could hear sobs from inside as they neared the building. He hoped he could handle whatever they found inside. It couldn't be as bad as battling, could it?

He knocked on the locked door of the Kirk, night having settled in. He stared up at the stars hoping he could finish this mission and hurry back to continue his search for Caralyn's daughters.

The door opened a crack and a priest stared out at him. "State your purpose."

Once Robbie convinced him they had been sent by Dundonald to help, the priest led them through the front door and into a room in the back primarily used for storage. As he drew closer, he could hear a painful chorus of moans and groans from the back room. Robbie shook his head, praying for strength. Whatever he was about to discover, he knew he wouldn't rest until he found the bastard responsible for sending a ship full of women out alone for such a dark purpose.

They stepped into the small chamber and Robbie made a slow assessment of the inhabitants. Six cots were spread around the room, young women resting on them in various stages of recovery. Cuts, bruises, bloody lips, broken bones, and worst of all, broken spirits. Some sobbed openly while others stared into space. A couple of priests assisted with cleaning the women's wounds and offering comfort where they could, but it was obvious that these wounds would be a long time in healing. Seeing the mistreated women brought memories of Caralyn the day he'd found her in the hands of the

Norseman. Mayhap the same group of beasts had found this ship.

Robbie turned to the priest, uncertain how to best proceed with transporting the women to Glasgow.

Father MacLaren spoke in a soft whisper. "Probably better to move them tonight, lads. There is naught more we can do for them here. They need to be tended by women, and we just don't have the supplies for bandaging or the healers to set their broken bones to rights."

Robbie frowned, but searched the priest's face. "How shall we move them, Father?"

"Och, there are two carts. I believe we can get them comfortable for the most part. There are several mounds of hay in the back. My fear is if you wait until daylight, you will draw more attention to the women. If you leave soon, you should be able to make it to the priory by morning. At least you'll travel through the royal burgh in the dark."

Tomas and Logan entered the room behind him. Without speaking, Logan moved over to one of the beds where an alert woman was resting, watching their every move. He moved toward her a bit, Robbie didn't know why.

The woman hissed, "Touch me and I will rip your bollocks in two, you rutting bastard."

Father MacLaren pivoted toward the young lass, probably around twenty summers. "Gwyneth, these men are here to help. They aren't the enemy. Their mission is to transport you to the priory. Please be agreeable."

Gwyneth lifted her head into the light so she could survey the group. Robbie decided she had been a beautiful woman before she'd encountered the Norse, though it was hard to tell between the bruises.

She hoisted herself up tall enough to almost look Logan eye to eye. Logan was still a mite bit above her, but she was close. Long legs supported her and she clutched a small plaid to her torso.

She cocked her head at Robbie. "Take me back to Glasgow and I will be eternally grateful, but I won't go to the priory. Fair warning for any of you, if you try to touch me, I'll stick a knife between your ribs when your head is turned."

Father MacLaren said, "Gwyneth, these are the men who fight for the Scottish crown. They aren't here to hurt you."

"Your pardon, Father. Other than you, all men are the same. Get me to Glasgow and you'll never have to see me again. Just give me my bow and arrows and my knife, and I will leave a happy lass. And don't try to tell me they aren't here, because I know the rotten bastard intended to sell my weapons, too."

Logan checked the woman over from head to toe, smiling when her gaze caught his.

"Do that again, and 'twill be the last thing you do, warrior or not." She leaned in so she was nose to nose with Logan. "You don't frighten me. I could kill you easily."

Logan locked gazes with her, his smile gone now. "I have nae doubt you could, lass. I'll keep my hands to myself until you request otherwise."

The two stared at each other for a long pause, Gwyneth in a snarl, but Logan unrelenting. The air bristled with tension, though Robbie wasn't quite sure what type of tension it was. Had his impulsive, daredevil brother-in-law just met his match? Finally, Father MacLaren cleared his throat and said, "Come, lass, I will give you your things as long as you promise not to use any of your weapons on these men."

Gwyneth limped along behind the priest. "As long as no one touches me, you have my word, Father. If any man dares to lay a hand on me, believe me, his life will be in *my* hands." When she made this last statement, she turned to give a pointed look to Logan, who had yet to remove his gaze from her.

***

Caralyn's hands trembled as she awaited the arrival of the abbess. She had been unable to come last night, but this morning, as soon as Malcolm left, she had made her way over to the priory. Malcolm had given permission for her to go to two places only, either the Kirk or the priory, supposedly to pray with the nuns. He sent two escorts with her each time she left the keep to make sure she went nowhere else. Fortunately, the priory wasn't far from Malcolm's by horseback and the men were only too pleased to stand watch from the outside of the building.

Once at the priory, Caralyn had volunteered to contribute

her help to the priory in some way. Mother Mary had led her down a dark staircase to the basement. After leading her through a maze of corridors, Mother Mary stopped outside a doorway and turned to speak to her. "My dear, I know your life has been difficult. I could ask you to toil in the vegetable gardens or in the kitchen peeling potatoes, but my instinct tells me you can better serve our God down here. This is where our healers do their work, and what they do varies depending on the needs of the town. Not long ago, we treated men who had been hurt at the Battle of Largs. Now, we have the need to treat those who have been hurt by the war in a different way.

"Father MacLaren sent me a message yesterday informing me of a group of women who had been beaten and brutalized by a ship full of Norsemen. These women were on a ship when the Norsemen took control of it. They used the women as they saw fit and sent the longboat drifting out to sea. The ship was recovered by the Scottish crown and brought to shore south of Ayr.

"The females are being brought here for treatment. A small group of the king's Highland warriors have gone to escort them here in carts. This will be a challenging assignment for anyone in the room. I believe you are up to that challenge. Tell me now if I have misjudged you." Mother Mary crossed her hands in front of her body, awaiting Caralyn's response.

"Aye, you have judged correctly, Mother."

"You understand you may see females in the same condition you came to us or worse? We kept you upstairs at the time because this hall was filled with men. But now it will be all women. If at any time you feel this is inappropriate or painful for you, please return upstairs. I will take care of your escorts."

"I would like to do this, Mother Mary. Please."

"Follow me, child." The abbess strode into the long hall lined with small cots on both sides of the room. A large hearth was situated outside of the room and a small hearth where they heated water and broth sat against another wall. Tables sat in the middle covered with linen strips and salves. Storage chests sat at the foot of many of the beds.

The beds were empty. A couple of nuns fussed with supplies, but there was no one in need of care yet. A sister with a warm smile and a dimple strode toward them, opening her arms wide to Caralyn. "My dear, you have come to assist us in our care of the weak?"

Mother Mary's chin lifted a notch, commanding the sister's attention. "Sister Donna, this is Caralyn. You may remember her from a fortnight ago. She was here with her two daughters."

"Of course, I remember her. And how do your sweet lassies fare?"

Caralyn stole a glance at her fingertips before answering. "They are fine, Sister Donna. My thanks for your concern." How she wished she could be truthful and tell them she had no idea how her daughters fared, that they had been taken from her and were being held against their will. Their happiness was completely dependent on her submission to Malcolm.

Mother Mary said, "I will leave Caralyn with you, Sister. I hope she can be of assistance. My messengers tell me we should expect our visitors sometime this morning."

The abbess left and Sister Donna gave Caralyn a quick tour of the facility, explaining where the most used supplies were stored. She introduced her to another nun, Sister Elinor, a younger lass with golden hair and a sweet smile. Fortunately, Sister Elly, as she called herself, chattered on so much that Caralyn didn't need to speak. At present, her thoughts were with her girls. Tears threatened to slide down her cheeks, but a noise from above interrupted their thoughts.

"Och, they're here, my dear. Follow me and I'll tell you what to do." Sister Donna ushered her over to the doorway.

She waited in the background, which proved to be a wise move. It allowed her to cover her surprise when she recognized the first man to carry a wounded woman into the room as none other than Captain Robbie Grant. He actually came to a halt when he saw her, but then continued on after Sister Donna. Oh, how her heartbeat quickened at the sight of Robbie Grant. Aye, she wondered if he had located her daughters, but she had to admit her reaction to the sight of him was stronger than she ever would have guessed.

Robbie stopped on his way out the door and said with a smile, "'Tis nice to see you, Caralyn." He headed down the corridor, presumably to assist more women who needed care. His smile had a way of warming her to her core, causing her to blush with pleasure.

Sister Donna oversaw everything while Caralyn worked with Sister Elly who kept her so busy she didn't have the opportunity to seek Robbie out again. She hoped he would come speak with her again before he left since she was desperate to hear anything about her lasses. The location necessitated discretion, however, so she didn't know if the chance would come or not.

Occasional moans and groans could be heard from the group, but for the most part, the lasses were silent, visibly sighing when they reclined on the soft mattresses and gave in to the ministrations of the sisters around them. An argument interrupted the silence.

Caralyn spun around in time to see a brawny Highlander carrying a woman into the room. She was arguing with him the whole way.

"Put me down, Logan Ramsay. I told you that you were never to touch me. How dare you assume I need help when I don't. And I am not staying here either."

Logan grinned all the way across the chamber. "Just following orders, my lady. Want to make sure you have no serious injuries." Logan plopped her down on the nearest cot and she landed with a string of curses.

Caralyn froze. "Gwyneth?" She hobbled across the room, her ankle still a bit tender, her arms open wide. "Blessed saints, 'tis really you?"

"Caralyn? Hellfire! How I have missed you."

Gwyneth smiled and the two lasses threw themselves at each other, hugging as if they hadn't seen each other in years.

Caralyn stepped back and stroked Gwyneth's arm. "I was afraid I would never see you again. Where have you been? Are you unhurt?" She helped Gwyneth back onto the bed before she sat down next to her.

"I wouldn't sit here for anyone but you, Caralyn Crauford, especially not for this lout!" She waved her arm toward Logan, leaning against the wall, his arms crossed and a smile on his face. With a huff, she turned away from him, giving him her back. "Caralyn, I am so happy to see you. Where are your sweet lassies? Wee Gracie must be so big by now."

Caralyn's face twisted into a frown, and she shook her head. "I don't know. Please, may we talk about this later?" She glanced up just in time to see Robbie striding over to the bed, Logan at his side. Caralyn's gaze caught his and he shook his head.

He whispered so no one else could hear him but Logan, Caralyn, and Gwyneth. "Sorry, lass. We haven't yet found your wee ones."

CHAPTER FOURTEEN

Several hours later, Caralyn washed her hands in the basin at the end of the chamber full of cots, preparing to leave for the day. After Gwyneth fell fast asleep, Caralyn had assisted Sister Donna and Sister Elly wherever she was needed. It had been a busy morning and afternoon. Fortunately, Malcolm had said he would be gone for most of the day, which was the only reason she'd been allowed to remain at the priory for this long. She knew he would never have allowed it if he'd known what she was doing.

As she dried her hands on the linen towel, she glanced over her shoulder at the women in the beds. She had helped Sister Elly clean and bathe each woman, and dress her wounds. Then she helped comfort them in whatever way she could. She had rubbed backs, listened to their stories, and hugged them while they sobbed.

Tears slid down her cheeks and she turned back away from the cots. She could have been any one of those women or worse. Aye, she had been injured and bruised by the Norseman, but not brutalized or raped.

Captain Robbie Grant had seen to that. She wondered why she felt the need to cry now and not while she'd listened to their stories. Did it mean she'd gone hard and cold?

A gentle hand rested on her shoulder. She jerked to see Sister Donna's smiling face. "Lass, for everyone it is different. Some cry when it happens, some don't cry until after. You were a great help to me and your strength was a blessing for all these poor victims. They needed you to be strong for them, just as I did. Now, you can let go. 'Tis acceptable to be emotional about what you have seen." Sister Donna kissed her cheek. "Why not step outside a bit for some fresh air?"

Caralyn nodded and thanked the nun. She stepped into the passageway, and after hobbling a few steps, she found a stool and sat, resting her ankle for a bit, not ready to leave yet.

This experience had forced her to confront exactly what Captain Grant had prevented her from. She had verbally thanked him, but after tending to these ravaged victims, her words seemed pitifully inadequate. He had not only saved her, but her girls as well.

Aye, she had thanked him, too, but tremendous guilt had rocked her core after it happened. She felt guilty no longer. They had shared something beautiful. Unable to understand it at the time, she had allowed her guilt to overpower her. Now, she recognized their lovemaking for what it was—normal and special at the same time.

He had given her a taste of what could be. Most of her past experiences with sex were tainted, but every moment she'd shared with Robbie had been beautiful, loving, tender, full of caring, and so different than her life. He was everything she had been missing since her husband had passed. One night with a stranger had given her something naught else had ever given her—hope.

And while Robbie had saved her from the abuses of the Norseman, the toughest of realities had just hit her. The stories of many of the battered women sounded not unlike her life with Malcolm. They spoke of humiliation and degradation, something Malcolm made her feel every day. She was more convinced than ever that she had to do everything in her power to get away from him. Forever. All along, she had wanted to do this for her daughters, but now she grasped the truth—she needed to get away for herself.

Aye, she was ready to be untethered to Malcolm, the man who had stolen her life. She needed to be free, free of hate and humiliation, free to love and care for her daughters. For a man who cared for her and honored her.

Voices at the end of the corridor interrupted her thoughts. She glanced up in time to see Robbie enter from the staircase. One look at him and butterflies burst to flight in her belly. He was talking to Tomas and the lad who had brought Gwyneth into the sick room, but he stopped when he saw her. She swallowed, hoping he wouldn't turn away. His gaze caught hers and he smiled.

Robbie's smile had a way of heading straight to her heart. His boots echoed on the stone as he made his way straight toward her. She couldn't have moved if she'd wanted to, pinned to the spot by his handsome gaze.

"Caralyn, I'm glad you're still here." He stopped in front of her and introduced his friends. "You remember, Tomas?"

"Aye." She nodded, her hands folded in her lap in an attempt to hide the trembling.

"And this is Logan Ramsay of West Lothian. His brother is married to my sister."

Caralyn nodded. "Greetings, Lord Ramsay."

Logan laughed, "My lady, I am no lord, believe me."

She couldn't help but smile in response to his smirk and his crinkled eyes. "Captain Grant," she turned to Robbie. "My thanks for returning my friend, Gwyneth, to Glasgow. We had met at a Kirk not long ago. I was verra pleased to see her."

Robbie sighed. "I must apologize. Tomas and I had every intention of finding your daughters when we were sent on this assignment."

"Och, well, 'twas a verra important task."

Robbie whispered, "So is finding your daughters."

Caralyn closed her eyes and squeezed to attempt to stop tears from falling. She nodded but didn't speak.

"Caralyn, now there are three of us. Logan is one of the best trackers of all the Scots. We will find them. Having completed all we need to do for our commander, I promise to focus on saving your daughters."

"Aye, my thanks, Captain Grant."

"I am surprised Malcolm allows you to come to the priory."

"Aye, he allows me here or the Kirk with an escort when he's out of town. He knows I like to say my prayers when I can. However, he does not know that I am helping the sisters with their sick ones. Mother Mary has kept his men busy so I can be of assistance." Caralyn picked at her thumbnail, her eyes downcast.

"Have you learned anything else about where he may be keeping the wee lasses?" He grasped her hand in his, stopping her repetitive movement with his thumb.

"Nay, I have no idea." She brought her gaze up to his. "Find my daughters and I will go away with you. Anywhere." Shocked at what she had just said, she realized the statement reflected her deepest feelings. Sometimes, it was best not to think but to follow your heart. Robbie Grant was her heart.

Robbie nodded. "We'll find them."

CHAPTER FIFTEEN

Robbie stood outside the priory, staring up and down the street as if an idea would jump out at him. Logan and Tomas stood with him, all deep in thought.

"We need a plan," Robbie said.

"Aye. Do you have any idea where to start?" Logan asked.

"Nay. I don't know Glasgow any better than you or Tomas do. I suppose we'll start by questioning people, or spending time in the market talking to local vendors. What ideas do you two have?"

A fourth person joined the group. "I'll go with you," Gwyneth announced, hands on her hips as if daring someone to disagree.

Robbie asked, "Do you know Glasgow?"

Gwyneth nodded. "I know Glasgow and I'll find the lassies. I have a hunch as to where Murray would hide them within town."

"Then I welcome your assistance," Robbie said.

Logan stared at Robbie first, than at Gwyneth. "What? Are you daft, lass? You belong in on the pallet resting."

Gwyneth retorted, "Like hell I do. You think just because I'm a lass, I'm not strong enough to join you?"

Logan argued. "Nay, I think someone did a fine job of beating you, and you're bruised from head to toe."

Gwyneth didn't slow for a second. "That has naught to do with it. Those lassies need to be found, and I'm the one to find him. Or is your cock so small you fear women just because they might find out the size?"

Logan smiled as he grabbed his crotch. "Would you like to

see my cock and judge for yourself?"

Fire burned in Gwyneth's gaze. "Aye, bring it out, but let me grab my dagger first. I'll take one of your sacs as a trophy. The last one I cut off, I flung into the firth."

Dead silence hung in the air. Robbie was not about to interrupt their waiting game of who would speak first. Gwyneth was going with them, there was no doubt in his mind of that since they needed her expertise, but the two needed to come to terms with each other if they were all to work together as a team. Plus, he hadn't been this entertained in a very long time.

After a long moment, Logan whispered, "I don't doubt your strength on a good day, lass. But the Norse knocked the wind out of you. I can see the fine tremor in your hand. The only thing you need is rest."

Gwyneth took a step closer to Logan. "Fortunately, what you say doesn't mean anything to me. I do as I please, not what some man orders me to do."

Robbie held his hands up. "Och, lass. No one is trying to order you. You came to us, remember?"

"Aye," she said, her gaze never leaving Logan's. "And I'm going with you."

Logan's hands settled on his hips as he continued to meet her stare. "Give me one good reason why we should take you with us. I see you as a detriment to our mission. You'll be slow and we'll have to cater to your needs."

Gwyneth moved her face a few inches closer to Logan's. "I won't be slow, and you won't have to cater to my needs."

Still staring into Gwyneth's eyes, Logan said to Robbie, "Hmmph. Did you hear a reason for us to take her, Grant? Because I surely did not."

Gwyneth crossed her arms in front of her. "Because the lassies know me. They'll never go with you. And I don't think any of you wish to deal with a two-year-old's rags once you find them."

Robbie knew that reasoning wouldn't work on Logan. He had cared for his niece and nephew through rags and vomit.

Logan stepped back and peered at Tomas and Robbie, a strange look on his face. He finally dropped his hands from his hips and stalked away. "Guess she goes with us. Saddle up and let's move."

Robbie quirked his brow at Tomas, but then shrugged his shoulders in agreement. "Let's go before sundown."

Gwyneth smiled and jumped on Logan's horse.

Logan growled, "Lass, find your own horse."

"I did." She smiled and took off down the path.

Logan mounted Tomas's horse in a flash and headed down the path after her. When he was close enough, he grabbed the reins, winked at Gwyneth and said, "You better hang on." He whistled and his horse came to a screeching halt. Gwyneth almost flew off the front, though she somehow managed to hang on.

Gwyneth yelled. "Och, stop! I'll get off. Have your foolish horse."

Logan tossed his reins to Tomas who had come up on his other side with Robbie. Then dismounting Tomas's horse, he climbed up behind Gwyneth in the saddle.

Gwyneth squealed and swung at him. "Don't touch me, you brute."

Logan chuckled and took off, whispering just loud enough for Robbie to hear, "Should have thought of that before you stole my horse. Now you ride with me." He held her back against him in a death grip while he yelled over his shoulder. "Move on, Grant."

Robbie smiled. Gwyneth would have her hands full with Logan Ramsay. She'd chosen the wrong one to goad.

CHAPTER SIXTEEN

Robbie motioned to Gwyneth and Logan to take the lead. After they rode for a bit, they found themselves in an area that looked a bit suspicious and Gwyneth signaled for the group to stop and investigate. He dismounted near several rows of run-down cottages. The odor of sewage was ripe and piles of waste sat in front of every hut as if the owners cared naught about their homes. A creek ran behind the rows, probably their only source of water. Given the amount of sewage nearby, it was a wonder they still lived.

He glanced at Logan, who slid off his horse, too, pulling Gwyneth behind him. As soon as her feet hit the ground, she swung and clobbered Logan in the side of his head with her fist. Logan spun her around in a matter of seconds and held her in a vise grip in front of him. Gwyneth struggled to free herself, but Robbie knew she didn't stand a chance. Logan was big and broad-shouldered, with a body lined with solid muscle. Robbie trusted him to do the right thing, so he and Tomas stood aside to let them settle their differences.

"Leave me be, you rutting bull." Gwyneth struggled to maintain any sense of composure.

Logan squeezed her back against his chest and spoke into her ear. "Now, do I have complete control of you, lass?"

"Aye, leave off, you surly brute!" She fought until her face was beet red, spitting and kicking at anything she could reach.

"Remember that. I have complete control over you. You have no power over me without your weapons. Agreed?"

"Aye," she snarled.

"Then know this. I will never hurt you or force you. If I

wanted to, I could throw you down on that ground and rut all I wanted. But I won't. Do you know why?"

The only sound from Gwyneth was a low growl as she fought to free herself from Logan's grip.

"Verra well, I'll tell you though you are not inclined to listen, please hear me and heed me."

Gwyneth managed one kick to his shin as she continued to squirm.

"Lass, I'll never hurt you. I don't hurt women. 'Tis not in me, nor is it in my friends. You need to accept that. There are two kinds of men, those who hit lasses and those who don't. 'Tis unfortunate the only men you have met are rutting snipes, but I'm not one. I like my lasses willing and I never hit." He continued his soft whispers until she seemed less agitated.

"But I will protect myself. Can you promise not to hit me or my friends? I won't let you go until you agree."

She calmed but didn't agree.

Logan continued. "I'm here to save the wee lassies. I have a niece named Lily whom I adore. She is a bit older than Gracie, and I would kill any man who dared to hurt her. So you need to decide. Will you join us to help save the lassies or will you continue to try to make me pay for whatever atrocities you have been forced to endure which will slow down our rescue considerably?"

A tear slid down her cheek before she nodded.

"I am going to let you go, and I swear on the saints above, if you swing at me, I will tie you to that tree while we search for the lassies. We did not bring you along for you to attack us." Logan relaxed his arms and she shoved away from him.

Gwyneth swallowed three times before she spoke.

"Think hard, Gwyneth. I'll help him tie you to that tree if need be. I am here for Ashlyn and Gracie. Are you?" Robbie waited for her answer as he arranged his weapons.

"Aye. Tell me what to do. I can kill Logan while he sleeps tonight." She had her hands clasped behind her back as if she didn't trust herself.

"Is this the most likely area, Gwyneth?" Robbie asked.

"Aye, some are just poor, but many are questionable."

Robbie noticed she refused to look at Logan.

"Any particular row?" Tomas asked.

"Nay, they could be anywhere. We need to look closer."

Robbie noticed Gwyneth fought to maintain control, so he made his decision. He needed to separate Logan from her. "I want each of you to search around both rows of cottages to see if you see any sign of weans. Mayhap we'll hear voices or crying, anything. 'Tis an area with many cottages because of the creek. If you look in that direction, I think you'll find another row around the bend in the creek. Meet back here in the next hour." He assigned each person a row to search and they separated, each holding the reins of their horse as they advanced.

Robbie canvassed the area he had chosen but found nothing. He listened intently, but heard naught but arguments and snores. Darkness was almost upon them. He stared at the sky, thinking about Ashlyn and Gracie. Gracie never spoke and he had never heard her cry, unfortunately. Her elder sister clung to her, always taking on the role of guardian. Neither were noisy. How would they ever discover her whereabouts?

He headed back down the path, hoping someone else had experienced more success than he had, when he noticed Gwyneth running straight at him.

"What is it, Gwyneth?"

She paused to catch her breath. "Rags," she panted.

"What?" Robbie couldn't understand what in hellfire she was talking about.

"Raggies. A wean's rags." She pointed to a cottage. "A whole pile of urine drenched rags are in front of that hut."

Robbie made his bird call, and Tomas and Logan rushed to his side. "I think we may have them, if Gwyneth is correct." He pointed to the hut in question. "Gwyneth, you go to the door to see if the lasses are there and how many guards are watching them. Ask for the nearest pub and act as if you are lost. I promise to guard you while Tomas and Logan go around back."

Gwyneth stumbled up the front path, making a ruckus while Robbie and the others got in place.

A slim woman opened the door, a wee bairn on each hip. Gwyneth stood there staring, realizing they had chosen the wrong house. Her gaze searched the inside, but there were no other weans in sight. "Mistress, I seem to have made a mistake. Are there any other bairns in the area? Two wee lassies? I came to visit my friend."

The woman shook her head and started to close the door, then paused. "Aye, I did see two bairns outside taking care of their needs yesterday. One was brown-haired and the other blonde. They be at the end of the path." Her finger pointed down toward the creek.

"My thanks." Gwyneth nodded. As soon as the door closed, she turned to Robbie and he whistled for his friends to join them.

When Logan and Tomas returned, Tomas said, "Nay? Wrong place?"

Robbie said, "Aye, but she told us the cottage we need. Same plan, but down the path."

They made their way to the suspected cottage and set up the same scene. Robbie hoped this didn't play out through ten cottages before they found the girls. Gwyneth stumbled up the path again so Logan and Tomas could make it around back. The front door swung open, and an overweight dolt opened the door.

"Fingal, look what I found." He reached for Gwyneth. "A plaything. We have something to entertain us now."

Robbie could see it took all Gwyneth's control to allow the man to touch her and pull her inside. He crept up to the door to take a look. Just as he made it to the entrance, he heard a crashing sound from the back. Jumping inside the doorway, he saw the two girls huddled in the corner, Ashlyn's arms wrapped tight around Gracie. He held his hand up to Ashlyn to make sure they stayed out of the way.

The big lout had his arm around Gwyneth and a knife at her throat. Fingal reached for the girls, but Tomas twirled him around and backed him up against the wall with his sword at his throat.

Robbie spoke, "Let her go, and my friend will let your comrade go." He didn't see anyone else inside. There was just the two of them.

The big lout reeked of fear. "Nay, let Fingal go and we'll

leave. You can have the lassies. Let him go or I'll cut her throat."

Logan strode further into the room and stood to the side of Gwyneth and the dolt, still a distance away so as not to cause the fool to lose control. Robbie could tell his brother-in-law was positioning himself for a good strike.

"One more step and I'll kill her. Let us go and you can have all three bitches."

"That would be impossible." A smirk crossed Logan's face. "That's my lass you have your hands on."

Fingal said, "We don't want any trouble. You can have her. Let us go."

"Can't do it," Logan said.

"Why not?" His gaze darted back and forth between Logan and Tomas, whose sword was still positioned at his comrade's throat.

"Because you touched my lass and no one touches her." Logan flung his knife and it landed in his side between his ribs. A strange bubbling sound rose from the man's lips as he dropped his knife and stared at Logan, his eyes full of shock, then at the knife in his side. He crumpled to the ground.

Fingal screamed, "You killed my brother." He pulled his own knife and tried to stab Tomas, but Robbie's knife landed in his body just as Tomas pierced his neck with the sword.

Fingal fell to the ground, dead.

CHAPTER SEVENTEEN

Gwyneth tore over to the two lassies in the corner.

Ashlyn yelled, "Gwyneth!" before jumping into her arms.

But when Gwyneth leaned down to grab Gracie, too, the wee one ran right past her, straight into Robbie's arms. He picked her up, and she wrapped her arms around his neck and tucked her head down onto his shoulder.

Gwyneth's nose wrinkled and Ashlyn burst into tears. "We smell, Gwyneth. Other than changing Gracie's raggies once a day, they wouldn't allow us to clean ourselves. We are dirty. Mama would be so upset."

Robbie said, "We don't have time to clean you now, Ashlyn. We must leave."

Logan passed a jug to Tomas and said, "Grab some water from the creek."

"What in hellfire are you doing, Ramsay?" Robbie barked from over Gracie's head.

"My guess is you are sending them north, aye? To your clan?"

"Aye. So how does that change the situation?"

"Weans don't like to be dirty and we have a long trip ahead of us. The further we travel, the colder it will be for them. 'Tis better to clean them now, near the creek."

Robbie finally agreed and set Gracie down as Tomas raced off to get the water. If Logan wanted to take charge of this, then he would grant him his wish. "We need to clean you before we go," Robbie told the wee lassie. "Then I promise to take you both away from here."

A few moments later, Tomas came in with the water.

Robbie, Gwyneth, and Tomas all stared at the ewer, unsure of what to do next. Tomas finally set it on the floor, then he and Robbie dragged the two bodies out of the way, covering them up.

As they did their unseemly work, Logan grabbed a big basin and dumped the water into it. When the two men finished their task, he handed the other adults bowls and buckets and said, "More."

Robbie decided it was the best job for him. He knew nothing about washing bairns, and judging from the look of Tomas and Gwyneth, they were equally ignorant.

By the time they returned, Logan had ripped strips of linen from Ashlyn's shift and had both girls scrubbing their faces with the sliver of soap he had always carried. He dumped the new buckets of cool water into the basin, took Gracie's gown and rag off, picked her up under her arms, and said, "Ready, lass?" Gracie nodded and Logan dipped her bottom into the basin and swirled her around in it. She yelped and giggled while they all stared in disbelief. Robbie had never seen the lass even smile. Now she was giggling with Logan?

He took her out and handed her to Gwyneth with a linen strip. "Dry her." Then he turned his back, held his plaid out to the side, and said to Ashlyn, "There's another basin of fresh water. Go ahead and do what you need to, lass. We won't watch. Gwyneth can help if you need."

As they waited for Ashlyn, Logan's companions stared at him in disbelief. "What?"

Robbie laughed. "You have talents even I didn't expect, Ramsay."

"I told you I have a niece, but I also have a nephew, and both were sickly with no mother. I learned how to care for them. 'Tis not so difficult."

As soon as Ashlyn finished, they headed out to the horses. Ashlyn rode with Tomas and Gracie with Robbie. They headed north and outside of town. As soon as they found a clearing, Robbie stopped and they gathered a group of logs for a fire.

"Hellfire, Grant. I thought we'd go back to the priory to find Caralyn," Gwyneth said.

"Nay, 'tis after dark and she'll be with Murray by now. He

still controls her." He pulled both girls over to him and spoke directly to them. "Lassies, I know you wish to see your mama, but 'twould not be safe right now."

Ashlyn nodded but her shoulders slumped.

"Can you get her away from Malcolm, Captain Grant?" she asked in a small voice. "We don't like him."

Two wee faces stared up at him and his heart broke. He knew they wouldn't be happy about his decision, but Robbie had guessed his wishes correctly. He'd decided the best way forward was to send them to the Highlands. "That is exactly what I plan to do, Ashlyn, but I need to make sure you two are safe first so he can't come and steal you away again. Your mama is forced to do what he wants when he holds you away from her. Do you understand?"

Ashlyn nodded. "I think so. I always hear him tell mama he will hurt us, and he did paddle us both once while mama screamed and cried. She told him she would do whatever he wanted if he would stop hurting us. I don't want to go back with him ever again. Where will you hide us?"

"I am going to send you to a wonderful place, but it will take a while for you to get there so I need you both to be strong. And you won't see your mama for a wee bit, but everyone in this place will love you both and take care of you, and I promise we'll join you soon. There will be other weans for you to play with, but most of all, I know you'll be safe."

"Where is that?" Ashlyn stared at him, wide-eyed. "We have never played with other weans."

"I am sending you to my clan. You're going into the Highlands to the Grant keep, a big castle with lots of nice people to love and care for you."

"Will Mama come, too?"

"Aye, as soon as I rescue your mama, I'll bring her to you."

"Can we not wait for you?" Ashlyn whispered.

"Nay, Malcolm will try to find you again. I need to get you as far away from here as possible. I'm sorry, lass, but 'tis the only way."

Ashlyn pondered what he'd said, then nodded. She grabbed Gracie's hand. "As long as we go together."

"Aye, you'll go together."

"How will we get there?" She chewed her lip as she glanced at the group around her.

"Logan and Gwyneth will take you. Tomas and I will find your mama." Robbie knew he was still acting like the Captain of the Grant warriors by speaking before asking them, but he was willing to take a gamble.

Gwyneth made a strangling sound in her throat.

Ashlyn peered up at her. "Gwyneth, you'll go with us? Please?"

Gwyneth nodded, but she gave Robbie a hard look that he couldn't ignore.

"Tomas, take the girls and find them some oatcakes. Lassies? You're hungry, are you not?" Both nodded and followed Tomas over to the horses.

As soon as they left, Gwyneth got right up in his face, not stopping until she was no more than an inch from his nose. "You can't mean it. I will not travel with that lout."

"Gwyneth, I am trying to do what is the best for the lassies. I need people I trust to travel with them through the Highlands, which isn't going to be an easy trip this time of the year. I have four other guards near Glasgow I'll send with you as protection."

"Fine, then send Tomas with us. Logan can stay here."

Logan stood behind her, his arms crossed over his chest and a smirk on his face.

"Nay, Logan knows the Highlands the best of anyone I know, and he's the foremost tracker, too. I would feel better if he was with you. He won't just lead the group, but also track ahead and make sure no one is in the area. Traveling with two bairns is too much of a risk. There are wild boars and wolves. You will protect the lasses while Logan leads, tracks, and kills when necessary."

"But I have never been to the Highlands. I don't want to go that far north. 'Tis freezing up there." She swung her arms wide as she rambled.

"Didn't you tell me you are good with a bow and arrow?" Robbie asked.

"Aye, I am, but..."

"Then you can help find food, too. See how thin Ashlyn is?

Surely they haven't been fed much, and Ashlyn gives Gracie her share of whatever food they're given. I need you to watch over them both. 'Twill not be an easy journey, and the girls need you. And I think Caralyn will feel better if she knows you're with them. I'm asking you to put your problems with Logan aside for the lassies. Once there, you can do whatever you like, but I am sure Caralyn would appreciate it if you wait until she arrives before you take your leave, and I think the girls will feel safer with you around."

Gwyneth stared at Robbie, then at Logan, her hands on her hips.

"Lass, I think you might like the Highlands. 'Tis beautiful land, and you may stay as long as you like at the Grant clan. We'll reward you when I arrive. Take a trip to our armory; find new weapons for your arsenal. I'll pay you in wool garments for the winter. Whatever your needs, let me know."

Logan sighed, the smirk leaving his face. "Lass, I have pledged it before, and I'll do so again—you have my word of honor on the Ramsay clan that I won't touch you unless you ask. I will control my banter for the girls' sake. I think Ashlyn will feel more comfortable riding with you."

He strode over to his horse and pulled out one of his plaids. "Here, you can wear this when you get cold, and it will be cold, especially at night."

She stared at Logan, then walked over to take the plaid he offered, throwing it over her shoulders and tying it in a tangled mess around her waist. "Lord, give me strength. Grant, I need to borrow your horse before we go to alert my family of my plans." She strode into the trees before she yelled over her shoulder. "I'll need my own horse, and I'm not your lass, Ramsay."

Logan grinned and said to Robbie, so she couldn't hear him, "You are now with my plaid on you."

Tomas walked into the clearing with the two girls in tow, a stunned expression on his face. "Did I just see Gwyneth with your plaid on, Ramsay?"

"Aye, but she apparently doesn't know what it means, so be quiet about it. 'Twill be a cold ride and you know it." Logan said, giving him a wink. He stooped down to pick up wee

Gracie, who put up no fuss.

Robbie gave Tomas one more job to do before he sent Logan and Gwyneth to the Highlands. "I don't want to wait long, Tomas. Find some provisions and the guards fast and get back. We probably only have a couple of hours until Murray discovers the girls missing. He may send guards out right away."

Logan said, "Don't worry. We'll lose them if they do."

After Tomas left, Robbie smirked at Logan. "I doubt you gave Gwyneth your plaid just to protect her from the cold. Quade will love to hear this."

"Aye, I meant what I said in the cottage. She's mine and no one touches her. The plaid will guarantee that your guards know their bounds." Then he snickered. "Just don't inform her of its meaning. I don't understand why she doesn't know, but mayhap they don't do this in the Lowlands to the west of Glasgow. And I'll tell my brother when he needs to know."

Two hours later, the group was saddled and ready to go, guards included. Right before Gwyneth was about to mount, a somber faced Gracie ran over to Robbie and held her arms up to him. Robbie picked her up and she whispered in his ear. "Pweez save my mama." She cradled his face in her wee hands and gave him a kiss before hopping down and running back to Gwyneth.

Those four words were the first words he had ever heard Gracie utter.

CHAPTER EIGHTEEN

The next day, Caralyn was allowed to go to the priory again. She had come to help Sister Donna with more new arrivals, including one that was carrying, and suddenly found herself part way through the delivery of a new bairn. Fortunately, Caralyn hadn't had much time to think, elsewise she would have been too scared to assist. Just as well, because she had been disappointed to see that Gwyneth had left.

After cleaning and drying her hands, she returned to Sister Donna's side and took the newborn bairn in her arms. She had cleaned him up while the sister cleaned up the mother. Now she could only stare at the baby in wonder.

"May I hold him?" the new mother asked.

"Of course," Caralyn answered. She handed the wean over to his mama. How selfish of her to want to hold the lad. He was just so perfect. Caralyn had gotten there right before his dark shock of hair emerged from his mama, but a few pushes before he'd entered the world. She had helped Sister Donna tie off the cord, and watched in wonder as the new mother delivered the part that follows birth. Thrilled with her assigned task, she'd been more than happy to clean up the new lad as he continued to announce his presence to the world.

It was time to take her leave after the wondrous experience. She excused herself from Sister Donna, knowing that Malcolm would be home shortly. She didn't want to get there after he did.

Once back in Malcolm's keep, she crept up the steps to her chamber quietly, still savoring the magic and wonder of new life. The slamming of the door into the great hall was a shock to her system, and she needed to grab onto the railing to keep from tumbling down the stairs. When she glanced over her shoulder, Malcolm stood at the base of the stairs.

"Where are they?" he sneered.

A growing fear crept up her spine. "What? Who? What are you talking about, Malcolm?"

He followed her up the steps and pushed her the rest of the way up and through the door to her chamber. He twisted her arm behind her back. "Your daughters have disappeared and two of my best men are dead. Who did it?" He tightened his grip on her arm until each finger dug into her flesh.

"What are you talking about? My daughters? You have lost my bairns? Och, saints above, help me! Where are my lassies?"

"Do not lie to me, bitch. You know where they are." He leered at Caralyn, his fury so potent she could feel the force of it.

"Malcolm, I don't know where they are. Did you check everywhere? Gracie likes to hide. Mayhap they were hiding."

He jerked her tighter to him. "They are *not* hiding! I said my men were dead. One took a knife to the throat and the other took a knife in the ribs. The air was driven out of both of them. This is all your fault! That captain...what was his name? He wants you, I could tell."

"Captain Grant? Why would he steal two innocent lassies? Please, Malcolm. Let me go. You are hurting me."

"And just in case you have any foolish ideas, know that I'll never let you go. I'll follow you to the end of the earth and drag you back here to my side. You are mine and no savage Highlander frightens me. Wherever you go, I'll follow. And when I do find you, I will beat you until you are in so much pain, you can't move for three moons."

Malcolm tossed her on the bed before turning in place and heading back out the door. He closed the door and locked her in. "You will go nowhere. Do you hear me? Nowhere."

Caralyn forced three deep breaths to slow the blood shooting through her body in fear. She had never seen Malcolm this way. He had been angry before, but now he was crazed. It had to be Robbie. Aye, Malcolm knew who had taken her lassies. Now she was imprisoned.

Get them to safety, Robbie. Please protect them. She had to believe that the right thing had finally happened. Her girls were going to be safe.

Which meant Robbie would be coming for her soon.

***

In the middle of the next night, she heard a distant scratching against stone. She jumped out of bed, thankful Malcolm was still out, and rushed to the window, her heart beating fast in her chest as she pulled the furs back to see who was outside. She sighed as she peeked down the side of the stone wall.

Captain Robbie Grant was scaling the side of the castle again. She quickly changed her night rail to a gown and donned warm wool socks and boots. She always had a small sack with a few essentials at the ready, so she grabbed it and stood next to the window, her hands twisting in her skirts. Could this be happening? Would she finally be free of Malcolm?

Moments later, Robbie's hand pushed through the fur and his head popped into the room as he hung on to the ledge. "Are you ready, lass?"

Caralyn ran to the window. "Do you have my daughters?"

"Aye, I do. They're away from the brutes. I'm here to take you to them."

She couldn't stop herself. She cupped Robbie's face and kissed him quickly on the lips. "Thank you." When she lifted her lips, her gaze caught his and she blushed.

"I thank you, lass, but if you kiss me any more than that, you'll force me to lose my footing and fall."

Her hand flew to her mouth to cover a gasp. "Och, I'm so sorry."

Robbie grinned. "I'm not. You know I love the taste of you, lass, but don't make me lose my mind just yet."

She giggled and he jumped inside the room. Before she knew it, he had hoisted her into his arms and stepped back onto the ledge. "Ready, lass? Now hang on to my waist."

Caralyn nodded her head and gripped him tight. Her head fell against his chest and she tried to hide her sigh of happiness. Robbie was so strong and kind, everything she had ever wanted in a man. He smelled of the woods and pine, as well as the mint leaves he often chewed. His power should be enough to scare any man away. Safe, she just felt safe in his arms.

If ever she wanted a man, he would be the one.

Her mother's voice interrupted her thoughts. *I told you, a man like this would never stay interested in you. He would never marry you, especially since he knows your secret.*

She closed her eyes to will her mother away. *Please, Mama. Don't I deserve happiness, too?*

They landed with a soft thud and Robbie set her down carefully before leading her to his horse. She noticed Tomas wasn't far away, and there were another two warriors further down the path.

She settled in front of Robbie on his horse and leaned into him, allowing the intimacy of the contact to invade her senses. They rode for miles. The further they went, the more the darkness of the night against the bright moon increased her anxiety. Fear that they were being followed consumed her, and she kept thinking she heard other horses behind them. Several hours later, she couldn't hold back any longer.

"Stop. Please stop." She turned to glance at Robbie. "I need to stop for a moment."

Robbie found a small clearing and signaled to his men to stop.

"Lass, if you have to take care of your needs, just say so." He helped her down from her horse and motioned for his men to inspect the area for safety.

"Nay, I mean, aye. Please, wait. My girls. Where are my daughters?" She needed to know more; she couldn't stand the suspense a moment longer.

"Och, lass. We have your lassies. I sent them on ahead a couple of nights ago." He brushed a stray hair back from her forehead.

Caralyn held her face in her hands. "Och, thank the saints above, and thanks to you and your men, Captain Grant. They are unhurt?"

"Aye, they were dirty and hungry, but no harm had been done to them."

"And you fed them?" She knew it was a ridiculous question. Of course, he would have fed them, but she still had to know.

Robbie smiled. "Aye, of course. We fed them, and Logan and Gwyneth cleaned them up before we left."

"Logan washed my girls and they accepted that?" She couldn't believe her ears. Wee Gracie hated strange men.

"Aye, not many of us have much experience there. Ashlyn was upset they hadn't been allowed to bathe. Logan has a niece about Gracie's age. He took care of Gracie and Ashlyn took care of herself."

She sighed. "Thanks to you, again. Where did you take them?"

"Caralyn, relax. The lassies are fine, but 'twill be a time before we reach them."

For some reason, she didn't trust the expression on Robbie's face. He was anxious, but she couldn't decide why. "What do you mean? Where are they?" She wrung her hands, awaiting his answer.

Robbie grasped her hands in his, rubbing them to warm them in the cool night air. "I sent them to the only place I could ensure their safety—my home, Clan Grant."

"You don't mean the Highlands. Do you?" Her eyes widened as she spoke.

"Aye, lass. I sent them to my home in the Highlands."

Saints above, she would faint for sure. Her daughters were a long way away from her now. "What? With who? Who has my bairns? Och, saints above, my bairns will never make it through the Highlands. How could you do such a thing? They are but wee lassies." She jerked her hands from his and paced in a circle, her hands resting on her hips.

"Caralyn, they are with Logan Ramsay and Gwyneth and four of my warriors. I promise you they will get them there safely."

"How could you send my girls with five strange men?" The pitch of her voice had almost reached a scream. Her head pounded as all her fears raced through her mind.

Robbie strode over and grasped her by the shoulders. "Calm yourself and stop your screaming. We don't need to draw attention to ourselves."

Caralyn swiped at her mouth, recognizing the truth in his words. But she still feared for her girls—so far away, and with strangers. She held her head in her hands as the tears started. "Nay, nay."

Robbie gave her a puzzled look. "Lass, I promise you, naught bad will come to your lassies. I would trust those men with my life. Don't you trust Gwyneth?"

"Aye, I trust Gwyneth. But they have rarely been away from me. Only because of Malcolm, and he sent them with two bad men. Now they go with others." She reached for Robbie's arm. "I just worry about them. Did they seem accepting of this?"

Robbie wrapped his arms around her. "Caralyn, they are Highlanders. They live and breathe honor. The girls were fine with them. And Gracie was comfortable with Logan, believe it or not. The important thing is they are safe."

Caralyn grasped his wool tunic and sobbed into his chest. He was right, she knew it. She just couldn't handle being away from her girls any longer. She hadn't seen them in so long, and now it would be even longer. She had thought to see them in a day or so once Robbie had rescued her.

He held her close and ran his fingers through her hair, massaging her neck. "They are unhurt. Please listen to me before you yell anymore."

His soft voice soothed her and she clung to him, allowing his voice to lull her chaotic emotions.

"I sent them to the Highlands because Malcolm will follow us. I don't think he'll let you go easily. He'll be in pursuit as fast as he can gather a group of fighters. I wanted your girls to be safe. Logan is the best tracker and one of the best swordsmen of all the Scots. Gwyneth is talented with a bow and arrow, as are two of the other men. Don't you agree?"

"Aye, you're right." His hand had fallen down to her back and was caressing her softly there, his touch easing the tight muscles. Finally relaxing, she told herself to let him take over, to let this man take care of her and her bairns. Mayhap she could let him worry for a day so she could rest, hard as it was since she had been relying on herself for so long.

"As we ride, I'll tell you all about Clan Grant. Believe me, the lassies will love being there, and my sisters and my brother's wife will take good care of your daughters."

"They will?" her voice barely a whisper. She thought back

to all she knew about Robbie Grant—the man who had given her hope for the first time in years, like a blossom finally blooming within her, the man who had saved her and her girls from a life in hell. He had done all this, and she had screamed at him.

"I'll tell you two more things to settle your mind, and then we must go. Alex's wife, Maddie, was mistreated. Trust me when I say that she will not allow anything bad to happen to your girls. And second, Logan is uncle to two weans who were so sickly that he was forced to care for them at times. His brother said he cared for them better than any woman could. Logan loves wee ones. You can trust him."

She nodded her head lazily, but didn't let go of him.

"We will have a difficult enough journey with just the four of us. I gave Logan and Gwyneth a lead of two days to make sure they'd get the lassies to safety in time. We might have to deal with Malcolm, but they won't." Robbie pulled back and lifted her chin with his fingers. "Can we go so we can stay well ahead of Malcolm? I worry about you, as well."

Caralyn nodded and then pointed to the bushes. Robbie leaned down and kissed her lips, a soft, tender kiss that melted her heart. Had she ever been kissed by a man without intimacy on his mind? He gave her a light push toward the bushes as he walked in the opposite direction.

A few minutes later, she stepped out of the bushes into his waiting arms, giving herself up to him, allowing him to take care of her. He settled her in front of him on the horse and galloped into the distance with the others following.

She was asleep in seconds.

CHAPTER NINETEEN

Robbie quite liked the feel of Caralyn in front of him on his horse. Her curves fit perfectly in his arms. Everything had worked according to plan so far, and he trusted that Logan and the others would traverse the Highlands without difficulty and get the lassies safely to his clan.

What worried him was Malcolm.

He could tell by the hard glint in the man's eyes that he didn't give up easily. Everything was a competition to him, and he would follow Caralyn. His musings were interrupted when she repositioned herself in the saddle in front of him. Saints above, but every time she moved her bum, his shaft snapped to attention. He knew she was no innocent and could feel him against her, but she ignored it. Just as well. There was naught they could do while on horseback.

A few hours later, she awoke abruptly, grabbing his arm as if to make sure he was still there. He squeezed her lightly, and she instantly relaxed. After a moment of silence, she tipped her head back over her shoulder at him. "Tell me about your clan."

He smiled and nodded. "Aye, my brother, Alex, is laird and is married to Maddie. They have two lads about the same age as Gracie and a wee lass named Kyla. My other brother, Brodie, is younger than I am, but he is recently married and his wife, Celestina, is tied up in the Scottish and Norwegian politics. He lost her, then found her again, but that's a long story.

"My sister, Brenna, is a healer and usually lives in West Lothian with her husband, Quade Ramsay, but they are presently at the Grant keep in the north."

"Is he related to Logan?"

"Aye, Quade is Logan's brother and laird of the Ramsay clan, but many of his clan not old enough to fight are currently in residence at Clan Grant to be certain they were far away from the battle scenes. Quade and his men were called to fight, as were many clans, because the king had no idea how many Norse would be here. He sent Logan and his other brother, Micheil, in his stead and stayed back to protect his family. Brenna convinced him to head north to her home."

"Is it Brenna and Quade's bairns that are sickly?"

"Nay, Quade has two bairns by his first wife. They were verra sick, but Brenna has helped them. Now, they are well and hearty. They must be careful with what they eat. 'Twas before Brenna treated them that Logan helped take care of them. One of the other traits Logan also is known for is wandering off into the wilderness, and Quade believes 'tis the only way he could handle his niece and nephew's illness. He loves them both something fierce."

"How old are they?"

"Torrian would be about nine or ten summers and Lily around four. Brenna and Quade just had a daughter they christened Bethia. So the five of them are at Clan Grant for safety and because Alex asked Brenna to help any of the Grant warriors injured in the war. So you see, there will be many bairns for your two lassies to play with."

Caralyn rubbed her gloved hand over his big hand, which was wrapped around her waist. "Is there enough room for all of them?"

"Och, the Grant keep is huge. Our great hall handles everyone in the winter. My brother had another kitchen built just off the back of the hall with a covered walkway to protect the women from the snow. They needed more space to handle all the food. He feeds everyone he can in the winter. 'Tis cold up there and we get snowed in many times. But the keep has three stories full of chambers, and the wee girls all sleep together. I also have a younger sister, Jennie, and she is at the age to watch over the bairns, though not old enough to marry yet. Quade has a younger sister, Avelina, who is close to Jennie's age, and the two are oft in charge of the wee ones."

"Your brother and his wife must be verra busy."

"They are, but I promise they will welcome you and your weans with open arms. We all pitch in to help wherever we are needed. The warriors work in the lists, aye, but we also hunt and chop wood. The lasses do their needlework and make woolen socks and plaids to keep us warm. Even though the soil is not the best in the Highlands, we have been more than productive with our fields. We grow some oats, have an orchard of apple and pear trees and many gardens of grain. Our cook makes the best pastries. Ask my sister Jennie. She is in love with sweets."

"Robbie?"

"Aye?" He rubbed her arm and nuzzled her hair.

"I don't think we'll fit in."

"Och, do not be daft. Of course, you will. We even have dogs in the great hall, though Maddie and Brenna restrict them to certain areas only. But Jennie has three and Torrian has a big deerhound that helped him learn to walk again after his illness. The lassies will love the dogs."

"But what can we do to help out? I have no skills." She peered over her shoulder to gauge his reaction to her statement. "I don't know how to cook or sew."

"My sisters will teach you. Maddie does beautiful drawings as well, and is a wonderful storyteller. The bairns all love her."

Robbie patted her arm, but he could tell she didn't quite believe him. "Why don't you rest your eyes a bit? In a couple of hours, we'll stop again, but there is no reason for you to stay awake. I think you're tired."

She tucked her head under his chin, but didn't have much to say. He knew she was still awake, staring ahead with her eyes open, and he couldn't help but wonder what her thoughts were. He knew why she was concerned. Her life couldn't have been very normal with Malcolm in it, and she worried about how she'd adjust. Surely she would, though, with Malcolm gone.

He had to ask himself what exactly he wanted from this relationship. Something inside him was still unsure. Their one night of lovemaking had been wonderful. She had two daughters, but that didn't bother him. At nine and twenty summers, he was too old to try to find a virginal bride. Did he want her to stay at Clan Grant? His definite answer to that question was aye. But did he want her enough to consider marrying her?

He had often been jealous of what Maddie and Alex shared. When Brodie had told him he had found someone, it had taken him completely by surprise. Robbie was a year older than Brodie, so he had always expected to marry first. But Robbie hadn't found anyone yet, and his priority had been as Captain of the Highland warriors. He could be needed again, and what would he do with a wife if that happened?

He just didn't know.

***

A few hours later, they stopped just before dawn. Robbie and Tomas searched for food while Angus and Rory, two of his warriors, searched the area. Caralyn headed off into the bushes to take care of her needs.

When Robbie returned to the area where they'd left their horses, he froze. He had only left her for a moment, but that was all it had taken.

Malcolm stood in the clearing, his back against a tree with his arm around Caralyn and a knife pressed to her throat. An armed man stood on either side of him. "You don't take verra good care of your hostage, Grant. Wandering off while she tends to her needs in the bushes. It gave me the perfect opportunity to grab her. I knew you would fail."

Robbie stepped closer. "Let her go, Murray. She doesn't want you."

Malcolm grinned. "Och, but I want her. And I want her lassies, too. They'll be valuable property to me soon. Where are they?"

"The lassies are far, far from here. You'll never catch them. They are two days ahead of us."

"Then I guess we shall follow. They are my property."

"Take your hands off the lass, Murray. If you don't do as I ask, I'll drive my sword through your throat."

"Och, by the love-sick look in your eyes, Grant, I am guessing my little Cat never told you much about herself, did she?"

Robbie didn't react to the words, but glanced at Caralyn's

face for a second, just long enough for time to see the blush of embarrassment rush across her features. What could the blackguard mean?

"I know all I need to know about Caralyn." Robbie held a death grip on his sword.

"Is that true? Did she tell you what she does for me? Did she tell you how she has been my whore?"

Murray was trying to get in his head, and Robbie knew he had to ignore him. Still he glanced at Caralyn to see if Murray's words were true. She averted her eyes. *No matter, deal with the issue as your brother has taught you. This man is no threat to the Grants, just a daft fool who believes he holds the power.*

"Didn't she tell you she was the whore of South Ayr for a time?"

Robbie tried the best he could to mask the look of shock on his face, but he failed.

Malcolm chortled. "She didn't, did she?" He wrenched her hair and pulled her face back so she was forced to look Robbie in the eye. "You haven't told him that you worked on your back? That you did whatever I wanted with whomever I wanted?"

Robbie's vision tunneled. He wanted to choke the man with his bare hands. He wanted to cut out his insides and stuff them in his mouth. How could he be so vile in front of her? And was it true? Had she been a whore? Nay, he quelled such thoughts. Without a doubt, whatever she had done, she had done it only to guarantee the safety of her daughters. No other reason. She had been forced by the bastard who stood in front of him, and the man would die for his crimes. *Focus, Grant. He is no threat.*

"Gus and Sorley will follow you to find the lasses and I'll take my sweet one with me. She has work to do now that she has been disobedient." He whistled and five more brutes came out of the trees.

Tomas emerged from the woods and stood behind Robbie.

Malcolm shouted, "The odds are not in your favor, lads. Hop on your horses and lead the way to the lasses. Or mayhap first, we'll tie you up and take your weapons."

Tomas chuckled. "The odds look in our favor, Grant. What do you think?"

Robbie laughed as his four guards appeared from the cover of the trees. "Six of us and eight of them makes it almost too easy."

Malcolm yelled, "Get them!"

No one moved. His hired men looked at each other in confusion. Malcolm lowered the knife from Caralyn's throat for a second to chastise his men, and she kicked his shin.

Robbie charged, Tomas right behind him.

The six battled Malcolm's seven men, while Malcolm ran off with Caralyn in tow.

Tomas yelled, "Go after him, Grant. We've got this."

Sorley lunged for Robbie just as he was about to make his way over to his horse. The clash of striking steel echoed in the still morning. Sorley parleyed with Robbie, but he didn't stand a chance against a Grant. When Robbie saw him gasp for a breath, he plunged his sword into his heart, then pulled it out and climbed onto his horse without delay. Malcolm and Caralyn were already a few minutes time ahead of him.

Robbie charged out of the clearing and found the path Murray had taken. He was one person on a destrier pursuing two people on a small horse. He would catch the bastard. Riding his horse low, he forced himself to slow his breathing. All pumped and ready to fight, he had to regain control of himself. Alex had always taught him that. If he wanted to win, he had to keep control.

He was losing the battle. His gut clenched at the thought of Caralyn being in Malcolm's clutches once again. Blood raced through his body, sweat drenched him even in the cool air of the Highlands night. Caralyn was his. He could not lose her now, not after all they had been through, and he couldn't even bear the thought of giving bad news to her daughters. Caralyn's strength had brought the three of them this far; he wouldn't let her down.

He noticed small clouds of dust ahead, evidence that he was gaining on him. He and his horse tore through bushes and tree limbs, around curves and up small inclines. He pulled his bow out with an arrow, hoping to get the chance to use it.

Finally, the opportunity arrived. He was on a straight path, Murray clearly visible in front of him. He fired his first arrow and missed. Taking a deep breath to steady himself, he aimed his second arrow and let it fly. The jerking movement in Malcolm's right shoulder indicated the arrow had flown true. A bellow followed the movement, and someone tumbled off the side of the horse.

As Robbie came closer, he realized Murray still sat on the horse. Caralyn must have fallen off. Now he faced a choice.

What would he do? Follow Malcolm and finish this or make sure Caralyn was alive?

CHAPTER TWENTY

Caralyn hit the ground hard and a shock of pain shot up her leg from her previously injured ankle. The speed of her fall sent her careening down an embankment, rolling through bushes, branches tearing the tender skin of her face. She buried her cheeks in her gloved hands as best she could, but then she needed her hands to stop her fall.

When she finally landed at the base of the small incline, she opened her eyes slowly, afraid to see where she was. Though she wasn't certain, she thought Malcolm had been hurt right before he shoved her off the horse.

Another horse's hooves echoed as they went by, flying after Malcolm. She had no idea if it was one of Robbie's men or one of Malcolm's lackeys. She braced her hand down into the scrub and pushed herself to a sitting position. Whoever had just flown by stopped and retreated, heading back in her direction. Though she was unable to see who it was, she heard the voice at the top of the hill as the rider dismounted.

"Caralyn?" Robbie shouted. "Caralyn, are you unhurt?"

She glanced up and gave a weak answer. "Here. I'm fine, I believe."

Robbie scrambled down the hill, sending small stones ricocheting toward her. She covered her face again and turned away.

"Och, sweeting, I'm sorry. I didn't intend to make things worse." He slowed his steps and dropped to her side as soon as he found her. His hand brushed the tangled curls away from her face. "Are you sure you're good?"

"I think so. I may have hurt my ankle again."

"The same one you hurt before?" He reached for her leg and lifted it. "Och, 'tis swelling again."

He turned his head back to her and she caught herself staring at him.

"What is it?" he whispered.

"You came for me." She could barely get the words out, choking on her sobs. When Malcolm threw her over his horse, she had thought her life was over. After what Robbie had learned about her, she was sure he would want nothing to do with her ever again.

"Of course, I came for you."

She gazed into his eyes, lost in the warmth she saw there. So, he didn't hate her for what she had done?

He set her leg down and took her hands in his. "Och, I understand. You thought I would stop caring about you because of what Malcolm said about your past?"

Unable to speak, she nodded her head as she swiped at the tears burning her cheeks.

He lifted her chin and held it. "Did you allow them to use your body because you wanted to?"

"Nay!" she shouted.

"I didn't think so. My guess is you were forced to do his bidding, though I do wonder why your clan didn't do a better job of protecting you."

She could not stop her breath from hitching. "We were so far away, and they were having their own trouble with a neighboring clan. So many died in our wee area. There was no one left for us. I didn't know what to do."

"And you had a daughter to protect. Is that how he got you to go along with him from the start? He threatened to take your lassie from you?"

"Aye. I only had…" she hiccupped. "…Ashlyn. I had Gracie after." She hiccupped again. "I don't know who Gracie's father is and that makes me the worst mama in the world."

Caralyn wailed, unable to hold her emotions in any longer. "I hated everything he made me do. I hated him. I hated every…" hiccup "…man…" hiccup "…he made me touch. They were disgusting men. That's why the girls are afraid of men. Except for you."

Robbie picked her up and settled her in his warm embrace, kissing each cheek before he kissed her forehead.

"Malcolm won't come back, will he?" she whispered, clinging to him.

"If he does, I'll take care of him. I haven't heard any other horses head this way, so my warriors must have taken care of his men. Malcolm is alone now and he won't come back to fight without more men. He is foolish to try to go against the Grants."

She buried her face in his chest and sobbed. The most important thing about this man? He never let go. He held her until she had no more tears. She drenched his tunic and he still held her, rubbing her back and kissing the top of her head. How she wished they could stay this way forever. Nowhere in this land felt safer than his arms.

When her crying slowed, he leaned down and cupped her cheeks. "I don't fault you for doing what you needed to in order to protect yourself and your lassies. Now is there aught else you need to tell me?"

She swiped the tears from her eyes, finally able to see again. What she saw took her breath away. Robbie was gazing at her with a warmth and concern she had never seen before.

She shook her head.

"Then we move forward." He kissed her lips and she sighed. His tongue swept inside her mouth and she melted into him. When he ended the kiss, she couldn't move.

He set her off his lap and stood, holding his hand out to her. "Come, let's go find your lassies."

She gave him her hand and she stood, but stumbled on her weak ankle. Without a word, Robbie swept her up into his arms and carried her up the small incline before settling her on his horse.

They headed back to the small clearing. Tomas and his men stood in the middle, smiles on their faces.

Robbie reined his horse in. "Och, you made quick work of the rest of them?"

Tomas chuckled. "Next time, leave us with a bit of a challenge, would you? This was too easy. Did you take care of

Murray?"

Robbie sighed. "Nay."

"What? What in hell happened? You couldn't handle one man?" Tomas asked.

"Aye, he has one of my arrows in his shoulder, but he pushed Caralyn off his horse and she rolled down an incline. She was my first concern." Robbie squeezed her arm as he talked.

Had he truly chosen her? He had been concerned enough to save her instead of going after Malcolm. Her mind was totally overwhelmed by everything that had just taken place, and she couldn't even consider the implications. Malcolm lived, so fear still crawled in her, too. She leaned into him and closed her eyes, searching for mindless bliss.

Robbie nodded to Angus. "Bring two of their horses. We may need them since we'll soon be deep in the Highlands." The men mounted their horses and they headed back to their original route. All she could do was lean back against Robbie's rock hard torso and close her eyes. She was so tired, but she couldn't get Robbie out of her mind. Malcolm was still out there and would probably cause more trouble. What would they do?

The one night in the priory she and Robbie had shared crept back into her mind. The time they'd shared together was the best she had ever experienced with anyone. She had gone in with the intentions of letting him know how much she appreciated all he had done for her, but the night had ended up proving something to her. There was a reason she had hated all those other men. And while she had appreciated her husband, she now understood that she hadn't loved him.

But Captain Robbie Grant? Everything about Robbie was different, and there was no sense trying to lie to herself. She loved him, without a doubt.

But how could they have a relationship after everything she had done? He wouldn't marry a woman who had been a whore, but would he be willing to keep her as his mistress?

CHAPTER TWENTY-ONE

They rode for a full day before Robbie found a clearing off the beaten path that he felt was safe enough for a resting place. He didn't believe Malcolm would be back for a while. He would head back to Glasgow and get his shoulder tended to before finding more men to hire. If they managed to get far enough ahead of him, he would have difficulty with some of his mercenaries. Highland air took some getting used to, especially in November.

The men killed a few rabbits and roasted them in the center of the clearing. Tomas even found a few apples for them to share. This could be the only chance they had to cook and get a solid amount of food in them. Caralyn's foot was quite swollen and her face was a mass of cuts from the brambles she'd hurtled through, though her injuries didn't seem to bother her. He wanted one night of nourishment and rest before pushing ahead as far as possible. They had ridden for almost a day and a half, and the horses needed a rest as much as they did.

Robbie wondered how Caralyn would sleep. He wanted her in his arms, but he didn't think she was ready to accept that yet. He didn't want to move too far away from her, though, because by the middle of the night, she would be so cold she would be searching for warmth. There was no way he would allow her to gain heat from anyone but him.

He set a plaid on the ground for her, not far from him and close to the fire. She stared at it, clearly contemplating what she should do. Pivoting around to check the area, she saw where the other three had settled. When she got to him, she stopped.

Robbie tipped his head toward the blanket. "I didn't want you too far away. You're welcome to sleep next to me for my heat if you would like."

Her brow furrowed, but she shook her head. "I'll be fine here near the embers."

"If you change your mind, just say so. I'll be right behind you."

She nodded and tried to settle on the plaid, wrapping it around her.

"Caralyn, you have my word I'll be honorable. 'Twill be cold."

She glanced over her shoulder at him. "My thanks, but I'll be fine here."

He watched her toss and turn, but finally he closed his eyes when she finally settled.

In the middle of the night, he awoke to a strange sound. He surveyed the area, before realizing the sound came from Caralyn. She was shivering so hard that her teeth rattled. She had to be freezing. He moved up close to her and set his hand on her shoulder.

She jerked in response to his touch. "Nay. I'll be fine."

"Lass, don't be foolish." He settled his hand on her face to show her the difference. "Trust me, Caralyn. I only offer warmth."

She rolled onto her back and gazed into his eyes with such a forlorn look his heart broke. "Promise me? Naught else with all these guards around?"

"You have my word of honor as a Grant." It would surely kill him and test all his self control, but he didn't wish to wake up to a corpse in the morning. She was too thin to withstand the Highland nights alone.

She nodded her head in agreement and rolled over onto her side. Robbie slid up behind her and tucked her body next to his, opening his plaid to wrap around her.

A small moan escaped her lips as his heat settled around her, slowing the shaking of her body. She tucked in closer, rubbing her bottom against his groin. Unfortunately, he sprang to life underneath her and she froze in response. She was no innocent; she knew exactly what had happened.

"Lass, don't fash yourself. I am human and you have a lovely bum, but I promise not to act on it. You need to stay warm." He could feel her muscles relax against him. "May I ask a question?"

"Aye," she whispered.

"That night in the priory. To me, 'twas verra special. We definitely have something between us, but you pushed me away at the end. Why?"

Caralyn cleared her throat before she answered. "Guilt."

"For what? You're a grown woman. Why would you feel guilty for what we shared?"

"Robbie, first you have to understand something about me. I came to you that night because I needed to thank you for all you had done for me and for my daughters."

"You had already thanked me. You didn't need to come to me. I thought it was something more. I thought you wanted me."

"Please don't be offended, but 'tis the only way I know how to thank men. The first reason was for what you did for me against the Norseman and second, for returning to find my daughters. The words *thank you* didn't seem enough. And I know what men want. So I gave you what you wanted."

Robbie stiffened. Was that all it had been to her? A task of appreciation? "But I never asked you for your body."

"I know, but 'tis what all men want."

"It didn't occur to you that I might be different?"

"Nay, not then. Since then, I have discovered you *are* different. But I shamed myself by going to you in the priory. I could have been severely punished. And quite simply, when I thought about what I had done, I was embarrassed." *And I just can't admit to you how much I did enjoy it. I want you to love me.*

"I don't believe you when you say you couldn't tell what we shared was different. You had to feel it. Mayhap those were your intentions when you came to me, but you have to admit we are special together. Nay?"

"Aye, Robbie, 'twas a verra special night for me, too. But where do we go from here? I am a whore, and I don't think your clan will approve of me."

"Enough. I don't want to ever hear those words from you again. You are *not* a whore. You were forced to make a choice in order to save your daughters." He gritted his teeth before he continued, "Go to sleep, we have a long day tomorrow." Hellfire, she made him so furious, he couldn't speak. If he heard that word one more time, he would be bellowing loud enough to rile all the animals in the forest.

The woman infuriated him.

***

When Caralyn awoke, the first thing she did was shiver and pull the plaid around her even tighter. Robbie must have left, taking his delicious warmth with him. She glanced around the clearing and noticed all four men were up and moving. They munched on oatcakes and drank from skeins.

She sat up and rubbed her eyes. Her face ached and she touched it carefully, sighing when she felt all the dried crusted blood there again. What a sight her face must be. Robbie strode over to her and handed her a skein of water.

"Have a drink and take care of your needs. Might be a good idea to wash your face. You have many cuts from the bushes." He handed her a small piece of soap.

She took the soap and the skein and thanked him, dampening a piece of her skirt so she could scrub her face. Something was different about Robbie this morn. His demeanor had changed. Gone was his effervescent smile and his good mood. He seemed almost angry with her.

It had to be related to their conversation. He'd said he thought there was something special between them, that their night together at the priory was like none he'd ever had, and she'd claimed it had been no more than her way of thanking him.

He had gotten really angry after she had said she was a whore and she was afraid his clan wouldn't accept her. Had he seen the truth in her words when he had bellowed? Or was it because she hadn't told him her true feelings?

Why hadn't she admitted the truth? True, she had gone to him with the intent of thanking him, but the night had meant so much more to her. The way he'd held her, the way he'd looked at her, and the way he'd made her feel...It had been a revelation.

Her heart fluttered at the thought that their night together had meant something to him as well, but she knew she couldn't explain her true feelings. There were two problems they would never be able to get past. First, she was a whore. No matter how angry he became over the thought, it was the truth. And second, she knew his clan would not accept her. It was probably for the best they separate now.

Last night had been so difficult for her. How she had wanted to roll over and face him; share her body with him again. She had dreamt of having him buried deep inside her, holding her while she cried out in pleasure, then calling her name out as he found his release.

But she could not allow her body the chance to betray her again. Her mother's voice rang through her mind again. *Aye, you know it. You were bad, verra bad that night. Ask the Lord for forgiveness.* She chewed on her thumbnail while she searched for the right cut on her arm. It needed to be the deepest. When she was satisfied with the one she chose, she drove her fingernail right into the middle of it. How it hurt! She didn't cry out, but pushed harder. She was so ashamed of her behavior. *That's right, my dear, you were bad.*

Robbie stopped in front of her, his eyes cold and distant. "Are you ready? We need to keep moving. 'Tis best if we get deep in the Highlands as soon as we can."

She pointed to the bushes.

"Aye, five minutes to take care of your needs. Then we move."

Tomas shouted across the clearing. "What in hellfire is your problem today, Grant? Don't take it out on a wee lass."

Robbie stared at her for a moment, his hands on his hips, his angry gaze raking her. Now *that* she was used to.

CHAPTER TWENTY-TWO

They didn't talk for most of the morning. He could tell by her stiff spine in front of him that she was upset about the way he had treated her. She had to have expected it. You don't insult people without retaliation. At least, most people didn't. But what had angered him most was her careless use of the term *whore*. How could anyone speak of themselves in such a way?

But Caralyn was not most people. She didn't act like any other lass he had ever met. Her entire focus was her daughters; that he understood. Mothers became very protective. Even his sister-in-law, who had seemed meek to him before she had children, became a wild cat around her weans. No one dared to cross Maddie when it came to the twins or Kyla. Even Alex treaded lightly. He grinned at a fond memory. The twins, John and Jamie, had come into the great hall one day tugging real swords bigger than they were. All Maddie had said was, "Alex!" and his brother had jumped. The lads were playing with their own toy wooden swords within a day.

So what was different about Caralyn? For one thing, Robbie had never had to worry about a lass before. Truth be known, they had fallen at his feet at Clan Grant. Aye, partly because he was a Grant, but there was more to it. He had learned at a young age all he had to do was flash his smile at a lass, and she would do whatever he wanted. Brodie claimed it was the color of his fair hair, but he believed it was his smile.

His smile didn't work on Caralyn. When he looked at her that way, she didn't give him the admiring looks he was used to from the lasses. He could only come to one conclusion—

Caralyn did not find him attractive.

Even if that was the case, he longed to understand her better. He racked his brain while they rode, trying to think of someone he knew who had gone through something similar to Caralyn, someone he could compare her to.

She had mentioned being accepted by his clan. Why would she be concerned about such a thing? His clan wasn't like that. Something bothered him in the back of his mind; something similar. Aye, his family would accept her for what she was, but would the others? Hadn't Maddie been accused of not being good enough for Alex after the Comming had spread lies about her? *Och, aye! Wee Tommy had thrown stones at Maddie.* They had all apologized after she had saved Jennie and wee Emma, and he hadn't even known there was anything happening out of the ordinary. The world was different for women. Mayhap he had been too judgmental.

Her spine still sat ramrod straight in the saddle ahead of him. "Lass, you may lean against me."

She glanced over her shoulder before looking back at her hands. "I thought you wanted naught to do with me after this morn."

"Aye, well, I can be pig-headed at times, but 'tis nae reason for you to give yourself a backache." He rubbed her arm lightly, hoping she would understand his mood had changed.

She leaned into him. "'Tis a long path to your land, is it not?"

"Aye, another day mayhap."

"'Tis the same path Logan and Gwyneth would have taken with the lassies?"

He could tell she waited anxiously for his answer. Logan was a hell of a tracker and would go his own way, but in some areas, there were no other choices. "Aye, for the most part, but Logan is exceptional. He may know a different path than I do. He would have taken them the fastest way, without a doubt. 'Tis chilly in the Highlands this time of year for your girls."

"Have you noticed any signs of trouble? If aught had happened, you would know it, wouldn't you?"

"I haven't seen any signs of aught."

She nodded and relaxed a bit more. "Och, but the land is

breathtaking, Robbie. I have never seen such beauty." Caralyn lifted her face to the sun, sighing when the rays danced across her features. Her beauty moved him, especially with the slight smile that he rarely saw.

"Did you always live in South Ayrshire?" Robbie hoped he could get her talking about her past. He wanted to know as much as he could about what had made this woman who she was.

"For the most part. When I was young, we lived inland near the clan keep, but my sire wanted to fish, so we moved to the coastline and he and a couple of friends built a small boat. My da loved to go fishing and took me often."

"Not your mother?"

"Nay, she didn't like it. When I grew up, his friend's son offered for me and my da accepted. We got along well enough. He fished with my da and his friends as well."

"Do you still like to fish? We have a lovely loch not far from us. The fish are incredible there."

"Aye, I do and so does Ashlyn. She doesn't remember her da well, but she loves the smell of fish, and even helps me clean them. I have taken her with me before while Gracie played in the water."

"What happened to your parents and your husband?"

"My parents passed from the fever not long after we were married. We lived in their house. When Ashlyn was three summers, my husband and his friend went out fishing one day and never came back. 'Twas in October when the gale winds blow in quick and they were caught in a storm. We never knew what happened to them until sections of their boat washed up on shore a fortnight later."

"Och, lass, I am sorry for such a loss." She had been left alone with a three year old. No parents, no husband. "How did you survive alone?"

"There were a couple of other friends who helped out for a while, but one friend was the father of the man who'd died with my husband, and he moved away, unable to cope."

Caralyn said naught for several miles. Robbie decided that she would talk about Malcolm when she was ready. He saw her swiping at her eyes. "Lass, you don't need to talk about it.

Forgive me for bringing up something so painful. I'm just trying to understand."

"I want you to know. There was a period that winter when Ashlyn and I had gone without food for almost a sennight." She squeezed his hand. "Do you know how hard it is to watch your bairn starve? I searched everywhere for food, even started walking in the snow and begging our neighbors, but 'twas a tough winter."

Robbie held her hand and let her go on. Truth was, he couldn't imagine such a thing—a lass alone with no one to turn to, no clan to protect her.

"Malcolm often passed our cottage when he was delivering crates down the path. One day, he came along with a bag of turnips and oatcakes. He brought them inside and just left them. I was afraid to accept the food, but Ashlyn was so hungry. We rationed it out, but it still wasn't enough."

He didn't know what to do for her other than to listen.

"He came one more time and left food again, but the next time, he brought two friends. I found out what I owed him for the food. I only agreed because he promised more food and clothing for Ashlyn, and it broke my heart to see her starve, Robbie." She hung her head and swiped at her cheeks. "I didn't know what else to do. We were so hungry."

"Every week he came with other men, but usually his same friends. Every week I paid for my daughter to eat. Then he would get back on his boat and head up the firth toward Glasgow. Had I anywhere to go, I would have. After a while, he started to leave men to protect us, or so he said. I found out it was to keep me from leaving."

Robbie couldn't handle anymore. He twisted her in the saddle and settled her so he could hold her while she cried.

"A couple of times, he took us to the royal burgh when he had business. 'Twas where I met Gwyneth. I often went to the Kirk with an escort, and she was there frequently because her brother is a priest. Malcolm always had someone watching us. I tried to escape to the abbey before Gracie was born, but his men caught us. 'Twas too difficult after I had Gracie, and his visits had decreased. I had hoped they would stop altogether. Then the Norse came along and ruined everything."

Robbie kissed the top of her head. "Mayhap you will someday consider it to have been a blessing. 'Twas the Norseman who got you into my arms."

"Robbie, how I wish things could work out between us. I just don't know how it could happen. We have much going against us."

She leaned into him and the soft mounds of her breasts settled against his arm. He inhaled her scent and sighed, wishing they were somewhere else, anywhere but atop a horse. She moved and must have discovered how hard he was, but she didn't move away. Instead she rested her chin on his other shoulder so she could press her beautiful breasts against his chest. All he could think of was how she had looked standing in the middle of a sea of warriors with naught but a shift on and her rosy nipples fully visible. His next thought was the sweet memory of how she had cried out when he had been buried deep inside her.

They didn't have much going against them, at least, not in his mind. He would find a way.

CHAPTER TWENTY-THREE

Caralyn couldn't sleep. Robbie had her cocooned in his warm embrace on the cold ground, and for some unknown reason, she enjoyed listening to his rhythmic breathing. She had to admit that sleeping with him like this was probably one of her greatest pleasures. Who would have guessed sleeping with a man could be so enjoyable? Aye, she had detected his occasional erection, but she did her best not to inflame him and he had kept his word about not pursuing sex.

Every day she spent with Captain Robbie Grant made her love him even more. She loved riding so close to him, talking to him, and listening to him talk about his clan. He was a proud man who loved his family dearly, and he would do anything for them. His smile could light up the world and her heart as well. She didn't think she would ever find another man she cared for as much as Robbie.

In fact, naught would make her happier than to marry Robbie Grant. But she knew it could never happen with her background. Could she live with him as his mistress? Did he want her that much or did he have another waiting for him?

The closer they came to his home, the more nervous she grew. She had so many questions. Were her girls safe and unhurt? Where would they go once they arrived? She didn't know what Robbie planned for her and her daughters. They would have to stay in the Highlands, but where?

"Are you excited about seeing your lassies again?" A soft whisper tickled her ear and she smiled.

"Aye, but I am nervous." The Grants sounded so wonderful, her girls would probably never want to leave, especially after the hard life they'd endured. They deserved happiness for a change, instead of going hungry and dealing with rude men.

"Why? Trust me that Logan got them there ahead of us safely."

She rolled onto her back and stared up at the stars through the treetops. "What if they prefer living with your clan than living with me?" She gazed at him, hoping he understood the severity of her concern. "My girls have never had the opportunity to play with other bairns. They will never want to leave."

"Playing with others and loving and missing their mama are two different things. They are probably just as anxious to see you as you are to see them." His thumb brushed her cheek. "Trust me, I have two wee nephews who love to play and battle with all the warriors, but when they want their mama, there is no substitute."

"I thank you, Captain Robbie Grant, for all you have done for us. I can never repay you." She leaned forward to kiss his lips.

Robbie pulled back and she stared at him in shock. "Lass, I don't want your kisses if they are just to thank me. I only want them if they come from your heart and they are for me, not for my honorable actions."

Caralyn thought for a moment and then nodded her head. "Then I would like to kiss you for you, Robbie. For your tenderness, your kindness, and because of all we have shared."

"Are you sure about that?"

She paused before answering. "Aye, I am sure. I kiss you for how you make me feel, special and protected, but you must understand that you also confuse me. I don't know what to make of you yet. You are so different to me, and yet I don't wish to lose you. Will you accept under those terms?"

"Aye."

He cupped her cheek and kissed her with a tenderness that drove right to her core. His lips were soft, warm, and tantalizing all at once. She didn't want it to end. She sighed and her lips parted, offering him more, giving him a taste of her she didn't often offer. His tongue swept into her mouth and teased her, beckoning her to dance with him. So she did, wanting to see how it felt to *want* to kiss, to enjoy the person you shared such intimacy with, and she couldn't get enough of him. She wanted to drink of this sweet pleasure for as long as she could, without enticing him to go further.

Because she still couldn't go there yet. Just not yet. He ended the kiss as if he sensed her conflicted thoughts. If she was to draw him to her, she had to be good. Her mother had been insistent. *Men don't marry bad girls.* She loved her mother and always tried to be good. *Mama, I will try to be good so he will stay with me.*

He smiled and she returned it, wanting him to know how much such a small gesture meant to her. He had allowed her to set the pace for their kiss. A small tug on her heart almost pushed her back for more, but she couldn't risk it. *I'll be good, you'll see. I won't ruin this.*

She was very happy with what she considered to be their first real kiss, not a kiss of gratitude or desperation, but a kiss of hope; a kiss from her heart.

Robbie stood and helped her up. "Shouldn't be much longer to the Grant keep, lass. Come, let's get on our way. I hope to make it before nightfall."

***

Many hours later, Caralyn awoke to a brush on her arm. Darkness would be here soon. She shook the cobwebs from her brain, amazed at how fast she could fall asleep in Robbie's arms. When she finally made sense of what was in her line of vision, her breath caught.

A fortress, one of the largest she had ever seen, sat atop a hill in the distance, surrounded by rows of neat thatched cottages.

"My home, lass. Welcome to the Grant castle." Robbie's eyes glowed with a sense of pride and a joy. Would she ever have a home that inspired such feelings in her?

"Robbie, 'tis immense. You have so many people here." A bustle of clan members moved about, busy in their daily work. A serene loch sat off in the distance. A cluster of buildings sat inside the bailey, and droves of warriors practiced in a side field, the clang of metal ringing out for all to hear. A bloom of hope sprang anew in her heart. "He'll never get to me here, will he?" she whispered.

Robbie leaned down to listen to her. "What did you say?"

She glanced at him over her shoulder. "Malcolm. He would never be able to get enough men together to kidnap my girls from this place. We'll be safe, won't we?"

Robbie rubbed her arm. "Cara, he'll never get to you here. Do you see all the men in the parapets near the towers? Do you see all the warriors working in the lists? Even all the men working in the bailey will protect you. We don't allow men to hurt women here, or kidnap them either."

They continued down the hill and rode up to the portcullis, Caralyn staring in wonder at all that transpired around her. Her voice trembled. "Do you think my lassies will be glad to see me?" Despite what he had said to her, the impact his comforting words had made, she still feared they would not.

Robbie headed toward the stables and halted, helping her dismount. He inclined his head toward the keep. "See for yourself, lass."

The most beautiful sound she had ever heard greeted her, Gracie's voice. She turned and saw her girls rushing toward her. "Mama! Mama!" *Both* girls called to her, not just Ashlyn. What a sweet sound it was! Gracie tumbled to the ground and Ashlyn helped her back up before they continued to run. Caralyn hobbled as fast as she could, tears streaming down her eyes at the vision of her weans in front of her.

Both lassies were smiling, arms outstretched, waiting for her. When she finally reached them, she lifted Gracie in one arm and wrapped the other around Ashlyn. Unable to speak through her tears, she hugged and kissed them both.

A booming voice interrupted them, and she looked up to see the biggest man she had ever seen crush Robbie in his arms. Another large man stood close behind him. "About time you arrived home, brother."

The second man limped over and grabbed Robbie in a full bear hug. "Glad to see you made it whole, Robbie."

"And Brenna didn't take your leg, I see?" He peered down at his brother's plaid to make sure all was well.

"Nay, our sister took good care of me." Brodie clasped Robbie's shoulder, still grinning.

Following them was a stream of lads, lasses, and bairns, all of them trying to make their way to Robbie.

Caralyn stared down at Gracie's smiling face and kissed her cheek. "You are happy, my wee one?"

Gracie's smile grew wider, and she placed her wee hands on Caralyn's cheeks before leaning over to kiss her cheek. "Lu you, Mama."

Caralyn eyes misted at the sweet words, but reached down and ruffled Ashlyn's dark hair before kissing her cheek. "And you, Ashlyn? They have been good to you here?"

"Aye, Mama. We have so much fun. We have many new friends and Gracie has been talking more and more every day. She loves Logan."

A voice called her name from behind her and she whirled around to see Gwyneth coming toward her, arms outstretched. "Gwyneth, thank you for guarding my daughters."

Gwyneth smiled and hugged her. "Och, 'twas no trouble at all. Your lassies are so sweet."

Caralyn's searched her friend's face. "No problems here, Gwyneth?"

"Nay." She smiled. "They are all wonderful, Caralyn. You'll see. 'Tis a different world here. They work hard, but everyone is kind. I am so glad you made it." She reached up and ran her fingers across the cuts on her face. "Trouble along the way?"

"Aye," Caralyn said. She gave a pointed look at her daughters. "We'll talk later. I am verra weary today. 'Twas a long journey and I worried so about my lassies."

A large hand wrapped around her waist and Robbie Grant tugged her toward him. "I want to introduce you all to Caralyn, Gracie and Ashlyn's mother."

Caralyn gazed into a sea of smiling faces. The names all flew by her: Laird Alex and Lady Madeline, Brodie, Celestina, Brenna, Quade, Torrian, Jennie, Avelina, Lily, Jamie, John, Kyla, Bethia, and the very last person she met stood with his chest puffed out like a peacock.

"And my name is Loki Grant."

Caralyn was hugged by so many, she lost count. It was almost dark, and her stomach rumbled with hunger.

Robbie finally stopped them and said, "Could we go inside for a bite to eat? We are verra hungry since we were forced to travel so fast."

Once inside, Caralyn sat on a bench at the longest table she had ever seen in the middle of the great hall. The laird had ushered them to this table so everyone could sit together. Servants brought out chunks of cheese and trenchers of stew and brown bread. A bowl full of fat apples sat in the middle of the table.

She couldn't help but stare at the hall. A large dais sat behind them. While it wasn't quite as regal as the one she had been in Glasgow, Caralyn liked it better. Beautiful tapestries representing the change of the seasons decorated the walls. A large hearth took up one wall with cushioned chairs arranged in a semi-circle in front. Fragrant rushes sat on the floor and a group of dogs played over near the door.

Gracie sat down on the bench and held a piece of cheese out to her mother. "Mama. Cheese."

Caralyn took a bite. She marveled at the change in her wean. Her eyes were bright, not haunted, and she ate everything within her reach. Ashlyn giggled and said, "Mama, they have the best cook here. You should meet her. And she gives us apple tarts sometimes."

A wean ran over and said, "I'm Lily. Gracie and I play together because she is my new friend. She likes to find my stones when I hide them." She climbed up on Caralyn's lap and kissed her cheek. "I'm glad you are here. Gracie missed you."

Just like that, tears blurred Caralyn's vision. Goodness, but everything in her life made her cry lately. Had she finally found what she had always wished for? She hadn't asked for much—a family to love and food for her daughters' bellies. Well, now both lassies smiled with exuberance. She peeked at the rest of the faces at the table, all babbling at one another, sharing food, laughing, hugging, touching. Caralyn couldn't seem to stop her tears. Robbie, who was sitting beside her, rubbed her back and stood, nodding to the woman next to Alex.

The laird's wife came over to her side. "I am Maddie. I am sure you didn't remember all our names," the woman whispered in her ear. "Come upstairs with me. I will show you to your chamber. Grab a couple of apples to take with you. You look exhausted."

"Lady Madeline, may my daughters come along?"

"Hush, call me Maddie. You're almost family. Of course the lassies may come along. I assumed you would want them to sleep with you."

Caralyn nodded, but reached out for Robbie. "Robbie?"

He leaned down and kissed her cheek. "You'll be fine. Maddie will take care of you. She understands." He gazed into her eyes. "Trust me. She knows what you need more than I do. I will be here if you need me."

CHAPTER TWENTY-FOUR

Caralyn picked Gracie up in her arms and followed Ashlyn to the end of the great hall. Lady Madeline led them up the staircase to the second floor and down the passageway almost to the end. She opened a door to the left and stood back. "I think this chamber will suit you. The bed is large enough for the three of you to sleep together if you'd like. The lassies were sleeping together in one room before you arrived."

Ashlyn grabbed her mother's hand. "Mama, we'll stay with you tonight. 'Tis a big castle."

Caralyn stepped into the beautiful chamber, marveling over the simple yet comfortable space. A large bed plump with warm plaids and thick furs sat on one wall while the hearth graced the outside wall. A chest sat at the end of the bed and a table and two chairs were arranged near the hearth. Dried flowers decorated the feminine room and fresh rushes had been added to the floor. One window sat on the side, thick fur coverings providing protection from the cold.

"Fiona will visit you often to see what you need. I will have someone start a fire in the hearth to take the chill out of the room while I show you to our bathing room."

"A bathing room?" Caralyn had never seen one before and wasn't sure what to expect.

"Mama, you will love it." Ashlyn grinned. Gracie tugged on Caralyn's arm to be let down, and once she was on the floor, she raced ahead of them to the room at the end of the hall.

Maddie rolled her eyes sheepishly when she opened the door. "My husband spoils me and had this room built for me. They have a large bathing room for the men outside near the stables, but I was always uncomfortable in it and he didn't want me walking outside with my hair wet. I admit I enjoy bathing more often than everyone else." Maddie rubbed her belly as she walked inside.

"How soon for your bairn, my lady?" Caralyn couldn't help but stare at Maddie's blond hair and beautiful blue eyes. No wonder the laird had married her—she was stunning.

"Och, not more than a fortnight, I think." She led the way around the grand chamber with three separate hearths. Four tubs of different sizes graced the room and stacks of linen squares sat piled neatly on the shelves. She moved to the outside wall. "These rope pulls will bring small buckets of water. 'Tis a lovely design in the summer because the small pool outside is warmed by the sun. Now, however, the water is quite cool, which is why we have three hearths. My husband has the men bring water up at night to heat for bathing.

"Over here, on this shelf, we have bathing oils, which are Celestina's creations. Her lavender oil is exquisite. Please use whatever you like." She turned and pointed to a door in the corner of the room. "Over there, my husband has again spoiled me by having a garderobe built as well with a door on it for privacy. If you'd like, you may bathe now to clean yourself of the dirt and grime of traveling. Then I'm sure you would like to rest from your journey."

A room dedicated to bathing was a decadence Caralyn would never have imagined, but at this moment she couldn't think of anything she'd like better than a bath. Nodding, she said, "I'd like that. A bath would be lovely and Gracie can bathe with me, but..."

"Aye, 'twas a long trip and you didn't bring much to wear. Ashlyn, be a dear and send Fiona up, would you? And please take Gracie along to assist you."

The girls ran to do as they were bid. Caralyn gazed at the regal woman in front of her, unsure of how to talk to her. She stared at the floor, deciding the best approach would be to wait for her companion to speak.

Lady Madeline gathered towels and oils for her and found a screen to settle around one of the tubs. "So have you been in the Highlands before??"

"Nay, 'tis my first journey to the Highlands. 'Tis magnificent. I had no idea of the beauty in the hills and valleys here." Caralyn helped Lady Madeline move the screen.

"Mayhap that is good. We hope you'll decide to stay. Your daughters are lovely. Gwyneth told us you are from South Ayrshire. 'Tis true?"

"Aye, and 'tis beautiful on the coastline, but 'tis more lovely here. Seems more peaceful." Oh, how she hoped Gwyneth hadn't said anything else about Caralyn and her life. She trusted Gwyneth.

"Och, wait until you see our snow." Maddie chuckled, then strode over and clasped Caralyn's hands in hers. "I want you to know that you will always be welcome here at Clan Grant. When I first came here, I had the foolish idea that I didn't belong and I didn't deserve to be in such a place. Can you imagine?"

Caralyn *could* imagine since that was exactly how she felt at that moment and it was what she had been afraid of all along. She gazed at Lady Madeline, wondering how she knew. Moments later, Ashlyn burst in the door with Fiona and Gracie at her heels.

"Och, here is Fiona now." Maddie turned to her maid. "Please have the men tote hot water upstairs for the lady. We must also find her something clean to wear."

Maddie kissed Caralyn's cheek and said, "Welcome to Clan Grant. We're verra happy to have you here. Please let me know if I can be of any assistance. I will leave you alone with your delightful daughters. I am sure they have much to tell you." She left with a smile.

Caralyn waited on the bench while the men brought up the water and Fiona left to find her serviceable clothing. More energetic than Caralyn had ever seen her, Gracie ran over and jumped into the smaller tub. She peeked her head over the edge and shouted, "Find me, Mama."

Ashlyn whispered in her ear. "Gracie likes to hide, and you have to pretend you don't see her. Then she'll jump out and scare you. 'Tis her favorite new game. Come, I'll show you."

Ashlyn tiptoed around the room, speaking all the while as she tugged her mother behind her. "Where is Gracie? I can't find her, can you, Mama?"

A fitful of giggles erupted from the tub.

"Is she here in this tub?" Ashlyn peeked in the first one. "Nay." She continued around the perimeter of the room.

More giggles came from Gracie, and Caralyn's eyes misted over. Had she ever heard a more beautiful sound than her youngest daughter's delight?

"Is she under this bench? Nay."

"Ashlyn, I can't find Gracie. Where is she?" Caralyn joined in Gracie's game.

More laughter erupted from her once silent daughter. Caralyn's heart filled with joy, a feeling of breathless glee radiating through her.

As they came near the tub that Gracie hid in, she jumped up with her hands in the air and shouted, "Rarrrrrr!"

Ashlyn jumped and Caralyn laughed and picked Gracie up and hugged her. "There you are."

Gracie peered at her mother and placed her wee hand on her wet cheek. "Mama, we stay here?"

"Aye, we stay here." How could she take her daughters away? Though she still didn't know what the future held for her and Robbie, she would do anything to see her daughters this happy all the time.

Gracie clapped her hands, pushed away from her mother to get down, then tore over to the same tub and jumped in again. She peeked her head over the side and said, "Mama, find me." Then her head disappeared again.

Ashlyn nodded with a quirk in her grin and glanced at her mother. "Aye, same game. She needs to find some new hiding places."

***

Caralyn glanced at her slumbering daughters in the middle of the large, soft bed. Gracie used to sleep with her thumb in her mouth, but not at Clan Grant. The lassies appeared so peaceful and relaxed, and the sight of them this way warmed her heart.

She had already shed enough tears for the day. So grateful for all the Grants had done for them, she felt she needed to do something.

She had seen Robbie walk into his chamber when they left the bathing room. Smiling at the memory of Gracie padding down the passageway to give him a hug, Caralyn realized how much she missed him. His warm embrace had been so welcome in the cold outdoors.

Settling a kiss on each of her girl's foreheads, she grabbed a robe Fiona had left her to cover her night rail and crept out the door and down the cold stone passageway to Robbie's room. He had not barricaded the door, so she sneaked inside and closed the door behind her.

Huddled near the door, she waited until her eyes adjusted. She could tell he was awake.

A deep sigh came from the bed. He held the covers up and she scooted into bed next to him. "Aye, Caralyn? What do you need?"

Caralyn cleared her throat before responding. She wished she had thought this through before entering his chamber. "I am so grateful for all you have done. My lassies…"

Robbie set his fingers against her lips, stopping her midsentence. "If you are here to express your gratitude only, please remove yourself."

"I don't understand."

"Lass, you have said thank you many times, more than I can count. You don't need to thank me anymore."

"But I'm so grateful, you have no idea. My one wish has always been to rid my daughters of the haunted look in their eyes, and you've done that. I've never seen them so happy." She squeezed her eyes shut for a moment to try to stop the tears from flowing. "Robbie, what you have done for them deserves more than two words."

"Then what is your intent?"

"I only know how to thank you one way. Please allow me to service you to let you know how much I appreciate all you have done…"

Robbie hopped out of bed. "Nay. 'Tis not what I want, Caralyn." His voice turned harsh. "I don't want to be serviced. If that's the only reason you're here, please leave."

Tears gathered in her lashes. "Robbie, I don't understand. Why are you angry? What have I done wrong? Don't you want me?" She sat up in bed and stared at him.

He leaned over the bed, placing his hands on either side of her so he could gaze into her eyes. "Caralyn, I want you with every fiber of my being, but not like this. I want you when you want me."

"I do. I want to thank you."

"'Tis the problem. You don't want me for who I am, you want me for what I am. You want me because I have helped you. You want me for saving your girls. I know you don't understand because of your background, but you need to want me for who I am. Until then, I don't want you in my bed. 'Tis not for the right reasons."

She wiped the tears from her cheeks as she climbed out of bed. "But I miss you."

"I miss you, too. But I need more from you. Mayhap you can't give it. I need to know you are here because you have feelings for me, not because you want to service me. Do you understand the difference? Have you ever loved a man before?"

She shook her head in confusion. "Nay. I liked my husband well enough, but I don't think I loved him." *Please, Robbie, if I say I want to be here for any other reason, I am bad, bad. My mother will accuse me.* In truth, she had barely admitted her real reasons for coming to his room to herself, just like the first time she'd slipped into his bed.

"I want what my brothers and sister have. A relationship needs to be built on feelings for each other. You don't know how hard it is for me to turn you away, but this is wrong."

"I am sorry, I just wanted..."

"A relationship shouldn't exist only in bed. 'Twill not end well. I have had that sort of relationship with other women, and 'tis not what I want. Not with you. I want more. You tell me what to do."

Caralyn shook her head, so confused she didn't even know what to say to him.

She flung the door open and fled down the hall. Not wanting to wake her girls up, she fled up the stairway to the ramparts.

And ran straight into Gwyneth.

CHAPTER TWENTY-FIVE

Gwyneth took one look at her and held her arms out to her friend. "Caralyn, what is wrong? Aren't you happy here?"

"Aye, but…Robbie doesn't want me here." Caralyn fell into her friend's arms.

Gwyneth held her for a while before forcing her to look at her. "What do you mean, Robbie doesn't want you? From everything I can see, the man is besotted with you."

"I just came from his chamber and he turned me away."

Gwyneth pulled her down to a set of stones built into the wall where they could sit. "Caralyn. You must realize he is much different than Malcolm. You'll never be able to satisfy Robbie in the same way as you did Malcolm."

"I don't understand. All men want to rut. 'Twas what my husband wanted from me, too. He wanted to rut all the time."

"Did you have any feelings for your husband?"

"Nay. Well, I liked him for a time and he did protect me and catch food for us, but Robbie asked me if I had ever loved anyone before. I don't understand love. I love my daughters, but 'tis different.

Gwyneth brushed her hair away from her face. "Och, lass. I know where you are coming from. I recall the horrors you lived through. Makes me realize how glad I am I was able to fight off the Norseman who came at me on the ship. But 'tis different here. I have watched all these husbands and their wives every day since we arrived."

She glanced at Caralyn before staring up at the stars in the sky. "Alex, Brodie, and Quade, they all treat their wives different. They ask their opinions. They touch and laugh and do as their wives ask them to do. And the wives do things for their husbands with a smile on their face, as if they enjoy it. 'Tis new to me, as well. But I don't remember my mama, and I have little experience with married couples. As far as I can recall, I have said I would never marry. But you know what?"

Caralyn shook her head, trying to catch her breath.

"'Tis verra nice. Makes me almost want to be married. I didn't think I would ever say such a thing. They are all happy." Gwyneth stood at the wall and gazed out over the land. "Look at this, Caralyn. Have you ever seen a world like this? What are you going to do?"

Caralyn shook her head again. "I don't know, but I want to stay. My lassies are the happiest I have ever seen them. Gracie is talking and doesn't suck her thumb."

"Mayhap you can contribute in some way and find your own cottage."

"Och, what can I do? My only skills are when I'm on my back, and I don't think Laird Grant would be agreeable. I can't sew or cook. Mayhap I could be a maid. What will you do? Do you plan to stay?"

"Och, you know I have to finish something. I'll hunt down the man who put me on that boat and kill him with my bare hands if I must. I won't rest until I do."

"Will Logan help you?"

"Logan is an admirable man. He is wonderful with the weans, and your daughters love him, but he's too stubborn for me. I can't ask him to come with me and settle my business. I have my bow and arrows and you know how much I've trained for this. I'll be fine. He showed me how to mark my path back."

"What if Malcolm comes for me? What if he brings a whole garrison of warriors and attacks the Grants? They're so wonderful, I couldn't stand to see anyone hurt."

"The Grant has over four hundred men training in the lists, and others waiting to join. I think he can handle Malcolm Murray and his group of misfits," Gwyneth snorted. "And did you see the size of Alex Grant? Brodie and Robbie aren't small either. The three of them are massive, along with Quade and Logan. They grow lads big up here."

The two of them laughed until Caralyn's belly hurt. "Mayhap you are correct, but someone could still be injured. I should go, but I don't have the heart to take my lassies away. When will you leave?"

"Soon. I'll head back down to Glasgow and mayhap, back to Ayrshire. Depends on where I will find that lousy bastard, Duff Erskine. The man killed my father and my brother in front of my eyes. He needs to pay for what he did to me and my family."

"I hope you can find resolution to this, and I hope Logan helps you, whether you want him to or not. Will you come back after, at least for a visit? I understand why you must go. You handle things differently than I do. But I hope someday our paths will cross again. Thank you for all you have done. I know how hard it must have been for you to travel alone with three men, but I felt so much better knowing you were with them."

"They were all gentlemen. Even Logan can be quite decent. He taught me a few things. If I run into Malcolm on the way, I'll take care of him for you."

Caralyn hugged her friend. "Godspeed, Gwyneth. You know I will worry about you."

"And I, you."

"Do you think Malcolm will come for me? 'Tis a long way."

Gwyneth leaned over the ledge again and peered out over the land. Caralyn stood next to her. "For most men, I would say nay. But Malcolm? 'Tis a competition for him and he must always land on top. I fear he will come, but mayhap not until spring. 'Tis a long trail in the winter. I'll see what I can discover in Glasgow."

"Gwyneth, are you sure you can't stay here? I'll miss you. You can have a fresh start here. You were a true friend when I really needed one. Mayhap the only true friend I have ever had."

"Och, we'll meet again. Don't worry."

***

Two days later, Robbie sat at the table in the middle of the solar while Alex sat behind his desk with Maddie seated close to him. "Why did she wish to see you, Alex?"

"I don't know, but I granted her request. Do you wish to give us a little background on your relationship with Caralyn before she joins us?"

Robbie shrugged his shoulders as he walked over to pull the fur back from the window. "I found her after a Norseman beat her until she was unconscious. She was in bad shape and didn't awaken until the next morning. I brought her to my camp, then went back and rescued her daughters. Tomas and I took them all to the priory near Glasgow right before the Battle of Largs."

"And that's all?" Alex's eyebrows lifted as he watched his brother.

"That's what is most important." He turned back around from the window to face Alex and Maddie.

"Then how did you end up bringing her to our clan?"

"Och, 'tis a long story."

"We have the time." Alex glanced at his wee wife, methodically rubbing her rotund belly. "Is aught wrong, sweeting?"

Maddie smiled. "Nay, I am fine. Just a wee bit tired."

Alex leaned over and kissed her cheek.

"Would you two like me to leave?" Robbie asked.

"Nay! You will stay until you answer my questions." Alex glared at him.

A soft knock sounded at the door.

"Enter," Alex said.

Caralyn stepped in hesitantly before closing the door, pausing for a moment when she saw Robbie standing by the window. "Should I come back?"

"Nay." Alex stood and ushered her over to a chair. "I have asked my brother to attend. Is this agreeable to you, Caralyn?"

She nodded and smoothed her skirts as she waited for a prompt to begin.

Alex settled back into the chair behind his desk and nodded for her to begin.

"My laird, I have come to explain a bit about myself and to ask a favor."

Robbie couldn't guess what she was about. Nervous, he started pacing in front of the hearth.

"I have two things I wish to discuss with you, if I may."

"Go ahead, lass."

"My mother always taught me to be honest, so I feel the need to give you an explanation of my background. I don't know what Robbie has told you about me." She glanced from Robbie to Alex Grant.

"Verra little. You tell us whatever you need to tell us," Alex said.

Caralyn's hands gripped her skirts before she started. Robbie wanted nothing more than to walk over and hold her in his arms before she started, but he could tell how much it had cost her to come here to speak with Alex, and he needed to let her stand on her own.

"I have a verra different background. While I was married for a time, for the last five years I have been a mistress to a man who sometimes gave me to his friends."

Robbie barked. "What are you doing? They don't need to know this."

Alex held his hand up to his brother before taking his wife's hand. "Maddie, would you like to leave?"

"Nay, Alex, I am fine."

"Continue." Alex nodded to Caralyn.

Caralyn glanced up at Robbie before she spoke. "I realize it may not be best for me to be around all your weans due to my background, so I wanted to be completely honest with you. I would like to stay at your keep, if possible, but I realize I'm an imposition. Still, I wondered if you might have a cottage near the loch where I could stay with my daughters."

Robbie stopped pacing and crossed his arms.

"I apologize if this upsets you, but I can't change who I am." Caralyn kept her eyes fixed on Alex Grant as she spoke.

After taking a moment to reflect on her words, Alex cleared his throat. "Is this what you wish to do? Do you wish to continue to be a mistress to someone while you are at the Grant keep?"

"Nay!" Caralyn bolted out of her seat, but then sat down again. "Your pardon," she whispered.

"Was it your choice to be this man's mistress?" Alex asked.

"Nay." Caralyn shook her head adamantly, then bowed her

head. "I was forced. We were desperate for food, and the man made his price clear. Then he held my daughters and threatened to hurt them if I didn't comply with his instructions."

"Then I don't see its relevance to this discussion."

Caralyn's head jerked back up, and she glanced from Alex to Maddie.

Maddie stood and walked around the desk to her, grasping her hands in hers. "It does not matter to us what you have done in the past. I disagree with you. You *can* change who you are. What would you like to do to contribute to the clan?"

"Well, 'tis part of my problem. The only thing my husband taught me before he passed was how to fish. I thought if we lived near the loch, I could catch and clean fish for you. Ashlyn loves to fish, as well."

Alex nodded his head. "I see. And the second thing you wished to discuss with us?"

"The person who forced me has been searching for me. He followed us out of Glasgow, but Robbie and his men fought off his men. He was able to escape back to Glasgow. I fear he may come for me and I don't wish to risk any of your clan being hurt by him."

Alex turned toward his brother. "Robbie, the man got away?"

"Aye, he threw Caralyn on his horse while we fought off his guards. By the time I followed, he was far enough ahead to force me to use my arrow. I struck him in the shoulder and he pushed Caralyn off his horse down an incline. I had to make a choice, and it was more important to me to make sure she wasn't in danger."

Alex quirked an eyebrow, then returned his attention to Caralyn. "If he comes for you, you are safer here inside the keep than in a cottage."

"But I don't wish to endanger anyone here." Her voice was firm.

Maddie returned to her chair in time to hear Alex whisper to her out the corner of his mouth. "Hmmm, where have I heard that before, wife?"

Alex stood. "Thank you, Caralyn. I will give some thought

to your request. Until I make my decision, I expect you to stay in the keep."

Caralyn stood and thanked both Alex and Maddie. She opened the door to leave and Logan rushed in, stopping in his tracks when he recognized her. "Where's Gwyneth?"

Caralyn shrugged her shoulders. "I'm not sure. I haven't seen her yet today."

"Did she tell you she was leaving?" His tone was persistent.

Caralyn nodded. "She said she planned to leave shortly."

"Where was she going?"

"In search of someone in Glasgow."

"Who?" Logan inched closer to Caralyn, towering over her.

Robbie jumped in front of him. "Stay away from her."

"She has information I need," Logan declared, hands on his hips.

"Then ask her politely and mayhap she will answer." Robbie glared at his friend.

"Slud. Have it your way, Grant. Caralyn, would you please tell me where Gwyneth has gone?" He tipped his head back with a smirk, looking over Robbie's shoulder.

Robbie stepped back, satisfied Logan was treating Caralyn with the respect she deserved.

"She has gone after Duff Erskine, the man who drugged her and forced her onto the boat."

"She left alone?"

"Aye. She has her bow and arrows." Caralyn glanced from Robbie to Logan. "Gwyneth always travels alone."

"And what is her purpose?"

Caralyn stared at her feet, nervously shuffling them.

Robbie took a step toward her and tipped her chin up so their eyes met. "Caralyn?"

"She's gone to kill him."

Logan growled. "Foolish lass." He cursed a couple of times before he turned away.

Caralyn stopped him. "Logan?"

"Aye?"

"The man killed her brother and her father right in front of her. She will not quit until he is dead."

It was all the motivation Logan needed to pivot and run out

the door.

By the time the Grants and Caralyn returned to the great hall, Logan had finished with the preparations for his trip—having grabbed another plaid, a loaf of bread, a chunk of cheese, and his satchel. He headed out the door, swilling an ale on the way.

Quade, who was also in the great hall and had been brought up to speed on his mission, yelled after him. "Good luck, aye? See you, brother."

"Och, aye," Logan yelled over his shoulder as he ran down the steps and out of sight.

CHAPTER TWENTY-SIX

Later that night, the Grant brothers sat around the hearth drinking ale, along with their brother-in-law, Quade. The only female present was Maddie, fast asleep in Alex's lap, resting in their favorite chair together, the one Alex had made special for them. He kissed her forehead and she sighed and cuddled closer to him.

"So, Robbie, do you want to tell us exactly what this lass means to you?" Alex asked.

Brodie smiled, "Aye, I see a bit more interest than is usual with you. Most of the time, you just ignore the lasses until it suits your needs. Your eyes follow this one everywhere."

Robbie sighed. "'Struth, I am interested in her. But her past has been so difficult that I don't know if we will ever suit. Her life is focused around her bairns, and I don't know if she wants another man in her life."

Maddie sat up, brushing the sleep from her eyes. "Your pardon. May I, Robbie?"

"Och, aye. I was hoping for your input, Maddie. I seem to say and do all the wrong things."

"Based on what she has said, my guess is she won't want to be touched for awhile. She was forced for so long, she probably wants no part of a man's touch right now."

"She isn't afraid of a man's touch. But I don't think she understands the way things should be between a man and a woman. Again, her experiences have tainted her view of the world."

"Aye, because all she has learned is wrong. It has been five years for her since her husband passed. The years since sound like pure torture. I know this is hard, but you will have to be patient if you really wish to pursue her."

He paused for a moment before he admitted the truth. "Aye, I do."

Quade said, "Are you ready to be involved in her daughters' lives? I think that would be important for her. She needs to see you interact with her wee ones."

"Gracie accepted me right away, long before Caralyn did. So she isn't an issue. I guess I am not sure about Ashlyn. They are so tied up with their new friends, I haven't spent much time with them."

"You must court her," Alex said.

"What do you mean?" Robbie asked.

"Start from the beginning and do the things she has never had done for her. Take her for a walk, go for a picnic, go for a boat ride in the loch. She needs to know life with you will be different."

Maddie nodded. "Aye, she has to learn what a good relationship is all about."

"Mayhap we can set her up in a place so that she feels she has something of her own. What about the cottage by the loch? We could fix it up for her." Robbie looked at Quade for support.

Alex said, "The family cottage is still there and it needs fixing up, but she can't stay there alone until the issue with Murray is done. I don't think it will be long before he'll be here, so go ahead and work on it if you wish."

Quade said, "I'll help. Will give me something to do while we wait for our new niece to be born."

"Nephew," Maddie said.

"Another lad, wife?"

"Aye, another lad. I can tell from the way he carries. No blonde haired lassie yet, Alex."

"Hmmph. Then we'll just have to try again," he said with a smile.

***

Two days later, Caralyn raced up the stairs to get her mantle. Robbie had offered to take her for a walk down by the loch, and she had accepted. She was so excited to go, and found her heart was pounding like a young lassie's.

Ashlyn followed her into the chamber. "May I go with you, Mama?"

"Mayhap this afternoon, Ashlyn. I think 'twould be too far for Gracie, and I need you to stay and watch her. I'm hoping to find our own cottage for us to live in."

"We can no' stay here?"

She knelt down in front of her daughter, "I need to find a place where I can make a contribution to the clan. I thought we could fish and clean the fish for Cook to use for midday meal. Remember how we used to fish with Papa?"

"Aye, I like fishing. That sounds like fun. And we do need to help, though I do care for the wee bairns, Mama."

"Aye, and I am proud of you. You are doing a great job with the weans. There will be a brand new one soon."

Caralyn fussed with her plait and then headed back to the staircase, Ashlyn trailing behind her. She stopped at the top and just stared over the railing. Robbie sat on a stool in the middle of the great hall while Gracie and Lily ran circles around him. Even though Lily was two summers the elder, both girls squealed and giggled as if it was the best game they ever played. Caralyn's heart melted at the sight of this big, braw Highlander playing with two wee lassies.

Robbie shouted, "Halt!"

The girls froze and didn't move at all. Caralyn leaned her chin into her hand, her elbow on the railing, so entranced with the way the two lassies gazed up at him, cherubic expressions on their faces as they awaited further instructions. She wondered what game they were playing.

He reached over and turned them so they were facing the opposite direction. "Ready. Now, Gracie you have to chase Lily and try to catch her. One-two-three, go!" The girls took off in a flash, arms swinging with glee, their laughter filling the hall as Gracie raced to catch Lily while everyone in the hall stopped to watch their antics. A simple game of chase and the bairns were having the time of their lives.

Ashlyn stood next to her mother and giggled. "Lily and Gracie play chase all the time, Mama. They love it."

"You like having new friends, don't you?" Caralyn smiled

as she tucked a few of Ashlyn's stray hairs back behind her ears.

Ashlyn nodded. "Aye, we never had friends before."

Caralyn descended the steps with Ashlyn and walked over to Robbie with purpose. Ashlyn ran off to play with the others.

Robbie quirked his brow at her when she bent down and kissed him on the cheek.

She blushed. "That kiss is for your talent with the wee ones. 'Tis part of who you are, I think, and I deem it a most noteworthy skill."

Robbie smiled and kissed her on the lips, careful not to move into the path of the rushing weans. "Kiss accepted and returned. Loving bairns *is* part of who I am and I thank you for noticing. I adore all my nieces and nephews, but mostly when they are a bit older and out of rags." He stood and held his arm out to her.

Caralyn caught Gracie as she raced by and picked her up to kiss her cheek. "Bye, my sweet. Mama will be back in a wee bit." Gracie gave her a kiss and scooted back down to continue with her game.

Loki came running over and jumped into the melee. "I'll help watch them, Master Robbie. I will make sure no surly pig-nuts bother them." He held up his fist to give impact to his words.

"Aye, I'm sure Ashlyn could use your help, but try not to teach the weans any bad name calling. Keep that between warriors." Robbie ruffled the lad's hair.

Loki covered his mouth and sheepishly apologized to Caralyn. "Sorry, my lady."

Caralyn smiled and said, "You may call me Caralyn, Loki. I'm not of noble birth."

"Nay, he can call you my lady. 'Tis proper respect."

Robbie took Caralyn's hand and tucked it inside his elbow as he escorted her to the door. Before leaving, they turned and blew the wee ones a kiss, though the only one who noticed was Ashlyn. A crisp autumn breeze caused Caralyn's skirts to billow as soon as they stepped outside.

"Are you still enjoying the Highlands, my lady?" Robbie gazed into her eyes as they strolled through the courtyard toward the gates.

"They seem to become more beautiful each day. The leaves are stunning. I am glad they hadn't all turned before we arrived. But I also love the sound of the wind through the pines."

"I'm glad to hear it." Once they were outside the gates, he took her hand in his. "I want you to see our loch before you decide where you would like to live."

"Do you think Alex will approve my request?"

"There are a couple of issues to be resolved and considered. First, there is only an old, run down cottage here. I want to check inside to see if it can be repaired. Second, and this is for both of us to think about, you will be a short distance from the village, so 'twould be harder to keep you safe. I don't think 'twould be wise for you to be here alone, and Alex won't approve your move until we know what will happen with Murray. It just wouldn't be safe for you and the girls."

They meandered for a short time, but soon came to a hill. The loch came into view when they reached the top. Caralyn stopped, awestruck by the sight in front of them. "Robbie, 'tis so beautiful." The hills and valleys ran in every direction, and the colors of orange and red decorated the landscape in sheer splendor. Golden leaves rippled in the breeze and Caralyn held her face up to the sun, drinking in the warmth of the rays. She smiled at the way the water sparkled, reflecting the sunlight across its small waves.

Caralyn stared up at Robbie, a smirk on her face. "Race you."

"How can you run with your bad ankle?"

"Och, 'tis much better now."

Robbie grinned his handsome smile, but she could read the question in his eyes. "Where to?"

Caralyn pointed to a stone building on the other side of the loch. "Isn't that the cottage?"

"Aye. You want to race me that far?" Robbie's eyes widened.

"Aye, I have my boots on. Race you to the cottage." Off she went, laughing in sheer delight as she scuttled down the hill, trying to maintain her balance. Her arms windmilled a couple of times just to stay upright, but she didn't let that stop her. She had started with quite a lead on him, but she could hear his heavy footsteps getting closer. A hand reached over and squeezed her waist as he came along beside her and she squealed, pushing him away and running in front of him.

She lost her footing and was about to fall head over heels when a strong arm grabbed her around the middle and righted her, pulling her in next to him. "Nay!" she screamed, shoving against his chest, her mood suddenly shifting to desperation.

Robbie's hands fell away from her and he held them up in the air. "Caralyn, nay. I will never hurt you or force you to do anything. I was just trying to keep you from falling."

Caralyn panted, mostly from running, but also a bit from fear. Stopping a distance away from him, she settled her hands on her hips in order to catch her breath. She gazed into his eyes and saw the hurt there, and something more. Concern.

And she did the only thing she could think of doing, she strode over to him and wrapped her arms around his broad chest and whispered, "I'm sorry. I know you would never hurt me."

Burying her face in his chest, she gripped his biceps while she chastised herself. *Bad, why must you continue to be bad?* But she was having so much fun and what was the harm? Racing with Robbie had made her smile again.

Her mother's voice echoed in her mind. *Do not be bad with your husband or he will get rid of you. Good women do not like it, only bad women. Do you hear me? Be a good and proper wife.*

Every time she thought she had a chance with Robbie, her mother reminded her of all the reasons it wouldn't work, all the reasons why Caralyn wasn't a good, virtuous woman. Something inside her was bad, that had to be it.

She was rotten, right to her core.

Robbie stepped back and lifted her chin. "Caralyn, don't look so frustrated and forlorn. I know you have issues you must deal with. We will work through them together. Just tell me what makes you uncomfortable."

She stared at him, fighting back tears, wanting to tell him, wanting to confess all. But she couldn't. If she did, he would hate her.

CHAPTER TWENTY-SEVEN

Robbie held his hand out to Caralyn. "Come, what's done is done. I won't let it ruin our day. We're almost to the cottage."

Caralyn put her hand in his and smiled. "Aye, I would like to see it."

They walked around the edge of the loch until they reached the small stone cottage.

Robbie still held her hand in his. He tilted his head toward the hut, overgrown weeds lining the exterior. "What do you think?"

Caralyn perused the area. A small dock sat over the water, mostly still in good shape. She gasped as they made their way closer to the building, thatches of wildflowers in plots arranged around the outside of the building. Groups of trees sat behind it. She glanced up at the thatched roof, where there were a few holes clearly in need of patching.

She stopped when they were directly in front of the house. A covered entrance was attached to the front with a wide railing on one side, probably for cleaning fish. Three stone steps beckoned them inside. "Robbie, 'tis beautiful." She turned her head to glance at him and her eyes sparkled with hope. "May we go inside?"

He nodded, pleased to see the glimmer of hope in her gaze. He had always loved this cottage, though he hadn't been inside in years. It was often just used for fishing in the summer, but he and his brothers had spent many warm months swimming in the loch.

He opened the thick oak door with a shove and it creaked as it swung open. As they walked through the front room, he was surprised to see the floor was also made of stone. He had remembered it as a dirt floor, but it was solid—quite dirty, though some soap and water would clean it up nicely. It made sense for the cottage to have a stone floor with water so close.

Caralyn's eyes lit up as they took in the front room, clearly the main room. A large hearth sat on the side wall with a big kettle hung to the side. Utensils hung from a row across the back, a few pots mixed in. A table and four chairs sat in the middle and a work bench of sorts stood in the back near the utensils. An assortment of stools sat in various spots along with two large chests. They had to brush some cobwebs away, and everything was coated with dust, but the place held promise.

Robbie tugged her hand toward the passageway. He had to duck to walk through it, but it led to a good sized chamber with a large bed. Two doors were at the back of the room. A quick examination revealed that one led to a smaller bedroom with one nightstand. The other was another small passageway that led to a garderobe and the outside.

"Robbie, I love it. Aye, it needs work, but it could be a lovely place to live. Right near the loch where you could listen to the frogs at night."

Robbie glanced at the ceiling. "The roof needs quite a bit of repair. And we would need to replace the bedding. Seems there are a few critters that won't be happy about that, but I agree with you. There aren't many three room cottages with such a large main room. I wonder why no one else is here, except 'tis a wee distance from the village."

"Aye, but I like my privacy."

"'Twould be mighty cold here. You don't have many pines for protection. A few out back, but the snow must drift terrible here."

"Could we transplant some pines to help with the snow?"

"Aye, I don't see why not." Robbie couldn't help but share her enthusiasm. He could absolutely picture living here with Caralyn as his wife, especially with the extra room for their bairns. They could sit outside at night and enjoy the peace and quiet of the loch, and fish and swim when the water was warm. They weren't far from the keep and he could protect her.

He glanced at her beaming face. Somehow, he didn't

believe they shared the same vision.

***

Malcolm stood in the middle of the clearing, bellowing at the four men with him. "I told you we were heading into the Highlands. Why would I pay you so much coin otherwise? I wouldn't pay you this kind of coin to run around Glasgow. I knew it would be tough."

The biggest man stood opposite Malcolm. "Aye, but you never told us we would have trouble breathing up here. I can hardly sleep in this air. We're out of here. C'mon Duncan."

He beckoned to the man next to him and headed for his horse. "We're getting the hell out of these Highlands. You can keep your coin. This 'ere place will kill me if I keep on."

"Wait," Malcolm yelled. "I'll double your pay."

"Nay, 'tis not worth it to me. You're daft." The two jumped on their horses and galloped back down the path.

Malcolm had known this would be a tough journey for anyone not used to the Highlands, but he wouldn't give up. Not now. Finally, he was almost exactly where he had always wanted to be. Trading in anticipation of a possible war had earned him more coin than he had ever wanted. The sale of weaponry, especially the bows and the Irish bills had reaped great wealth for him. He had put his parents in a nice cottage and his father was proud of him.

Erskine had tried to talk him into selling slaves, but he had turned him down. Malcolm didn't have much of a heart, but one existed. And Erskine had wanted to sell Caralyn along with her friend. Nay, never. Caralyn was his, he had trained her well and she had become quite the delight the way her mother's guilt nagged at her.

He rubbed his shoulder where the arrow had pierced him. Damn, but Grant had good aim. Caralyn had been right where he wanted her till Grant had interfered.

He still had two men left, Ross and Bruce. Three men ought to be able to steal Caralyn away.

"How can we kidnap three of them when there are only three of us?" Ross asked.

"We don't need all three of them. We only need one daughter to get her to do what I want. Hell, I'll be happy if I just steal Caralyn. We'll just need to change our plans a bit."

This satisfied Ross and Bruce, but he had to give it some thought. Malcolm paced around the grove of trees while he thought the situation through. Mayhap he should give it all up and go back. He had several others he liked. Why did he need Caralyn?

Aye, she was a beauty, but it was the way he could make her moan that forced him to go after her—that and his other purpose. He chuckled. The true reason he liked her so much was because of her mother. She had filled Caralyn's head with madness, and he used it to his advantage. Why, he never had to punish the lass, she spent all her time punishing herself. He had seen her cut herself once, just to stick her own fingernail in the wound to cause herself more pain. The girl was daft, even if she was passionate.

Then Robbie Grant popped into his mind. How could he forget him? That was reason enough for him not to turn around. He wouldn't let the little weasel have his woman. Captain Grant couldn't win. He had stared down his nose at him as if he was better or of noble blood.

He would take care of that look in Captain Grant's eyes. He would show him who was best. The hell with the daughters. Malcolm Murray would kidnap Caralyn to make the captain pay.

CHAPTER TWENTY-EIGHT

Caralyn sat brushing her hair in front of the hearth. She had just come in from the bathing room and had gotten the lassies settled in bed. Rubbing Gracie's back always put her to sleep in a hurry. Caralyn sighed when she thought of how happy Gracie was here. Ashlyn was, too—she loved having lasses her age to play with—but she could tell that her eldest still worried about her.

The afternoon with Robbie had been wonderful, except for her outburst. She couldn't believe how she had treated him, but it had been instinctive for her...and the biggest miracle of all was that he'd seemed to understand.

Every day her feelings grew for Captain Robbie Grant. She loved the way he held her hand and protected her. He was so good with wee Gracie, who adored him. His heart was kind and giving—despite his great physical strength, he wasn't one to issue orders or insist on getting his own way.

When they had stood inside the cottage, she found herself wondering what it would be like to live with Robbie as her husband, to live with him in the cottage, fish with him, cook for him, and spend their days playing with their bairns. She knew Robbie had to work in the lists every day or do whatever his laird required, but how wonderful it would be to be wrapped in his arms every night just the way she had been under the stars.

She checked the girls again before grabbing her robe and putting on her slippers. Heading out the door, she turned to the right and padded down the stairs. She had asked Maddie if she could chat with her privately after the girls were settled, and she agreed. As soon as she hit the bottom of the staircase, Maddie popped her head out of the solar and beckoned her inside. Alex, Brodie, Robbie, and Quade all sat in front of the hearth in the great hall, laughing about something. Loki and Torrian played with Growley, Torrian's big hound, on the floor.

Caralyn stepped inside and closed the door. "Thank you for meeting with me."

Maddie smiled and wrapped her arm around her from the side. "Of course, I will help you in any way I can." She stepped back and lowered herself into a seat in front of the hearth. "I had Alex build the fire up a bit. He worries about me so when I'm carrying, but it will not be much longer now."

Caralyn sat down and folded her hands in her lap. She stared down at them, not quite sure how to start.

"Robbie told me that you have some things in common with me…" she stammered. "But I don't know where to start."

She paused for a moment, then said, "Today, Robbie and I were racing, and I started to fall and he reached out and caught me. He was only trying to help me but I shoved him and screamed at him." She swiped at the tears threatening to fall down her cheeks. "How could he want to be around me when I act like that?"

"First of all, know that you are not alone. We are all here for you, and you always have someone to talk to in this keep," Maddie said. "The first time I met Alex, he rescued me in the middle of a whipping from my stepbrother. You would think I would trust him after that, wouldn't you?"

Caralyn nodded.

"Every time Alex took a step toward me, I took two steps back. And if you don't believe me, you may ask both of his brothers, because they noticed it."

Caralyn smiled. "I guess 'twould be noticeable."

Maddie reached over and patted Caralyn's arm. "What you're doing is normal. Robbie will get used to it."

"But I don't understand. How can you want to be married? After all I have been through, I'm not sure I can fully trust a man again…even Robbie. I have strong feelings for him, but I am confused."

Maddie said, "With the right man, you will. Mayhap it is Robbie, mayhap not."

"My biggest problem is that Malcolm is in my mind all the time. How do I stop that?"

Maddie pulled her chair next to Caralyn's and hugged her. "It will take time, especially since Malcolm is still a threat to you and your daughters. But as time goes by, you will think about the people you love more, and about the people who hurt you less." After a short silence, she added, "I actually had to make a commitment, and I made it for myself and for Alex."

"What was that?" Caralyn mopped her eyes with one of the linen squares that Celestina had given her the other day.

"My stepbrother was the worst person in my life, and the one I thought about most. I realized that if he were still alive, he would be verra happy to know he was still in my thoughts. By thinking of him, you give him that power over you, that control. You can't do it."

"How did you defeat him? 'Twill not be easy. I can't just make him go away or I would have done it already."

"I retrained my mind. Whenever my stepbrother popped into my mind, I forced myself to think of Alex. It took time, but it worked. The happy thoughts became stronger than the terrifying ones."

Maddie rubbed Caralyn's shoulder in encouragement. "Caralyn, this may be more difficult for you because from what you have told me, you are not sure how you feel about Robbie, correct?"

"Aye… nay. Och, sometimes I'm sure, and other times I'm not."

"Think of any pleasant thought. Did you enjoy your walk to the lake?"

"Aye, especially when we were racing." Caralyn smiled as she thought about Robbie running next to her, the sunlight reflecting off his hair and his smile that melted her heart.

"Then use that. Whenever you think of Malcolm, think of that race instead. It may make you smile." Maddie kissed her cheek. "Robbie is worth it, he is a wonderful man and we would love to have you in the family."

Although surprised to hear Maddie say they would love to

have her in the family, Caralyn nodded. She would try. She had to.

CHAPTER TWENTY-NINE

Caralyn awoke in the middle of the night to a soft knocking at her door. She fell out of bed and padded over to the door, holding it open just a crack to see who was on the other side. Robbie stood there with a look of urgency on his face that immediately caught her attention.

"Caralyn, Maddie's time is here and Brenna wondered if you would mind assisting her. They're in Maddie's chamber down the corridor."

"Aye, of course. Give me a moment to put something on." She rushed through the room, searching for a clean gown and her slippers. As soon as she was dressed, she fussed with her hair for a moment, trying to set the plaits to rights before joining Robbie and closing the door behind her. "The girls are sound asleep."

Robbie tugged her in close. "Lass, I can't resist you."

He kissed her, just long enough to invade her senses and make her forget her purpose. She leaned into him to savor his taste and the feel of his warm embrace. How she missed this man. She wanted him now and forever.

He ended the kiss and helped her to stand on her own again. "If I don't get you there, my sister and brother will have my hide." He cupped her face and kissed her quick. "You do distract me, Caralyn." As they headed down the corridor, Robbie asked, "Have you ever helped with a birth before?"

She nodded, hiding her smile at Robbie's declaration. "Aye, at the priory."

He guided her to Maddie's chamber and she slipped inside, surprised to see Alex still there, pacing frantically, along with

Maddie's maid, Alice.

"Och, good. Another set of hands," Brenna said. "You don't mind, Caralyn? You won't faint?"

"Nay, I helped the sisters with a birth at the priory. I am happy to assist any way I can."

"Wonderful. We need to ready the bed. Let's put Maddie in this chair and settle the bed with extra sheets. Robbie, take Alex downstairs for a wee bit, will you?"

Alex barked. "Nay, Brenna. I'll stay while my wife births the babe. You should know that by now."

"Aye, Alex, I remember. But you take up half the room, especially when you pace. Can't you leave so we can prepare for the arrival of your newest wean? You have a few minutes before the bairn arrives."

Robbie snickered. "Come along, Alex. An ale may help you. You had several before the twins were born."

"Fine. But I will return shortly." He helped Maddie out of bed and into a chair by the hearth. He kissed her on the lips and said, "I love you. I'll be back. Don't do anything without me."

"Go, Alex." She gritted her teeth as another wave of pain racked her body. "I'll be fine. Let them get everything settled. And please go find the cradle."

Alex left in a huff, and once he was gone, Caralyn turned to Brenna for guidance.

"Caralyn, you know Maddie's maid, Alice, who has been with her since she was a bairn. Will you help her ready the bed?"

"Of course." She settled to the task with Alice and watched as Brenna used a nearby chest to lay out her tools. Fiona came in the room with water and more linens. When they finished, she helped Maddie get back into bed, fluffing the pillows behind her back.

"I so wanted to have this bairn during the day hours so you could sleep, Brenna. This is all Alex's fault."

"Och, we all know that, Maddie." Brenna rolled her eyes at her sister-in-law.

"Nay, that's not what I meant. Alex cannot keep his hands away. I told him if we kept going on like that, we'd rush the babe out." She giggled as she told her story.

Caralyn couldn't hide the shock on her face. She had relations while she was carrying?

Brenna glanced at Caralyn. "Caralyn, are you well? You aren't going to drop on me, are you?"

"Nay." She picked up the linens and folded them, still puzzled by what she had just heard.

Brenna chuckled. "When I was carrying Bethia, Quade was afraid to touch me. I told him there was no way I could go nine months without my enjoyment. He finally relented. 'Tis fun to play with the different positions, isn't it?"

Brenna and Maddie both laughed at their own memories. Caralyn stared at them, mouth still agape.

"Caralyn, you were married when you had Ashlyn, aye?" Brenna said. "You didn't enjoy relations when you carried?"

Caralyn cleared her throat and swallowed before she sat on a nearby stool, puzzled. "My mother told me you couldn't have relations when you carried."

"Child, your mother was wrong," Alice spoke up. "Most women can have relations while they are carrying. Though many in England believe the same as your mum. Do you agree, Brenna?"

"Och, aye. Would have driven me daft if I couldn't hold my husband close and enjoy him. 'Tis the best part of marriage. But I did have one mother who I advised not to have relations near the end. She carried the bairn too low. But other than that, most continue to enjoy their husbands until the verra end."

In that one moment, Caralyn's world fell apart. Could everything she knew be wrong? Had her mother told her untruths? And both women were talking about enjoying relations…wanting them…like it was no sin. As if it was natural.

Maddie reached for her hand. "Come sit on the bed near me. You can hold my hand."

Caralyn sat next to her and gripped her hand, then whispered, "You enjoy relations with your husband?"

"Och, aye. I love relations with my husband. He takes such good care of me. But I have heard of some women who don't." Maddie's face turned to Brenna. "Brenna?"

"Aye for me as well. Caralyn? Why do you ask? You never

did?"

Her mother's voice echoed in her ears, loud and insistent. *Good wives do not enjoy marital relations. 'Tis a sin for a woman to enjoy it like a man. Do not let him try to make you take part in it. Just lie there until he is done and it won't take long. Women who enjoy relations are bad. You will be bad, bad, and your husband will get rid of you. Only whores like it. Remember what I tell you, Caralyn. Be a good wife, lie there and say naught. Elsewise you will be branded a whore.*

She massaged her temple as the truth wove its way through her memories.

Her mother had lied, and all these years Caralyn had believed her. She held the side of her head as she tried to make sense of how these deeply ingrained lies had impacted her thoughts, her actions, her everything. Malcolm had told her the same things, teasing her, telling her that her enjoyment of sex made her a great whore. Most of the time, she could ignore them and pretend it wasn't happening, but Malcolm had always known how to force her enjoyment. How to make her feel guilty. That's what he was about. Guilt. Control. How she hated him!

Lies, they were all lies.

Only one person had not made her feel bad in his bed.

Captain Robbie Grant.

She heard Brenna's voice before noticing her hand on her arm. "Caralyn, would you like to talk about it?"

Caralyn had to ask again—she had to *know*. "'Tis normal to enjoy it?" she whispered, praying the answer would still be aye.

"Aye." Brenna held her hand. "You don't look well."

"'No one thinks bad of a woman who likes it? My mother taught me only whores like it."

Alice gasped. "Nay, child. Pardon me, but your mama told you wrong. She could have been raised in one of the strict churches, though, so don't think poorly of her. She told you what she was taught is my guess."

"You are normal, Caralyn." Maddie squeezed her hand. A second later, a tighter squeeze came as another wave of pain and pressure hit Maddie's body, trying to prepare it for the birthing process.

The door burst open and Alex flew in, tugging Caralyn off the bed so he could climb up behind Maddie. "Sorry, lass," he gave Caralyn a sheepish look. "This helps when my wife has to push the bairn out. 'Tis all I can do for her." He began to massage Maddie's shoulders and Caralyn stepped back.

Robbie stood in the doorway, winked at her and said, "See you later, lass. Time for me to leave."

Time flew by over the next hour. Maddie worked hard to deliver her bairn, and Caralyn helped where she could. She forgot about everything they had discussed, devoting all her focus to Maddie and Brenna. Alex was a delight to watch as he took care of his wee wife, cradling her between pains, encouraging her when she needed him. He mopped her forehead and kissed her cheek. She had never heard of any man staying through a birthing. This was definitely something she would have to ask Robbie about.

Sometime in the following hour, Brenna yelled, "I can see the bairn's head, Maddie. Push now, push hard." Brenna pulled Caralyn down next to her and pointed to the babe's hair. "I think 'twill be yellow haired, Maddie. Push for your husband." Jennie popped her head in at the last minute and Brenna beckoned her inside. The lass stared at everything in wide-eyed wonder, but she knelt down on the floor to watch.

Alex held Maddie up while she pushed, her hands locked behind her knees for leverage. The bairn's head came closer to being ejected, but it fell back when Maddie took a breath. While Maddie relaxed, Brenna told Caralyn and Jennie about the life cord that came out with the baby, and showed them what she would use to tie it and then cut it when the time came. They waited for another wave of pressure to prompt Maddie into pushing.

When it came, Maddie pushed with all her might. Finally the head popped out and Brenna cradled the bairn's wee head in her hand, using a cloth to wipe off the wean's face. "Come on, Maddie, the head is out, you need to push and get the shoulders out."

"I cannot, I have no strength left." Maddie panted in exhaustion.

Brenna cleaned out the inside of the babe's mouth. "Alex, she needs to push. Get her to finish this."

Alex sat her up and when a new wave of contractions assaulted Maddie, she pushed until her face was beet red. The bairn's shoulders slipped through the small opening, and Maddie fell back against her husband, sighing in relief.

Brenna caught the wee one and Caralyn reached down to help her. The healer had just set the babe in Caralyn's waiting hands when he let out a loud yelp and turned bright red.

"You have another lad, Alex! Maddie, 'tis a beautiful lad. He has light hair and he is hopping mad right now. What a strong laddie!" Brenna's joy was contagious.

The bairn let out a feisty scream as he wiggled, his wee hands fisted with all his might, and they all smiled. Caralyn only realized there were tears streaming down her face when her vision blurred. She watched Brenna tie off and cut the life cord and wrap the bairn in a soft plaid before settling him in his mother's arms. Maddie cried when she saw her new wean and Alex kissed her.

Alice, who stood by Maddie's side, cried rivers and, in between, managed to say, "Four, my word, child, four healthy bairns. How I wish your mama could see you now."

Caralyn helped Brenna take care of the life piece that came out after the baby. They all worked together and cleaned the babe up enough to send Alex out the door to show off his new son. Finally, they cleaned Maddie up, dressed her in a fresh night rail, and she fell asleep.

Brenna hugged Caralyn and thanked her before sending her out the door. When she stepped into the passageway, she realized the sun had risen. She turned to see Robbie walking toward her, and she promptly ran into his arms sobbing.

CHAPTER THIRTY

Robbie wrapped his arms around Caralyn, uncertain what to say, but grateful to have her in his arms for any reason. He was quite happy whenever she was near.

"Sweeting, you are well?" he asked softly.

Caralyn picked her head up and blubbered, "Aye, 'twas so beautiful." Her breath hitched three times. "Nay, my mama lied to me all those years ago."

Robbie understood the first comment, but he had no guess as to the meaning of the second. He wrapped his arm around her shoulders and guided her toward her chamber. She sobbed all the way down the passageway, but he held her tight.

As soon as she stepped inside, she gave him a questioning look. "My bairns? Where are my bairns?" She hiccupped and waited for his answer.

"Sweeting, 'tis morn. The wee ones are all in the great hall eating and fussing over the new wean. When I left, they were trying to choose a name for the laddie." He patted her shoulder in assurance. "They're fine. Quade, Brodie, and Celestina are all with them. Come, sit and tell me why you cry so."

She sat on the bed and leaned into his shoulder. "Your brother was so wonderful the way he was there for Maddie. And 'twas beautiful when the wean was born, all red and messy, but still beautiful. I was so amazed watching Brenna deliver the bairn. She is a talented healer."

"Aye, she learned from our mama and is teaching Jennie now. She has saved many lives, including her husband's."

"And when Brenna wrapped the bairn in the plaid and handed him to Maddie, I wanted to cry on the spot, but I couldn't because I wanted to assist Brenna."

Robbie kissed her forehead. "You didn't have anyone to help you when you had your girls, did you?"

"Nay, just the midwife, but I didn't like her. And she told me awful things, not at all like the things said to Maddie. Brenna and Alex were both so encouraging. Alice, too."

"I am sorry, lass. But you still have two beautiful lassies." He brushed her hair away from her face, drinking in her beauty, enjoying this rare chance to be close to her. Somehow, he knew she still had secrets, but would she share them? He waited, hoping she would continue.

***

Caralyn picked up a fresh linen square and mopped her cheeks. She lifted her head from Robbie's shoulder and gazed into his eyes, so appreciative of the warmth she saw there. He really did care for her. He had to, or why would he be there holding her while she blubbered so? She suspected he would prove himself every bit as wonderful of a mate as his brother, Alex, if she would just give him the chance.

She sat next to him on the bed and faced him, crossing her legs in front of her as she gathered her thoughts and tried to calm her breathing. The tears had slowed and she took a deep breath, still clasping his hand as if she was afraid to let go.

"Robbie, I need to tell you something and 'tis an embarrassing subject. Mayhap 'tis not something I should discuss with a man, but as difficult as it is for me to admit it to myself...I trust you. I am so confused, I don't know who else to turn to." She chewed on her thumbnail as she glanced up at him to see his reaction.

"Go on. I will try to help if I can, Caralyn." He squeezed her hand and she held on tight.

"When we were together in the priory..." She paused and caught his gaze, hoping she would see anything but condemnation there, instead seeing the concern and something else—love? She could only hope. Glancing at the ceiling, she gathered her strength before she continued, then stared at their intertwined hands. "If you recall, before I left, I shoved you away, angry."

Robbie nodded. "I remember every moment of that night,

most of them wonderful." He ran his fingers down her cheek, caressing her skin beneath her tears. "What you speak of was the only bad part for me."

She glanced away, so afraid to see judgment in his face, but she forced herself to finish, even though she knew she couldn't handle looking in his eyes as she confessed. "The night before my wedding, my mother explained to me about the marriage bed. She told me to lie there for my husband and be quiet."

Robbie's brow furrowed, but he said naught.

"She told me that lasses didn't enjoy the marriage bed, that enjoyment meant you were a whore and your husband would send you away."

She dared a quick look at his face, and the shock she saw there encouraged her to continue. "That's what I did with my husband. I did what I was supposed to do, what I was taught. I didn't know any better." Her eyes misted again and she used the linen square to wipe them as she talked. "I don't think he was verra experienced either, but he never told me otherwise and I was carrying soon, so our lovemaking stopped." She squeezed her eyes shut as memories assaulted her mind, memories that she had shut out for so long.

Robbie reached for her and pulled her onto his lap.

She rested her head on his shoulder before continuing. "When Malcolm came along and forced me to have relations with him in exchange for food, he did things to me that brought me pleasure. I told him what my mother had said, and he laughed. I still recall exactly what he said. "Your mother is right, you are a whore, so you'll whore for me and my friends, and you'll still enjoy it. In return, I'll make sure your daughters don't go hungry. But be sure you always know what you are. A whore."

She kept her head on his shoulder, too embarrassed to look him in the eye. "I did what I had to do to fill my lassie's bellies, but all along, I chastised myself for being the whore my mother had warned me against being.

"That night with you was the most wonderful night of my life. You made me feel so special, and you never made me feel guilty. It was as if you enjoyed pleasuring me, and 'struth is I enjoyed pleasuring you. When we finished, my mother came back into my mind and told me how bad I had been. How wrong."

As she finished this last sentence, she sat up abruptly, as if under someone else's control, and her right hand grabbed her left wrist and she drove her fingernail into her skin. Robbie separated her hands. "Is this why you hurt yourself? I have seen you do it before."

"Aye." Tears welled in her eyes again, but she let them fall this time. "It's how I punish myself for being bad. But now, after talking to Brenna and Maddie, I know my mother lied. Mayhap I'm not bad after all." She pulled her fingernail away from her tender skin. "Mayhap, I don't need to do this anymore."

"Och, sweeting." He brought her wrist up to his lips and kissed the broken spot tenderly. "Aye, 'tis a lie of ignorance from your mother, and probably what she or her Kirk believed. She didn't tell you that to hurt you. I am certain your mother loved you. You believe that, don't you?"

Caralyn nodded as she stared at the spot on her wrist, knowing that in her heart she did believe her mother loved her. She had told her such because of her own beliefs, not because she wanted to hurt her. She returned her gaze to Robbie.

"But Malcolm? He told you to gain more control over you." He placed his hand under her chin. "You're not bad for enjoying relations with me. 'Tis the way it should be between a husband and wife, between two people who care about each other. Even though we aren't married, 'tis still normal."

She gazed into his gray eyes and touched his jaw with her finger, caressing his rough beard with her thumb and wanting to kiss him more than she had ever wanted to kiss anyone. "Do you care for me, Robbie Grant?"

"Aye, lass, I do. And I hope verra much you feel the same."

She smiled as she rubbed his bottom lip with her thumb. "I love you, Captain Grant. I just never understood what love with a man was until we met. I'm so scared of the way I feel, but there is no denying it."

"May I ask why?" He smiled, but the look in his eye told her he would not back down. He needed her to be honest with him now.

He wanted assurance from her, and somehow, this tickled her from the base of her spine all the way up to her neck. This big, brawny, handsome Highlander wanted to know if she had true feelings for him. "I love you for the way you make me feel, so special and so wanted. I love you for the way you are with my bairns. I love you for your tender touch, for your protectiveness of all of us, for your smile, and for the way you look at me. Does this meet with your approval?"

All she heard was a growl as he took her lips in his in a searing kiss, slanting his mouth over hers. He swept her sweet mouth with his tongue, tasting and tantalizing her at the same time.

He cupped her face with his hands and pulled back, leaning his forehead against hers and saying, "Aye, lass. 'Tis enough for now."

"Then make love to me, Robbie. I want to know how it feels to have no guilt about what we do."

CHAPTER THIRTY-ONE

Robbie couldn't be happier to oblige Caralyn, but first he got up to barricade the door. He had to make sure the girls wouldn't walk in on them. He removed his brooch and tossed his plaid on the ground before removing his leine. The musical sound of Caralyn's laughter rang out in the room.

He tugged her off the bed and pulled her to him, holding her tight against his chest. "Do you know how long I have waited for this? How long I have wanted you, lass?"

He nuzzled her neck before he helped her out of her gown. When they finally both stood with naught on, he paused to look at her, awestruck. "Caralyn," he reached over and ran his hand down her arm. "You are so beautiful. I knew it in the dark, but to see you now takes my breath away."

The blood raged through his body and he crushed her to him, capturing her lips with his so he could taste her again. His tongue stroked hers until a fever lit his body. He could feel his erection pressed against her belly and he moaned when her hand wrapped around him and stroked him in a wicked rhythm that threatened to unman him.

He lifted her into his arms and set her on the bed, taking another look at her gorgeous body, drinking in his fill of her before he leaned in to touch her. Settling himself on top of her, he brushed her hair back from her face and said, "You'll tell me if I do aught you don't like, sweeting?"

"Robbie, I don't think you could do anything I wouldn't like. You're so tender, yet so big and hard." She grasped his biceps in delight, smiling up at him. "Please don't stop."

He loved the feel of her breasts against his chest when he

leaned in to kiss her. Unable to restrain himself, he brought his head down to taste her, licking a path down the valley between her lovely mounds. With just a look, she had unleashed a hunger inside him. He kissed a hot trail over to each nipple, bringing them to a taut peak as she writhed underneath him in fevered passion. Bringing one into his mouth, he suckled her until she cried out. She reached down and grabbed his shaft, stroking him softly as a tease, touching the tip with the lightest of caresses.

He stilled her hand to keep from spilling his hot seed into her hand. A wave of emotion swept through him—how amazing what one small lass could do to him, could make him feel. His hand caressed her hip, gliding over across the soft skin of her thigh until he found her slit. Probing her soft folds, he groaned at the wetness and the slick flesh that met his touch, then pulsed his fingers inside her to make her ready for him.

"Please, Robbie, now. I want you now." She clutched his arms as she gazed at him, her features ripe with passion.

He grabbed her hips and thrust inside her as she spread her legs to welcome him. He stilled for a moment as he gazed into her eyes. "I didn't hurt you?"

"Nay," she cried out, tipping her pelvis up to him to bring him in further. "More, I want more."

Robbie leaned on his elbows and gave her what she wanted. She joined him in his rhythm, both ruled by the powerful force that pushed them to an edge. Her soft moans drove him into a pace he couldn't control. He plunged inside her and lifted her hips to take more of him groaning, gasping because of how good it felt to be inside her. She took all of him and rocked him, squeezing him until he wanted to lose it all, but he wouldn't go before her. Reaching down between them, he found her nub and caressed her until he heard her gasp, felt her cling to him as she went over the edge, her contractions milking him and he finally surrendered, calling her name as his seed shot into her and a searing ecstasy possessed him like he had never felt before.

He braced himself on his elbows and gazed into her eyes, the haze of her pleasure still evident on her face, a bliss that he had shared with her. He kissed her forehead and each cheek, before settling on her lips.

"Sweeting, that was wonderful," he whispered. "Nae guilt?"

She smiled in a languished pleasure. "No guilt. I love you, Robbie Grant."

An all-consuming peace settled over him and surprised him. "I love you, too, Caralyn."

***

The midday meal was full of giggling and happy chatter as the Grants welcomed the newest member of their family. After Caralyn had cleaned up and taken a nap, she came downstairs and her two daughters raced to see her, both tugging her toward the cradle set in the middle of the table, surrounded by weans of various sizes, all waiting to see what the babe would do next.

Now she sat on the bench and gazed at the beautiful wonder in front of her. The laddie slept as no other, oblivious to the stirrings around him.

Gracie pulled herself onto her lap. "Mama, see new bairn?"

Kissing her wee lassie's cheek, Caralyn said, "Aye, I saw him last night. He's beautiful."

Ashlyn stared at her mother. "You were there? Why didn't you come for me? I wanted to be there." Her face fell, full of disappointment.

"Och, lass, I needed you to stay in bed with Gracie. The chamber was full enough. Now is when you'll be most needed. You and Jennie and Avelina can help Maddie clean him and change him when he needs it."

Ashlyn's eyes grew big as saucers. "Mama, I saw him pish already. He pees straight up. And Loki says that's what lads do. Is that not odd? Loki says he and Torrian will care for the boy because he is a laddie and has to be a warrior someday."

"Someday, but I think he has a while yet." Robbie came inside with the twins, John and Jamie, and Brodie. Loki and Torrian trailed behind them, Growley stopping at the bowl near the door for a drink of water.

Without pausing, Robbie strode right over to her and kissed her cheek, then gazed at his new nephew with a smile. Gracie hopped down to play with the twins and Robbie sat on a nearby stool. "Och, those lads are busy. Jake never stops."

"Jake? I thought his name was John?"

"His real name is John after his grandsire, but sometimes we call him Jake. I don't remember how it started." He turned to Ashlyn. "What do you think of the new bairn?"

"I love him already, but he cries verra loud."

"Ashlyn, once things settle down in here, I thought I might take you and your mama out to see the cottage by the loch. Brodie and Quade said they would help me fix the roof, and you could mayhap help your mother sort out and straighten the inside?"

"Alex has given us permission to live there?" Caralyn could not believe the good news. Though their visit there had been short, she'd fallen in love with the cottage.

"Nay, not yet, but it'll take some time to fix it up proper. If we all help, we should be done before the heavy snow falls. We want to fix the roof first to help protect it against the weather. I also want to get Quade's help with the heavy work before he and Brenna return home. They want to beat the winter snows or they'll be staying with us for the winter."

"They aren't staying? That means Lily and Torrian and Bethia will leave, also." Ashlyn's disappointment spread across her features.

"Quade is laird of the Ramsay clan and Brenna is their healer. They are needed back home. They brought many of their clan with them, but they wish to settle at home. She promised Alex to remain until my return and Maddie's delivery. All are well, so she can go home now. Quade's mother and brother are awaiting their return."

"But then who is the healer here?" Ashlyn asked.

"Alice can deliver bairns, and though Jennie is still young, Brenna has been training her. There is an auld healer in the village as well."

Just then, bairn Grant began squalling. "Have they settled on a name yet, Robbie?" Caralyn reached into the cradle to pick him up. She loved to rock weans in her arms.

"Connor is the lad's name. What do you think?" He smiled at his new nephew. "He'll have to be a tough one to handle his two older brothers."

Connor continued to yell after she wrapped him tight in his

plaid. "Mayhap I will take him to Maddie. Could be time for his feeding." Sensing that he would be soon taken away, Gracie ran over to kiss the bairn's cheek before turning back to play with the lads. Suddenly, she whirled around and rushed to Caralyn's side. She placed her hands on her mama's knees and said, "Lu you, Mama."

Caralyn said, "I love you, too, Gracie."

Without hesitating, Ashlyn came over and whispered in her ear. "Mama, do *you* love you?"

Caralyn didn't know how to answer that question.

Robbie looked at her as she stood with the babe wrapped in her arms. "The lass has a good point. Do you love yourself after all you have been through? 'Twould be difficult after all the wrong things you have been told about yourself."

Caralyn headed to the staircase, her mind totally confused. She had never given it a thought.

CHAPTER THIRTY-TWO

Two days later, the work crew hustled around the cottage at the loch. Quade, Brodie, Tomas, and Robbie had brought what they needed to fix the roof. Loki had brought Growley with him because Torrian was having a bad day with his belly and had sent him to play with the girls. Ashlyn and Gracie had come with Caralyn to see the cottage.

When Ashlyn stepped inside, she gasped in excitement. "Mama, this cottage is so big." She raced through the passageway to the back and yelled to her mother. "And look, Gracie and I can have our own chamber." She was still babbling when she remerged in the front room. "And there is even a garderobe in the back. But no bathing room, is there?"

Loki laughed. "What do you need a bathing room for when you have the loch?"

Ashlyn retorted with a huff that made Caralyn chuckle. "Because the loch is cold this time of year."

Loki said, "Och, you only need two dunkings in the winter. Just pick a day when the sun shines. I'm going out to pick stones for my slinger. Do you want Gracie to come with me or stay inside?"

"Two dunkings all winter? That's dirty, Loki Grant."

"Hush, Ashlyn. Loki had a different upbringing."

"Aye," he said with a grin. "I used to be Lucky Loki and I lived under a crate, but now I am Loki Grant and," he patted his chest, "I am a mighty Grant warrior and Brodie Grant is my sire." He turned and ran down the water's edge, stopping occasionally to pick up a stone to slide into his pocket.

"Mayhap we'll work outside in the gardens today," Caralyn

said to her daughter as she moved her onto the porch. Right before she stepped outside, she glanced up at a hole in the roof and caught Robbie staring at her with a grin on his face. He winked and she blushed, catching up with Ashlyn.

"Let's see what we find in the weeds. If we're lucky, there's an old vegetable garden underneath." She took the girls with her and found a couple of patches of different growth. "Let's look around here, Ashlyn. Much is dead, but we could find some seedlings for next year."

Caralyn and her daughters set to work on the huge patch of overgrown grasses and weeds. Every once in a while, Caralyn would check on Robbie up on the roof. At one point, she wandered over and yelled up. "How bad does it look? Is there much that needs repairing?"

Brodie stuck his head over the edge. "Och, a few critters need to find new homes, but won't be too bad. We should be able to fix this within a sennight."

Caralyn shuddered at the thought of what could be living in the roof, but walked back to the large patch of grass the girls were still wandering through. Once there, she took a step back and spent a minute perusing the area. "Ashlyn, this entire patch is in the sun. The rest of the weedy areas are under the trees. This must be a garden. I wonder who lived here."

Robbie came up behind her and wrapped his arms around her waist. "My grandparents loved it here. Brodie and I are heading back for supplies. Quade and Tomas will stay with you. We should be back in less than an hour." He nuzzled her neck and whispered in her ear. "Do you know what the sight of you bending over that garden does to me, lass?"

Caralyn slapped his arm and giggled, then glanced at Ashlyn to make sure she hadn't overheard.

He rubbed her bum before he headed over to his horse and mounted, flicking his reins to catch up with Brodie.

Caralyn watched him go and sighed. How this one lad had changed her life, and all for the better.

Ashlyn whispered, "You love him, Mama, don't you? He loves you, I think."

Caralyn blushed. "Aye."

"Will you marry him?"

"Och, Ashlyn, he hasn't asked me. But Robbie should have a noble wife, one who can contribute. 'Tis little I can do to help Maddie and Brenna with all they do to run the clan and the keep. I know naught of such things."

"Mama, you are clever enough and noble. You are as good as Maddie and Brenna. Why would you say such a thing?"

The innocence on her daughter's face brought her back to younger days. How she hoped Ashlyn would never know why she was so different.

Echoing her words from the other day, Ashlyn blurted out, "Mama, do you love yourself? If you did, you couldn't say such a thing. You are always telling me to believe in myself."

Gracie stood up with a handful of weeds and dropped them in their growing pile. "Mama, you lu you?" she asked.

Slud. How did her wean know just when to ask such a question. "Thank you, Gracie. Let's keep working."

She glanced down at the edge of the loch as Loki ran off to the bushes. "Got to pish."

The lad always seemed to wait till the last minute. She chuckled and bent over the garden patch. Noticing Loki's departure, Grace ran off to follow him.

"Gracie, come back. Loki doesn't need your help."

The sound of approaching horses caught her attention. Since Robbie had just left, she doubted it would be him. Quade's voice bellowed out, "Caralyn! Get to the horses. Get the lasses on the horses!"

The sound of Quade's voice was enough to send a chill up her spine. She spun around and saw there were three horses headed straight for them. Malcolm. Malcolm with two others on horseback streaked across the meadow toward them.

Quade and Tomas jumped off the roof and mounted their own horses, readying themselves for a confrontation. Ashlyn screamed and started running toward the horses while Gracie was still headed toward Loki, oblivious to the approaching danger.

Caralyn dropped everything and raced for Gracie. *Oh Lord, help us.* She tore past Ashlyn, trying to reach Gracie. Only when it was too late did it occur to her that Ashlyn could not mount a horse on her own.

Tomas and Quade bellowed the Grant whoop as they galloped toward the intruders. Approaching the first horseman, Tomas swung his sword but missed. The second horsemen came behind him and swung a club and hit him in the back of his head, knocking him off his horse. Caralyn's gut clenched in panic when Tomas fell to the ground. Hard. *Get up, Tomas, get up.* He didn't move.

She picked up her skirts and raced as fast as she could, screaming at her girls to run. One man headed straight for Gracie, the other two headed toward her and Ashlyn.

Everything seemed to be moving in slow motion as her life fell apart in front of her. The smallest man leaned over and scooped Gracie up and the other grabbed Ashlyn by the arm and threw her across his horse. Caralyn changed direction and ran back toward the horses.

She glanced over her shoulder to see Loki come flying out of the bushes with Growley at his side. Both chased after the man with Gracie on his lap. Tears ran down her cheeks as she heard her daughters' screams rent the air. Quade went after Ashlyn, Loki after Gracie, and all Caralyn could do was try to get on her horse in an attempt to evade Malcolm.

As she mounted, Loki pulled his slinger out, loaded his stones into it, and pelted the man who held Gracie on his horse.

The lout yelled and slapped himself in the face. "My eye! The wee bastard hit me in my eye." He dropped Gracie and Loki ran over to pick her up, throwing her on the giant deerhound's back in one smooth movement, latching her arms around Growley's neck and her legs around his back. He then gave the dog a shove toward the trees and yelled, "Go, Growley!"

Growley hurtled down the path into the woods and Malcolm yelled at the brute. "Get her, you fool! Are you planning to let a wee lad beat you, Ray?"

Ray set off after Growley, but the dog ran in between bushes where the horse couldn't go. Gracie hung on for dear life, but she managed to stay on him, at least as far as Caralyn could see. *Go Growley, go!* Loki followed the attacker and continued to pepper him with his stones from behind. Ray finally cursed and turned his horse around, charging after Loki, who took off into the forest again, easily evading his pursuer.

Quade followed the brute who had Ashlyn flat across his horse in front of him, and managed to stab him through the back. The big man fell sideways, tumbling off the horse. The animal reared and Ashlyn grabbed its mane, screaming for help. Caralyn kneed her horse directing it toward Ashlyn.

Quade jumped off his horse and, after a quick battle, killed the one interloper who was still on the ground. When his horse returned, he mounted and took off after Ashlyn, finally grabbing the reins of the horse and scooping the girl onto his lap.

Caralyn gasped a sigh of relief. Both girls were safe for the moment. She surveyed the area and noticed Malcolm was now following her.

"Ray, go after the wean, you halfwit!" He pointed down the meadow where Growley had just emerged from the forest with Gracie still clutching his fur, her face buried in the hound's back.

Ray retreated and headed after Gracie again. She watched in horror as Ray caught up with the dog and grabbed Gracie again just as Loki came tearing out of the woods.

Memories flooded Caralyn. In a matter of seconds, she saw the haunted look in Gracie's eyes change to joy at the Grant keep, Ashlyn's frown change to a smile as she played with Torrian, Jennie, and Avelina. She heard Robbie's chuckle as he stood at the hearth in the great hall with his brothers, Brodie and Alex.

And she made a decision. The choice had to be made quick, and she did not hesitate. She stopped her horse and held her arms out to Malcolm. "Leave my girls alone and I'll go with you willingly." She had no choice, her daughters were finally where they belonged. She wouldn't allow anything to take their happiness away. "Malcolm, leave Gracie behind and I'll go with you."

Malcolm smiled. "Let the wean go, Ray. I have what I want."

CHAPTER THIRTY-THREE

"Protect my back, Ray. Leave the girls." Malcolm smiled as he galloped toward her. Ray headed to the edge of the meadow and left Gracie near Loki, bypassing Quade and Ashlyn and veering away from the woods.

Caralyn let out a deep sigh. The bairns would be safe.

Following after her, Quade yelled, "Nay!"

Caralyn rode her horse over to Quade while Malcolm trailed behind her. Ray had already departed the area. "Quade, stay back. I don't want him getting my bairns. Let me go. 'Tis best for my girls."

Ashlyn screamed, "Nay, Mama! Don't leave us."

The Highlander stopped his horse, and started to set Ashlyn on the ground, but Caralyn wouldn't let him. "Nay! Protect her. And please help Gracie. She may be hurt from the ride in the forest." She could tell the indecision in Quade's mind, but he had to choose to protect Loki, Ashlyn, and Gracie. "Please, Quade."

His decision finally made, he rode over and dismounted to check on Tomas. Robbie's friend moaned as Quade rolled him over, his eyelashes fluttering. As soon as she saw Quade go check on wee Gracie and Loki, Caralyn turned her horse and cantered over to Malcolm, ignoring the pleas and sobs coming from her eldest.

Malcolm grabbed the reins of her horse. "Promise?"

"Aye." She nodded and glanced back over her shoulder to see Loki standing not far from her, watching Malcolm with his slinger in his hand. "Loki, tell Robbie to let me go and tell him to take care of my girls," Her voice hitched as she gave Loki instructions. He gave her a sad look before he chased after Quade.

As they headed down the path, Caralyn's heart sunk. She was doing what was best for her girls. After all, her dreams had almost come true. Her daughters were happy here, and the Grants would take good care of them. She couldn't contribute to the clan anyway. Everyone did their part; the men fought and built cottages, and the women cooked, cleaned, sewed, and healed. What did she have to offer? Nothing.

As much as she loved Robbie, she had naught to offer him, and she had Malcolm to thank for that. As they headed down the path, she glanced over her shoulder and noticed the line of Grant horses far in the distance, and all she could think was one thing. *Let me go, Robbie. Just let me go. I cannot endanger your clan anymore.*

She heard Quade's last words. "I'm only letting you go so Robbie Grant can have you, Murray. He won't be far behind you."

Malcolm spurred his horse.

***

Robbie cursed as soon as he heard the Grant war whoop. He bellowed as he tore back to the stables, Brodie right behind him. A flurry of lads from the lists ran in the same direction.

Once they were both mounted, he yelled to Brodie. "How many? Can you see?"

"Aye, three or four. Nay, three."

Robbie spurred his horse faster, trying to outrace the sinking feeling that it was already too late, that he'd already lost her. How could he have been so foolish? Slud, could he not make the right decisions? The lass would never trust him again. Now she and the three bairns were in danger. Why had he not taken ten guards with them? Because he was daft and had thought he could handle everything on his own. *Still trying to prove yourself to your brothers, fool.*

"Stop beating yourself up and get focused," Brodie said. "Can you tell who it is?"

Robbie pulled himself together. He had to. He would not let her go. "I can't tell who it is from this distance, but it could only be Murray. I don't know who is with him. We made sure his other helpers would never return. He must have hired more louts to help him."

"What's your plan when we get there?"

The fire returned to his eyes. "Malcolm is mine. You go after the other two if they're still standing. You'll have help soon enough." He tossed his head back toward the warriors who were following them. They'd outpaced them on their superior horses.

As soon as they made it to the loch, Robbie relaxed a bit. Two horses were heading toward the end of the meadow—he expected them to be Malcolm and his comrade, because the man's other assistant was clearly dead, face down on the ground. Quade was walking toward them with Ashlyn and Gracie in hand and Loki and Growley close behind him. Tomas lay on his side on the ground, moaning but alive.

Robbie made his way to Quade. "Where is Caralyn?" His gaze searched the area again, certain he must have missed her. "Caralyn?" he shouted. His pulse sped up as he checked the ground for another body.

"Malcolm made off with her. I'm sorry, Robbie. I had to make a choice. I had the two weans and Loki and Tomas on the ground." Quade wiped the sweat and grime from his face as he set Gracie down. There were a couple of cuts on the wee one's face, but otherwise both lassies appeared unhurt.

"Tomas will live?" he asked.

"Aye." Quade nodded. "I knew you would want the honor of taking care of Murray yourself, so I let him go. He'll be easy to catch, though Caralyn decided the only way to save the three weans was to go with him." Then his face broke out into a huge grin. "She doesn't know you verra well yet, does she?"

"Captain Grant, please find our mama. I don't care what she says. I love her and want her back." Tears streamed down Ashlyn's face.

Robbie turned his gaze to Quade and shook his head.

Loki was the one who spoke up. "Master Robbie, she said to tell you to let her go and promise to take care of her girls."

"Did she really go on her own?" Robbie couldn't get that thought to register in his mind. Hellfire, she was a stubborn lass.

Quade nodded. "Aye, she told Murray she would go with him willingly if he promised to leave the weans alone. Grant, they are no' far ahead of you. You should be able to take a few men and catch them easily."

Robbie stared at Brodie. "Why are women so foolish?" How the hell could she do such a thing? He didn't need to think too hard about it. She would sacrifice herself for her daughters any day, any time. He had seen it on the beach; he had seen it in Murray's house.

Caralyn Crauford was a verra brave lass who would do anything to save her daughters. Slud, he could accept that, but she expected him not to follow her? Not a chance in hell.

"Loki, anything else I need to know?"

Loki shook his head. "Nay, but I can help." He looked up at Robbie expectantly.

He held his arm down for Loki. "Let's go. Do you have your slinger?"

Loki's eyes lit up as he grabbed Robbie's arm and flung his leg over the horse. "Aye, I am always ready. I pelted the bad man in the eye and he dropped Gracie. I am Loki Grant, a Grant warrior."

Robbie looked at Quade. "How many?"

"Just the two."

Robbie turned to his brother. "Brodie, you ready?"

Quade yelled, "You want me along?"

"Nay, get the weans back home. Brodie and I can handle two brutes." The rest of the guards came up behind them on their horses. Robbie turned to Angus, who was in the lead and had ridden up right behind him. "Allow Brodie and me to go on ahead before you follow. I want the element of surprise. You can follow at a distance in case there are more than we expect."

"And me, Master Robbie. I will help, too." Loki glanced up at him, hope in his eyes.

Quade smiled. "Loki saved Gracie all by himself. I had my hands tied with the lout in the middle." He pointed to the one body in the meadow.

"Aye, and Loki. Three to two, no problem. Ashlyn, we're going for your mama. You stay with your sister, she needs to see Brenna."

Ashlyn peered up at Robbie, her sobs finally slowing. "I trust you Captain Grant. I know you'll save her." Gracie blew him a kiss and they left, heading down the path until Robbie picked up their trail. As they got closer, he realized there were prints from three horses, not two, and they were staying on the main route. Good, that meant Caralyn was on her own horse, which would make it easier for him. He didn't want to risk her safety when he finally got close to Malcolm Murray.

"Brodie, we're taking the shorter path. I doubt he'll try it, he doesn't know the Highlands well enough. Mayhap we can catch up to them."

Brodie nodded.

The path they took joined with the main path a while later, just past a couple of large rocks. As soon as they returned to the main path, Robbie stopped short. "I don't see any fresh prints."

Brodie agreed. "It looks as if they haven't come through here yet."

"Caralyn doesn't ride fast. They must be behind us, so we'll backtrack, but we need a plan first. Brodie, you take the other fool. Malcolm is mine. Loki, when we get near them, I'll drop you off so you can roam around the perimeter and help out wherever you are needed most. I trust your judgment, lad."

"Aye, Captain Grant. I will fight like a true Grant warrior."

"And you must keep your eye on Caralyn at all times. Understood?" Robbie needed to make sure she was safe. When he caught Malcolm, he wanted no distractions.

"Aye. I will make sure she is safe."

Robbie wanted to chuckle at the wee lad's seriousness, but slud, he had seen him in action. He was a quick witted warrior, and he had great aim with his mighty slinger.

They cantered along the rocky trail until they hit a small meadow between the mountains. Nodding to each other, they settled in to wait for the others. Sure enough, three horses came bounding through the opening at the other side of the meadow a few minutes later. Murray held the reins of Caralyn's horse, keeping her behind him. Robbie set Loki down and pointed to a rock off to the side that would be perfect for him to hide behind. Then he nodded to Brodie.

"Full attack?"

Robbie nodded. He bellowed his war whoop, and galloped straight at Murray. He unsheathed his sword and yelled at Caralyn as he drew closer. "Caralyn, move out of the way."

"Nay, Robbie! Let me go. I don't want anyone else to get hurt! Please stop this."

Robbie ignored her and headed straight for Malcolm Murray. He wanted naught more than to drive his sword straight through the man's belly for all he had done to Caralyn.

"Robbie, let me go!" Her voice ricocheted off the rocks surrounding them.

"Never!" He didn't for one moment take his gaze off his target. He would enjoy every minute of pulverizing the fool.

Caralyn had moved her horse aside and out of the way, but she persisted with her foolishness. "Please, Robbie. I couldn't bear it if you were hurt. Let me go!"

Robbie turned to glance at Caralyn for a second. "Nay! I will never let you go! Don't you understand that yet? Never!"

Returning his gaze to his target, he bellowed as he met Murray in the middle of the meadow. He swung his sword arm directly at the blackguard with all his might, hoping to unhorse him with one brutal swing.

Caralyn screamed as the clang of steel rang out when Robbie's sword clashed against Murray's. He rode past him and turned around, surprised to see him still seated.

Malcolm chortled. "Och, she is a mighty sweet thing, Grant. Sorry we took so long, I had to have her once on the way."

His smirk ripped at Robbie's insides, but he funneled his rage into another charge at Murray.

Malcolm started toward him, but a rock struck him in the face. "That wee bugger is throwing rocks again, isn't he?" he yelled. Darting off the path, he headed straight toward Loki, who was standing on the outside of the meadow, as the brothers had bade him to do. Loki turned and fled, while Malcolm surged after him.

Caralyn screamed. "Malcolm, nay! Leave him alone." She jumped off her horse and ran toward wee Loki.

Robbie followed and was about to spear Malcolm in the

back when the man changed directions and spun around, his sword arm extended. Robbie blanched because he thought Malcolm's arm was aimed straight at Caralyn's heart, and he would never get there in time to stop him. But Malcolm's sword continued in its arc and the tip of the sword caught Robbie across the face as he flew by him. Blood spurted from the wound and Caralyn screamed.

Robbie's face burned from the impact. Slud, but he had panicked at the prospect of Caralyn getting stabbed and his inability to stop it when, in reality, Murray had not been close enough to her to make contact. The warm blood shot into his eye temporarily, blinding him. He had lost his focus for a split second and it may have cost him his eye. As soon as he wiped the blood off his face, he saw Murray closing in on him for another strike. Loki and Caralyn both grabbed Malcolm's leg and yanked it at the exact moment when his arms were raised over his head. Murray lost his balance and tumbled on the ground.

Dropping his shield, he rolled into a standing position, still holding his sword, and headed straight for Caralyn.

"You'll not have her!" Malcolm bellowed as he aimed for Caralyn's belly.

Praying he would get there in time, Robbie roared and spurred his horse, lunging toward Malcolm. Murray was seconds away from Caralyn on his sword, when Robbie surged forward and plunged his sword through the man's back.

Murray fell and Robbie jumped off his horse, to check on Murray and see if he was really dead. Caralyn screamed his name and ran to him, throwing her arms around him and sobbing into his shoulder. He wrapped his arms around her, holding her as she cried, kissing her forehead and cheeks. "Shush, sweeting, you're not hurt?" He noticed Loki was headed toward them, his head down, but no evidence of injuries.

"Robbie." Caralyn couldn't catch her breath, she sobbed so. "I'm fine, but I was so afraid when I saw him hurt you." Her breath hitched again and again. "You're bleeding so heavily. Where are you cut? Will you heal?"

He glanced over her shoulder to see Brodie walking toward

him, guiding his horse behind him. His opponent lay in the middle of the meadow, unmoving. Robbie heard a wee voice yell, "Papa!" and watched as Loki ran into Brodie's arms.

"Papa, Captain Robbie is bleeding bad. Is he going to die?" Loki asked as he clutched his sire.

Caralyn pulled back and held Robbie's face, kissing his lips and whispering, "I love you, Robbie Grant." She ripped a piece of her skirt off to mop at the blood still pouring down his face. "How frightened I was when I thought I was going to lose you. The thought of leaving the Highlands and never seeing you again broke my heart in two. Then I had to worry about you dying. Never do that again!"

"Och, my sweet, I'm fine." He kissed her sweet lips again, but she shoved him away.

"Nay, you're not fine. You have blood all over you." She continued to mop, searching for the wound.

Brodie came up next to Robbie and pulled Loki's head away from his side so the boy could see his uncle. "Look, lad. Captain Robbie will be fine." Brodie took the cloth from Caralyn's hand and wiped at Robbie's forehead. "I think 'tis up here, lass." Caralyn and Loki both looked on with wide eyes. "See, 'tis in his forehead. It'll bleed like a river up there, even when 'tis just a wee cut."

When Brodie finally slowed the bleeding down, Loki whispered to his father, "Papa, 'tis not a wee cut."

Robbie overheard him, smiled and ruffled Loki's hair. "Don't worry, lad. I don't plan on dying anytime soon. All warriors must get a scar now and again."

Taking Robbie's hand in hers, Caralyn rested her head on his shoulder, and wrapped her other arm around his waist. "Robbie, that was too close."

"Aye, but your troubles are over, lass. He will never bother you again. And I do believe I have to thank someone for saving my life."

Loki's brow furrowed as he stared at Robbie in confusion. "Who?"

"You, lad. You don't remember yanking on his leg and unbalancing him enough that he fell off his horse? I could barely see through the blood at that moment. You had mighty good timing, because you tugged on his leg just as his arms flew in the air. At any other moment, you wouldn't have been able to move him."

Loki's face lit up. "I did?" There was a puzzled look on his face for a moment, followed by a grin. "Aye, I did, now I remember. Caralyn and I unseated him. Aren't you proud of me, Papa?"

Brodie patted him on the back. "Aye, I am verra proud of you. Now let's get ourselves together so we can head back. Robbie, can you get Caralyn on your horse?"

"Och, I can manage."

CHAPTER THIRTY-FOUR

Before they mounted, Caralyn grabbed his wrist. "Robbie, my girls. Are they well?"

"Och, aye. Gracie has a few wee cuts, but she wasn't crying and Ashlyn begged me to go after you." He tucked a stray lock of her hair behind her ear. "Your daughters were heartbroken."

"But I didn't leave them because I wanted to. I had no choice, 'twas the only way to keep them safe." Her face fell.

"I think Ashlyn needs to hear that from you. She knows 'twas all Malcolm's fault, but she was quite upset."

Once Robbie mounted and she settled in front of him sideways, he asked, "Do you wish to tell *me* why you volunteered to go with Malcolm?"

Her head was settled on his shoulder. "You know why. 'Tis the same reason I wouldn't leave his keep with you when you first asked me." She clutched his bicep as they rode, not wanting to let go of him, hoping she would never have to let go of him again. The agony she had gone through when Malcolm's sword grazed his face was something she never cared to experience again.

"Would you mind repeating it for me?" His voice was barely a whisper above the sound of the horse's hooves on the rocks.

"Because of my lassies. You know that. When the brute had Gracie in his hands, I wanted to vomit. I had to do something." She played with the plaid he had partially wrapped around her.

"Is that the only reason?"

"I didn't want anyone else to get hurt. Tomas was already on the ground and I didn't know if he was dead or alive. Gracie was on Growley's back in the woods, while Ashlyn was sprawled across one lout's horse and Loki was being chased by the other. Quade saved Ashlyn, but then the brute grabbed Gracie again and…" She buried her face in Robbie's chest again. "I couldn't handle all the people I love at risk. Quade could have been hurt, 'twas two against one." There was another reason, of course, but she didn't feel ready to admit it to him.

Robbie chuckled. "Aye, those odds are good odds for Highlanders. The enemy can outnumber us two to one and we will still win. We know how to fight, love. Didn't you trust me to come save you? I'm sure my brother has over a hundred warriors mounted and ready to head this way."

"But you weren't there and once Tomas went down, Quade was fighting on his own for three bairns. Is Tomas alive?"

"He was moving when I left. He has a tough head, so he should be fine. He's more embarrassed than anything."

A moment of silence hung between them, then Caralyn said, "Mayhap it would be best if I wasn't here. My girls love it, but all I seem to do is draw trouble."

Robbie kissed the top of her head. "Your trouble is now dead. So do you wish to stay at Clan Grant? Or is there something else you need to tell me?"

She shook her head. "Nay, I just wish my girls to live a happy life." Moving her fingers back and forth on his arm, she couldn't bring herself to look at him. If she could just think of something of value to offer his clan, mayhap she would feel worthy of being his woman, his wife.

Robbie stopped his horse and forced her gaze to meet his. "Caralyn, your daughters need you. No one is more important to them than you. And after losing half my remaining years when Malcolm aimed his sword at your heart, I realize how much I need you. All three of us love you. Why can't you accept that? We would be lost without you."

Caralyn shook her head in confusion, but then kissed him on the lips because he was so dear to her. She knew she needed to say what he wanted to hear. "I love you, too. I find I am always thanking you and you don't like it, but I must thank you again. My mind will rest better now that Malcolm is gone."

"Och, good. 'Tis what I was hoping to hear you say. You can stop worrying about the bastard coming after you and your girls. 'Tis done." He kissed her cheek and kneed his horse to move on.

She leaned her head back against his chest and closed her eyes. Aye, she did love Robbie Grant; he was all she could ever ask for. He would make both a wonderful husband and father. But she, Caralyn Crauford, daughter of a fisherman, was not worthy of his love…and she didn't know if she ever could be.

Maddie ran the largest keep in the Highlands with the ease of any queen. Robbie's sister, Brenna, was a healer whose talents were lauded across the Highlands. Jennie, younger than Caralyn by far, assisted Brenna frequently and rarely became flustered at all the blood and gore. Celestina created the most wondrous bath oils and fragrance. Even Ashlyn had become a trusted assistant to Maddie and Brenna with their bairns. But what could Caralyn do?

Naught. She could do naught. Actually, she had two skills. She was able to bone a fish and cook it, and she knew how to see to a man's needs—hardly a skill she wished to advertise or put to use with anyone besides Robbie.

As soon as they traveled a bit further out of the narrow path, ten rows of Grant warriors came toward them. It was a powerful sight. Angus was in the lead. "Grant, you need any help? Did you take care of him this time?"

"Aye, Murray is dead. Probably wouldn't be a bad idea to search the area for any others who may be in hiding. We left the bodies if you wish to take care of them."

"Aye, I'll take care of the buffoon." Angus grinned and cantered around them, followed by the others.

When they arrived back at the keep, the others clustered around them, concern etched on their faces. All Caralyn wanted to do was find her lassies. Robbie held her hand tight as they searched the hall for her daughters. As soon as Celestina saw them, she took them to the chamber Brenna used for healing.

They entered the chamber and Caralyn noticed Brenna was busy working on a couple of warriors, while Tomas slept on a nearby pallet. Her heart broke when she saw wee Ashlyn on a pallet in the corner. Her eldest daughter was crying, her hand clutched around Gracie's even though the wee lassie was asleep. "Mama!" Ashlyn screamed as soon as she saw her mother. She tore across the room and threw herself into her mother's arms. "I was afraid you would never come back. Why would you say such a thing? We could never let you go."

Caralyn kissed her wet cheeks and said, "Hush, lass. I am here now. I'll explain later. Just know that naught makes me happier than to be back with my lassies."

Ashlyn clung to her skirts as she cried.

"Come, sit over here with me while Gracie sleeps." She ran her hands through her daughter's hair, surprised at how upset she still was. Ashlyn was usually the strong and courageous one, the one who always protected Gracie. Yet Gracie was sound asleep and Ashlyn was sobbing. Had her eldest daughter always been strong for her wean's sake?

Caralyn sat and patted the spot next to her, but Ashlyn couldn't sit. She ran over to Robbie and hugged him tight around his waist. "Thank you, Captain Grant, for saving our mama." Tears continued to flow down her cheeks. And Caralyn noticed something new. Ashlyn didn't want to let him go anymore than she did. He had won her over, too.

***

Robbie knelt down and wiped the tears from Ashlyn's cheeks. "You are welcome, lass. You know there is nowhere else your mama would rather be than here with you."

Ashlyn nodded her head and then leaned over to whisper to him. "Can't you marry my mama so we could stay forever? I don't want to go back to the place where we lived before. There were too many mean men. I hate Malcolm." She stopped as her sobs forced her breath to hitch. "He was mean to my mama and to Gracie. Please? Gracie and I promise we will always be good. I can take care of Gracie so she won't bother you."

"Malcolm will never bother you again. I think I would need to talk to your mama about marrying first. And now I have this ugly cut on my face. Do you think she'll still like a scarred man?"

Ashlyn tipped her head to get a better look at his face. "'Tis still bleeding a bit." Her face twisted into a grimace of concern. "I think you need to get it fixed."

Startled awake by the noise, Gracie hopped off her pallet and toddled over to her mother. "Mama!" She kissed her mother and then stepped back to show off all her wounds. "Mama, I have cuts. See? But Bwenna fix dem." Her wee finger pointed to her neck, where a couple of small scrapes were covered in salve. "And I ride Gwowley. Gwowley save me." Growley came up behind her, from where he'd been curled up in the corner of the room, and snuck a lick onto Gracie's face, causing a burst of giggles to erupt from her. "Gwowley lu me." She wrapped her arms around the big deerhound's neck and gave him a kiss.

Caralyn smiled as she petted Growley. "Aye, I will have to find you a big bone, my friend, for saving my lass."

Leaning over, Robbie kissed Caralyn's cheek. "I need to go see my brother. Will it bother you if I leave you here alone?"

She gazed up at him and shook her head. "I'm fine, but shouldn't you get that cut fixed first?" Not waiting for an answer, she rushed off and said something to Brenna. When she returned, she mopped his forehead with a dampened cloth.

Robbie grinned. "I have to say I could get quite used to you tending my needs, lass."

Caralyn's eyes sparkled. "I like it better when you tend mine."

Robbie laughed before giving her a quick kiss on the lips. "I'll have to remember that."

Moments later, Brenna came over to check his injury. "Och, Robbie will be fine. I'll put some salve on it to stop the bleeding, but I don't think it needs stitching."

***

While Brenna applied the salve, Caralyn glanced around the room at the different men who were being treated. Tomas was still sound asleep on his pallet. Another lad sat on a stool with his boots off, waiting for Brenna to wrap his swollen foot, while another held a piece of cloth to his bloody arm.

"Brenna, how is Tomas?" Robbie asked.

"Och, he'll be fine. He has a nice bruise on the back of his head from the club, but I think once he sleeps a bit, he'll be able to return to everything."

A commotion sounded at the door and Alex Grant stepped in with a bundle wrapped around the front of him. His arm was around a dazed and bloody warrior, clearly the victim of an injury in the lists. "Brenna, Tavish was dreaming about a lass out in the lists. Could you take care of him please?"

Brenna let her hand fall away from Robbie's forehead and shook her head. "Alex, what are you doing out there? Can't you slow down? I will never get home at this rate."

A smile spread across Alex's face as he turned his attention to his brother. "Och, Robbie, all is taken care of?" Then he peeked inside the bundle strapped to his chest and kissed a wee blond head.

That was when Caralyn realized he was carrying Connor bundled up against his bare chest. The bairn was sound asleep, even with all the loud noises his sire was making. She couldn't help but smile.

Alex returned her smile. "Never too early to have a Grant lad hard at work in the lists. Maddie says I keep him warm with my blast of heat, and this helps ease her burden." He rubbed Connor's head as he spoke.

"Aye, all is fine," Robbie answered. "As soon as Brenna finishes with my head that does not really need tending, I'll explain everything to you." He pointed to the girls. "The lasses want it tended."

Alex smirked and headed out the door. "Brenna, take good care of my warriors. Robbie, I'll be in my chair by the hearth as soon as I check on my wife. Nice to see you are safe, Caralyn."

As soon as Brenna finished her ministrations and moved on to Tavish, Robbie kissed Caralyn's cheek. "I need to talk with my brother," he said in an undertone.

Caralyn nodded and sat back on the pallet. She couldn't take her eyes from the lad with the gash on his shoulder. "Brenna, may I be of assistance?"

"If you don't mind. You could wrap Gavin's ankle or just clean up Tavish's blood so I can have a look at the wound underneath."

"Aye, I can clean him up for you."

Brenna moved on to the lad with the swollen ankle. "That would be wonderful. As soon as I finish wrapping Gavin up, I'll check to see if Tavish needs stitching."

After finding a stool for Tavish, she grabbed a cloth and basin. Gracie played with Growley, but Ashlyn stood at Caralyn's side. "Mama, may I help?"

Caralyn stayed and helped Brenna for another couple of hours. All the time she worked, she thought about how nice it was to actually feel useful, to be giving and not just taking. Where did she fit in?

CHAPTER THIRTY-FIVE

Robbie strolled into the great hall after meeting with his brothers in the lists. He had asked for some time to himself.

He needed to make things right with Caralyn.

Two days had passed since their confrontation with Malcolm. The two lasses had settled back in and had stopped clinging to their mama, so he hoped today would be a perfect day to carry out his plan.

This idea had been in the back of his mind all along, but the conversation he and Alex had after Malcolm's attack had made him realize he needed to act quickly.

Saints above, he was grateful no one else had been around the hearth when he met his brother there that day. As soon as he sat down, his brother barked, "When's the wedding to take place?"

Robbie just stared at Alex, so wrapped up in everything that had just taken place with Malcolm and Caralyn that his brother's comment totally took him off guard.

"Wedding?"

"Och, aye. After the sounds coming from Caralyn's chamber a few hours after my son was born the other morning, I am surprised the wedding wasn't the next day."

Robbie turned beet red, embarrassed by his brother's crude comment, "I have plans to ask the lass to be my wife."

"Get on with it."

All he could do was scowl when Alex quirked his brow at him, his expression making it clear that he thought the discussion was over. Robbie should have realized someone would have figured out what they were about. He had counted on the birth of the new lad to distract his family. Apparently, it hadn't distracted his brother, though Robbie had to admit that Alex rarely missed much.

They had finished their talk with a brief exchange about Malcolm, but Alex was too wrapped up in his wife and the new bairn to sit still for long. Maddie was slow in coming out of confinement this time, and Alex was totally distraught.

Alex and Maddie would return to normal soon, but Robbie needed to complete his plan now. When he found Caralyn with the girls at noon day meal, he hurried over to their table. He picked up Gracie and gave her a kiss before stooping to kiss Ashlyn on the cheek. "Good morn to you all. Caralyn, I wondered if you would like to ride to the cottage near the loch after you finish eating."

Ashlyn clapped her hands. "May we come along?"

"Och, not this time, lass," he said. "Your mama needs to let me know what she wants done with the inside of the cottage."

Ashlyn glanced down at her hands. "Mayhap I don't want to go after all. 'Twould remind me of the other day."

"Shush," Caralyn said, running a comforting hand through her daughter's hair. "That man will never bother us again."

As if something had suddenly occurred to her, Ashlyn grinned at her mother, then at Robbie. "'Tis fine if you two go alone."

Caralyn's expression was unreadable and Robbie thought she would turn him down, but she said, "I'm ready now. I'm sure the girls can stay with Celestina. They can help her with Maddie's lads and wee Kyla."

Celestina was seated further down the table but she had overheard. "Aye, they can help me." The girls scrambled over to join her.

Caralyn ran upstairs to grab her cloak and met Robbie at the door. He took her hand in his with a smile, and a loud giggle came from her daughters as they watched the two with glee.

As they made their way out to the stables, Robbie said, "I think your daughters would like to see us together."

Caralyn laughed. "They aren't being the least bit subtle about it, are they?"

Once mounted atop their horses, they crossed the meadow

at a canter, enjoying the crisp autumn day.

Robbie lifted his gaze to the sky. "'Twill not be long before snow is falling. Do you like snow, Caralyn?"

"Aye, my lassies love it."

"'Tis not what I asked you. Do you like snow?" He raised an eyebrow at her, grinning.

Her brow furrowed before she answered. "I don't like to walk in it much, but it is pretty."

"Have you ever gone sliding down a hill over the snow?"

"Nay, but the girls like to make balls out of snow and try to throw them at things."

"Then we must plan to go sliding this winter. Alex's lads love it."

When they arrived at the cottage, Robbie helped her dismount. He couldn't help but be a bit nervous because he had no idea what she would say. Though he knew she cared about him, he wasn't sure it was enough to overcome the scars of her past. And he also had a hunch there was some unspoken reason why she'd offered to go with Malcolm the other day, though he didn't know what it could be.

He took her hand in his and led her up the porch and in through the front door. Caralyn's look of surprise was worth all the work.

"There are no holes!" she said, peering up at the new roof. "When did you fix them, Robbie?"

Saints above, she was lovely. He could understand why Malcolm had followed her all the way to the Highlands. There were not many natural beauties like Caralyn, and even fewer who were beautiful inside and out. But he knew she didn't see herself the way everyone saw her. "Quade and Brodie came back with me yesterday. Didn't take us long. Then I brought a couple of young lads to clean out the hearth, and they also brought a new mattress for the bed." He led her by the hand to the back of the cottage.

She laughed as she bounced on the new mattress and linens, then lay flat on her back, staring up at the new roof. "Robbie, 'tis lovely. You have worked so hard on this. So Alex is willing to let me move out here with the girls even after what happened?"

"Well," Robbie cleared his throat. "'Tis why I brought you here alone. I wanted to ask you if you would do me the honor of becoming my wife."

Caralyn sat up and stared at him.

Lowering himself onto the bed next to her, Robbie took her hand in his. "I promise to treat your lassies as my own. You know I love them already."

Caralyn blushed and glanced down at their interwoven hands. "Robbie, I don't know what to say."

"Aye, say aye and make me a verra happy man."

Somehow, he knew this wasn't going to turn out the way he had hoped.

She stood and walked over to a window, pulling the fur aside to look out over the loch.

"Caralyn, what is it? You don't love me? You said you did."

When she spun around, her eyes were filled with tears. "That is not it. I do love you, Robbie. It's just…"

"What? What is it?"

"Robbie, I'm not worthy of you. You are Captain Robbie Grant of the Grant warriors. You are brother to Laird Alexander Grant. You should be marrying a young lass who will give you many bairns, one who has noble blood like you. I am seven and twenty summers. I may not be able to have more bairns. You need someone who can manage your household, who can make you proud. What can I do?"

She wrung her hands as she talked, to the point he was afraid she would start hurting herself again. Robbie walked over and grabbed her hands. "Caralyn, don't be foolish. I love you for who you are. You are an unbelievable mother to your bairns. Look how you have protected them. You have raised two wonderful lassies and that isn't an easy thing to do alone. I have seen you fight for your life, for their lives. You are honest and sweet. I couldn't think of a finer woman."

"But Robbie, I have said it before, and I will say it again. I can do naught. I can't heal people, I can't cook or manage a keep, I can't make fragrant oils or pastries or create fine needlework. Do you understand?"

"Caralyn, I don't care about pastries and oils. You'll manage our keep or cottage or wherever we choose to live just fine. Why don't you believe in yourself? Malcolm is gone. He'll never bother you again."

"But he has already ruined my life. Don't you see? I am only good for one thing and that is all I can offer you."

Fury shot through him. She couldn't mean what she just said, could she?

"Don't tell me we are back to this again. What are you trying to tell me?" His voice came out in a roar, louder than he intended, but he couldn't stop himself.

"The only skill I have. I know how to please you. That's all I was ever taught—how to service a man. I have naught else to offer. 'Tis why I can't marry you. Sometimes, I don't even know whether I should be around my own daughters."

"So what does that mean?"

Her voice raised a level. "Mayhap I will raise them poorly. I can't read, I can't write. How could I be a respectable wife to you or a mother to them when my only skill is in the bedroom?"

"So let me make sure I understand you correctly. You are turning me down. You refuse to marry me. Are you willing to service me, then? Is that what you offer?"

Caralyn paused before she answered. She stared at her feet. "Aye, I will service you if that is what you wish. But I will only do it here in the cottage when the girls aren't here."

He could feel the blood pulsing over a spot in his temple, but he forced himself to continue. "And shall we have the girls live in the keep so they won't be embarrassed about what you do?"

He could see the confusion in her eyes, but he said nothing. If this is what she thought of herself, then he would force her to see the truth. There was no other alternative. He would have to enlist the help of his sisters-in-law, but he thought he could make it work. *Just say aye, Caralyn, and you'll see for sure. Say it.*

"Aye." Her voice was barely a whisper, but she agreed.

"Good, so starting tomorrow, you and I will live here so you can service me and we'll arrange for someone to watch the girls. You say you have no skills, but didn't you tell me could catch and cook fish?"

"Aye."

He felt so guilty when he saw the defeat in her eyes, but he thought his plan might be the only way to prove her own importance to her. "Perfect, because I love fish. So you can fish and clean our cottage during the day, cook me fish for dinner and service me at night. I will bring you to see the girls once a week. That way, there is no chance you will corrupt them. Do we have a suitable arrangement?"

Caralyn hesitated, but she finally answered, her shoulders so slumped it broke his heart. "Aye."

Slud, why could the lass not see her own value? Would he really have to go through with this charade in order to help her see her significance? Based on the look in her eyes, the answer to that question was aye.

Robbie hoped he hadn't just made the biggest mistake of his life.

CHAPTER THIRTY-SIX

What the hell had just happened? Caralyn rode her horse back to the keep, riding in silence next to Robbie. First of all, she couldn't believe he had asked her to marry him. Though every bit of her had wanted to say aye, she couldn't. She had come far since arriving at the Grant keep, but she still knew she wasn't good enough for Robbie.

Now she was to do as he wished. Somehow, she was living the the same life she had lived before the Norseman's attack, with two exceptions. One was that she wouldn't see her lassies every day, and the other was that Robbie would be her man and not Malcolm. Mayhap it wouldn't be so bad. At least if she took care of Robbie, she would feel like she was doing something for her daughters. Hadn't Malcolm always said something to her about earning her keep? Well, she would give the lassies the right to live at the castle.

Her daughters would be happy and well-fed, and they'd have many friends. The Grants would treat them as family, and she, Caralyn Crauford, will have accomplished something on her own. She would miss them terribly, but this would be best for them.

Gracie was still little, but Ashlyn was the age to start asking questions. And Caralyn did not want her daughter to ever know the details of her past. Though she had lived through it, perhaps Ashlyn was too young to have fully understood.

When they arrived at the keep, Robbie helped her down. He was in a different mood, but then she had just rejected him. Men probably did not take that sort of thing well.

"Get your things ready. I will move you to the cottage on

the morrow. Decide who you would like to watch over your bairns and have a talk with them. If you need my help, let me know. Is there anything else you require at the cottage?"

Caralyn shook out her skirts and said, "Nay. Och, mayhap a fishing pole if you can locate one, and a good dagger for filleting the fish."

Robbie said, "I will see to it." He nodded to her and headed off to the lists.

Caralyn managed to drag one foot in front of the other and made her way up to the great hall. Who would she ask? And even worse, what would she say? She moved by countless people in the courtyard who waved to her or spoke, but she could do little but move forward. Her heart was broken. The man who held her heart had just broken it, but somehow, she knew it was her fault. All her dreams could have come true, but she ruined them out of a desire to be true to her feelings.

She considered two possible protectors: Maddie and Celestina. She rejected Maddie because she had just given birth and now had four weans to care for, even though Alex often helped. It would have to be Celestina. She and Brodie didn't have any bairns of their own, though they had adopted Loki.

Not seeing Celestina in the great hall, she headed up the staircase and down the passageway until she heard Gracie's voice in Maddie's chamber. She knocked on the door and stepped inside. Gracie was kissing wee Connor on the bed while Ashlyn helped Avelina change his rags. Maddie had Kyla on her hip. It seemed as though Brenna was headed out the door, her wee daughter sleeping cradled in her arms, but she stopped to smile at Caralyn.

"How do you fare after that horrible fight, Caralyn? By the way, your lassies are delightful." Brenna hugged her.

"I am fine. I was looking for Celestina, actually. Does anyone know where I can find her?" She glanced at Maddie. "Would you mind if the girls stay with you for a while longer until I return?"

"Och, nay, they're such a big help to me." Maddie smiled and waved her hand at Caralyn.

Gracie and Ashlyn rushed over to give her a hug before returning to wee Connor's side, both of them transfixed.

Putting out a finger for him to grab, Gracie giggled when he squeezed it tight. "Lu you, Connor."

"I think she is in her chamber repairing Brodie's leine," Brenna said. "Come, we'll see if we can locate her."

As Caralyn followed Brenna down the passageway, wee Bethia awoke and started chattering and smiling. They knocked on Celestina's door.

Celestina opened it wide, "Come in, please. How lovely to see you, Caralyn. Brenna, how is wee Bethia? May I hold her?"

Caralyn stood to the side watching Celestina and Brenna fuss over the wean.

"May I help you with something, Caralyn?" Celestina asked as she bounced Bethia on her hip until she smiled.

"I just wanted to ask you about something, if I may." Caralyn stayed off to the side.

Brenna took Bethia back and turned to leave, "I'll leave you two alone so I can get Bethia down for her nap." She latched the door behind her after she stepped into the corridor.

Celestina returned to her seat in front of the window, the fur pulled back to give her light to work by. She patted the chair next to her. "Come in, come in, Caralyn. You have had such a difficult week, haven't you?"

All Caralyn could think was that Celestina had no idea how hard it had been. She sat on a stool and straightened her skirts, wondering how to phrase her request. Blushing in embarrassment, she fought the urge to cry as she stammered out, "I have a favor to ask. I know I don't know you well, but I'm hoping you can help me."

"Of course, I would be happy to help." Celestina continued to work the needle and thread into her husband's shirt. "What is it?"

"I wondered if you would be willing to watch my bairns for a while." She thought very hard before framing her next sentence. She didn't want to lie, but it didn't feel right to describe their situation in crude words. "Robbie and I have agreed to live in the cottage near the loch together for a short time without my lassies."

Celestina's eyes widened with surprise, but she didn't hesitate before saying, "Of course, I love your daughters. I'll help in any way possible." A moment passed, then she added, "Pardon my intrusion, but this doesn't sound like something Robbie Grant would do. What will you tell the girls?"

Caralyn swiped at the tears forming in her lashes. "Well, I thought to tell them that it was too dangerous for them to join us. Ashlyn may be uncomfortable there, anyway, after everything that has happened."

Silence settled between the two. Celestina said, "Is this what you want or what Robbie wants? Forgive me if I pry too much."

"We both agreed." Caralyn didn't know what else to say, because she couldn't find the words to explain the situation.

Celestina stood and tugged her to her feet, wrapping her arms around her. "You do what you need to do because you are so deserving of happiness. You have had a traumatic fortnight at least. Bairns are so resilient; they will be fine without you for a moon."

Caralyn could only nod and say, "Thank you."

"Caralyn, you don't look as though you are pleased with the situation. May I do anything else to help?"

Caralyn shook her head, unable to speak for fear she would fall apart in front of the young girl.

When she turned to leave, Celestina called out her name again. She sniffled and tipped her head to look at the other woman.

"By the way, Ashlyn asked me if I would teach her to read and write. Would that be acceptable to you?"

"Of course," Caralyn said.

"I'd be happy to teach you, too, if you are interested, Caralyn. Ashlyn said she didn't think you could read."

Caralyn nodded and ran out the door down the passageway, heading straight to her chamber. She fell onto her bed and wept uncontrollably.

CHAPTER THIRTY-SEVEN

Robbie had taken a beating from Brodie and Quade, both of whom thought he was daft and his scheme would never work. But Alex hadn't disagreed with him. He thought the idea had merit.

Tomas had just stood to the side shaking his head with a grin on his face. "You're a fool and you'll regret this."

He hadn't wanted to ask his friend why. What other choice did he have? He wouldn't give up on her.

It was hard to watch Caralyn say her tearful goodbyes to her daughters, but they had just waved her off with smiles, eager to run back to their game. Gracie, Jake, Jamie, Lily, and Loki were playing a game of chase, all shrieking loud enough to shake the rafters.

"Mama, I'll miss you." Ashlyn stared at the two of them, uncertainty and questions written all over her face, but somehow, the lass didn't share what was on her mind.

Robbie's guilt nagged at him a bit, but he reminded himself if his plan worked, Ashlyn would be much happier.

He helped her move her things into the cottage just before dusk. Caralyn had checked the shelves and cupboards, surprised to see everything that had already been stocked there. She had brought several sacks of cloth with her, though he had no idea what she planned for them. After she had situated her belongings, she came back into the main room and sat across from him at the table.

Robbie could see the anxiety in her face. "Relax, Caralyn. We won't start anything this eve. I just wanted to get the cabin arranged for us. On the morrow, I'll go to the lists to train, and you'll have the day to yourself."

"Will you be back to eat the noonday meal or will you go to the keep?"

"I'll come here. I don't want you alone all day. Does that suit you?"

"Aye."

When they settled in bed, Caralyn rolled on her side, facing out, but he wouldn't let her get away with that. He knew it would be cold in the middle of the night, so he tugged her up next to him. Right now, he knew Caralyn was a bit angry with him and missed her bairns. She would need his heat, and he needed her warmth next to him, too. It would be difficult to control his urges with her soft bottom nestled up against him, but he was determined to stick to his plan. He had even discussed it with Maddie, who had given him a few ideas.

He slept like a rock all night, but headed off to the lists in the morning as planned. Caralyn was still asleep, so he kissed her cheek, grabbed an oatcake, and headed out the door after starting a fire in the hearth in the main room.

When he returned at midday, he was a bit afraid of what he might find. Half expecting to see the cottage empty, he was surprised to be greeted by a sweet aroma of apples when he opened the door. Caralyn gave him a charming smile as he sat at the table and she brought him a tankard of ale and a plate of cooked fish, along with a brown concoction all mushed up. He knew better from his brother's tales than to say anything about it and he was half starved, besides, so dug into everything.

A few moments later, he stopped and looked at her. "What is this?"

"What? The apple mush?"

"Aye, I have never had it before but 'tis delicious."

"Och, 'tis the only way I can get Gracie to eat sometimes. I have to cook it until it is verra soft. It is both apple and parsnips mashed together. She loves it."

"The fish is tasty. How many were you able to catch?"

Caralyn played with her food a bit before she answered. "I caught four and boned them, but they are small. I saved two to use in soup for the meal tonight. Is that acceptable? I have parsnips and carrots to add. I can't believe it, but I found a few underground outside. That place where Ashlyn and I were weeding the other day? I thought it might have once been a garden because it was in the sun. I found some parsnips there, and some of the herbs I used as well."

"Caralyn, you told me you couldn't cook."

"Aye, I said I could cook fish. I have always cooked for my girls, but I could never cook for all the men in the keep."

"Well, this is delicious. You can cook for me anytime." He was quite serious. Wait until he informed his brothers. Knowing that Caralyn denied any knowledge of cooking, they were all putting in bets as to whether he would come back sick or starving.

Before he left, he kissed her sweet lips and said, "Thank you. I enjoyed the meal."

She chuckled. "Have I ever heard you thank me for something? 'Tis usually the other way around."

Dinner went just as well. The idea of fish soup hadn't sounded appealing, but he made himself taste everything she put in front of him...and he loved it. He had two bowls and brown bread. "You baked the bread here?"

"Nay, I brought it from the keep yesterday. I didn't think I could make it without an oven."

"Good thinking, my sweet. And the soup is excellent. Do you think the garden will produce much next year?"

"I picked and pulled what I could from what's left in the plot. There's enough to use for flavoring broth. I could probably add seeds from Brenna's garden for whatever isn't here. The soil is good and dark in that spot."

"Caralyn, I know naught about gardening."

She smiled. "I was on my own for a long time, Robbie. Remember I was desperate to do anything to feed my girls. We ate fish and turnips for a long time and I learned to search out apple trees and pear trees."

After they ate, they sat on the front steps for a while, listening to the frogs and talking, enjoying the serenity of the loch. Somehow, he thought he would never tire of talking to her. Her eyes lit up with excitement about the simplest things. He could tell how much she loved the loch and the water—she said it combined what she loved about her old home with what she loved about the Highlands. Next summer would be delightful here—if she was still with him.

How he hoped she would be. His gut clenched with the thought of what he had planned for the evening, but he had to do it. He had to know how she would respond. She wouldn't like him, but that wasn't why they were here.

He stood up and held his hand out to her. "Come. 'Tis time for bed." Her hand tensed in his, a moistness dampening her palm.

He walked into the bed chamber and dropped his plaid on the floor. He removed his tunic and turned to her. "Remove your gown, lass. 'Tis time for you to do your part. You promised, aye?" He couldn't stop himself from reacting to the sight of her beautiful body when she stood in front of him in naught but her shift, her rosy nipples standing pert in the cool night. "Lass, you do have a lovely body."

"What exactly is it you would like?" she whispered with her head down.

Hellfire, this was going to be difficult. But it was also the only thing that might work. "I'm not sure. What's your specialty?"

Her gaze shot up to meet his and he noticed the fire in her eyes. Good. It was exactly what he had hoped to see. He had to continue. She took a step closer to him, so they were close enough to touch. He glanced down his nose at her and said, "Mayhap I would like you down on your knees sucking me."

Her hand flew out and slapped his cheek. "How dare you talk to me that way!"

He reacted instantly, grabbing both her hands and pinning her against the wall so that her hands were locked in his above her head. He had expected anger from her, but not a physical blow. He forced himself to be happy. She *did* respect herself. She just didn't realize it yet. He spoke slowly, his lips close to her face. "Remember, wee one, this is what you wanted, not me. I want you in my bed proper. I want you with me because I love you. 'Tis *you* who does not accept *me.*"

The fire still burned in her gaze. She was furious he had control of her, and she bucked at him and struggled against his binding of her hands. He had one more point to make before he would set her free. "Do you think I am strong enough to force you? Can I make you do whatever I want at this moment?"

"Aye," she whispered as she attempted to kick him.

He had seen Logan do something similar with Gwyneth, and he thought the move held merit. She needed to trust him. "You are correct. I can do whatever I want with you right now." Her eyes were cast downward. "Look at me, Caralyn." He could tell she didn't want to, but he waited until she did. "This is to let you know I will never hurt you. I can, but I'll never raise a hand to you. That is not who I am. No matter what you say or do, even when you strike me, I will never strike back."

When he released her hands, she flew at him, shoving at his chest. "Mayhap you didn't strike me, but what you said to me? 'Twas like a slap in my face. I won't allow you to treat me as a whore. Do you hear me? I am done with that life. Done!"

He stared at her, allowing her own words to sink in, knowing she'd said it all without first thinking about her words. He locked his gaze on hers. "Good. That is just what I would expect of a strong woman, of a woman worthy of being my wife. Now, get into bed, we're done for tonight."

Caralyn flung herself into the bed and turned away from him before the tears started. He tucked her inside him again, kissing her shoulder and holding her hand until she fell asleep.

Thus far, all had worked exactly as planned.

CHAPTER THIRTY-EIGHT

Caralyn awoke the next morning to a quiet cottage. She padded out to the main room and discovered he had already left, but not before starting a warm fire in the front hearth. Wrapping a plaid around herself she sat in a chair in front of the hearth, her mind a storm of confusion.

It had quite surprised her that Robbie enjoyed her cooking. She knew he hadn't lied because he ate everything so fast and with such relish. Mayhap she wasn't such a bad cook after all.

Last night had unleashed a whirlwind of feelings deep from her gut. How angry she had become, more so than she'd believed herself capable. It was a sign of how tired she was of her old life—being controlled by Malcolm, having no say in whatever they did—being forced to service a man she hated. Everything she had done and said to Robbie had been on instinct.

She couldn't help but think of the first time she'd slapped Malcolm for calling her a whore—her face had been bruised for a week from his retaliation. Robbie hadn't so much as scratched her. He was indeed a special man.

And Robbie hadn't forced her to uphold her end of the agreement. Aye, she had cared for him all day, but men had particular needs. She knew that very well, had seen the evidence of it in Robbie when she undressed to her shift.

But rather than forcing her, he had held her in his arms until she cried herself to sleep. She had to admit, it was her favorite way to sleep. Aye, she missed her girls, but there was no place she would rather be at night than encased in Robbie Grant's strong arms.

She glanced around the room and decided the cottage would be perfect with just a few more feminine touches. It was something she could accomplish today. But first she had to catch lunch, so she finished her ablutions and headed out the door to the beautiful loch. She had briefly considered sneaking up to the keep to see the girls, but she knew it would be wrong. She would not go back on her word, and it would be too difficult for the lassies.

Robbie came back for a quick midday meal. When he walked in the door, she took one look at his tousled hair and the sweat visibly making a pathway down his chest, and she froze. She licked her lips as visions of him with naught on danced through her mind, but she forced herself to stop and move to get his trencher of fish for him.

He surprised her by tugging her close and kissing her. It was just a quick kiss, but she pulled him back and tasted him with her tongue, inspiring a large groan from him that sent a shiver through her all the way to her toes.

To her delight, his hand ran up her skirts and caressed her bum, and she lost all ability to think. She reached under his kilt and found his hardness and teased him by caressing him back and forth with a feather light touch.

"Lass, I can't stop. Do you want this as much as I do?"

She moaned as his hand found her nub and he rubbed his thumb across her, causing her to lean back on the table and spread wide for him. "Robbie, aye," was all she could say, and it came out in a moan that didn't stop.

Robbie shoved everything off the table and helped her lie back on the table before positioning himself at her entrance. "Lass, you make me lose all control." He entered her swiftly and leaned over to capture her lips in a deep kiss, melding his body against hers as she rocked her pelvis to pick up his rhythm.

Minutes later, she shattered and he followed her, shouting her name as he finished.

Robbie picked her up and settled in the chair with her on his lap, still nuzzling her neck. "I made a mess of my food, lass. But you were the best meal I have had in a verra long time. Let me help you clean up."

She rested her head on his shoulder and drank in his essence; his scent, his warmth, everything she knew to be Robbie, the man she adored. Somehow, she had to make this work.

Caralyn managed to find an apple for him and a piece of bread before he darted back out the door with the explanation that Alex was in a rant that day.

The afternoon flew by as memories of their lovemaking kept a smile on her face. When he walked through the door at the end of the day, he looked exhausted. His forehead had bled again at some point, but it was now crusting over. It didn't stop him from noticing the few extra touches she had added during the day.

"Lass, where did you find the cushions for the chairs?"

"I made them. I do love this cottage, but it needed a couple of things to brighten and soften it. Maddie told me I could take any cloth that I needed from the storage. I wanted to make the girls a couple of new gowns."

"And the flowers?" He pointed to the centerpiece on the table and the flowers hanging from the rafters.

"I foraged to see what I could find to dry for the winter. Mama and I had a beautiful flower garden when I was a wee lass."

He ate everything she set on the table, complimenting her as he went, but she could tell he was overtired.

"Did you not say you had no sewing skills?"

"Well, I had to sew clothing for my girls from whatever scraps of material I could find. I wish I could make the beautiful wool gowns Madeline crafts, but I don't know how."

"Caralyn, she would be happy to show you."

She stood and carried the dishes to the basin to wash them. "Do you think Logan has found Gwyneth by now?" It had been on her mind for quite some time since Malcolm was no longer a threat.

"I don't know, but I hope so." Robbie wrapped his arms around her waist.

"I don't think she'll ever rest until Duff Erskine pays for killing her brother and father. I worry about her. She is a stubborn lass."

"Logan will find her and protect her, don't worry about that."

She paused to gaze at Robbie and thought about how fortunate she was to have her own protector, not just for her, but for her daughters.

After they finished cleaning up, he stared into her eyes with a grin on his face.

"What is it?" she asked, confused by his look.

"I could go straight to bed, I am so tired, but I can no longer stand the smell of myself. I am going in the loch. Care to join me?"

"Och, nay! 'Tis way too cold."

"Lass, come, 'tis good for your skin. Cleans it fine."

"You should go in to clean off your wound, but 'tis too cold for me."

He swooped over and picked her up in his arms, laughing. "What if I throw you in?"

She squealed as he carried her out the door. "Robbie, nay. The gown will drag me down."

"Then take it off. I am throwing you in. If you wish to live near a loch, you must learn how to enjoy it...all year round. I went swimming in this loch many a winter month when I was a wee lad. 'Tis not that cold yet. I'll keep you warm."

He set her down and she ran from him. Sure enough, he followed, chasing her halfway around the loch, their laughter echoing off the hills. When he finally caught her, he gently tugged her arm, leading her toward the lake.

"Stop, stop!" Caralyn squealed and finally decided to join him. When had she ever laughed this much? His grin was contagious. "Let go and I'll remove my gown."

"Promise?"

"I promise. Now let me go."

He released her hand and she removed her gown while he stripped down to naught. She giggled.

"If you are wise, you'll remove the chemise, as well. 'Twill only make you colder when you come out."

She stared at him for a moment as she considered his advice. Finally deciding he was correct, she peeled off her chemise.

Robbie stared at her and said, "Och, lass, you know how to bring a man to his knees."

"Now or never, Robbie Grant. I won't stand here with naught on for long." She put her hands on her hips and waited.

He grasped her hand and together they ran into the loch, jumping at the last minute. She came up sputtering. "Cold! 'Tis cold, Robbie! Why did I let you talk me into this?"

She started shivering and he pulled her in close, his body still blasting heat. She didn't know how it was possible, but he did. He took the soap he had brought out with them and lathered her back and her hair, handing it to her to clean her front. Hell, but the lad was a gentleman through and through. She was shaking so much from the cold that she headed for the shore as soon as she had washed off. One glance back at Robbie turned her right around.

"Robbie, let me wash your forehead. You have so much dirt in the cut." She gently washed out the gravel. "Were you rolling in the dirt today in the lists? How did you get so much grit in it?"

He smirked. "The only rolling I did was with you on the table. Do you have a sore bum tonight? Mayhap I should check for splinters."

"Nay," she giggled. "You didn't hurt me. But you need to take better care of your wounds."

"Lass, can you still love a scarred lad? I always had lassies chasing me, but only because of my looks. Now my looks are gone. Will you still love me?"

"Och, Robbie," she sighed. "I love you for so many reasons, but not just because of your looks."

His brow furrowed. "I am ugly to you?"

She finished her task and gave the soap back to him, turning her back to walk out of the loch. Right before she ran out, she turned and splashed him. "Nay, not ugly, but I won't feed your feelings of self-importance."

She ran out and he chased her all the way back to the front steps of the cottage. "'Tis freezing!" As she shivered at the door, she said, "My gown, I forgot my gown."

"Hellfire." He tore back down the shoreline, picked up their clothing and sprinted back.

Once they were inside, he wrapped her in his plaid and they sat in front of the fire so she could dry her hair. Robbie pulled his fingers through the long tresses, helping her to dry it. "Caralyn, have you given any more thought to my offer? You must see how well we suit each other. Our time has been wonderful here."

"Aye, I have. What does your family say? I am worried they won't accept me as your wife."

"Hold on, let me go find something and I'll plait your hair for you." He left the room for their chamber.

Caralyn stared at her hands. Her wrists were healing because she hadn't needed to punish herself lately, just now realizing it. A few minutes later, when Robbie didn't return, she walked back into the room and found him sound asleep on the bed.

She crawled in beside him and snuggled up against him.

CHAPTER THIRTY-NINE

In the middle of the night, a loud banging on the door awakened them both. Robbie got up and threw his plaid on before answering it.

"Brenna needs Caralyn's help."

Quade was at the door, and Caralyn overheard him, so she jumped out of bed to get dressed. She flew into the main room and stared at Quade. "Not my lassies?"

"Nay, the girls are fine. There are two women ready to deliver and she can't be in both huts at the same time. Brenna was hoping the two would deliver before we left, but not at the same time. Anyway, she wondered if you would help Jennie."

"Of course." She grabbed her boots and Robbie finished dressing.

"I'll bring her. Where?"

"Gavin's wife." Quade nodded to them, then left. Moments later, Caralyn burst out of the cottage and headed for her horse, but Robbie stopped her. "You are barely awake and 'tis confusing in the dark. I'll take you on my horse since I know the way."

She didn't argue, too lost in her thoughts, trying to remember everything about the two births she had witnessed. Of course, she had her own to remind her of everything, but she wouldn't wish the midwives who had attended her births on anyone.

When they arrived at Gavin's, Robbie helped her down and gave her a kiss on the cheek.

"You are strong enough to do this," he reminded her.

She gazed into his eyes realizing how much his comment

meant to her. Then she nodded glumly, trying to tell herself the exact same thing. Could she? She placed her hand on his arm. "Thank you for the escort, but you don't need to wait. Could be a long time. I'll find my way back."

"I'll be right out here when you're done." He gave her a slight push toward the door before joining Gavin, who was waiting on a nearby log, jiggling his knee up and down.

Caralyn stepped inside to find a small group of people clustered around the bed. Brenna and Jennie were at the end while two maids handled water and linens, swaddling a nearby cradle.

Brenna turned to her as soon as she stepped inside. "Och, great. Caralyn, my thanks for coming. I have another woman birthing a few rows over and she is having a difficult time since it is her first. This is Nessa's third, so she should be fine. Jennie knows what to do, but I'll feel better knowing she has some assistance. Can you handle it?"

"Aye, I remember what to do. If aught happens I don't understand, Robbie is outside. I will send him for you."

"Gavin can come for me as well. If everything goes fine, I could be back before Nessa delivers. Here is the tie for the cord, a clean knife, and don't forget to clean out the bairn's mouth." Brenna gave her a hug and flew out the door.

Caralyn took a deep breath and introduced herself to Nessa and the maids just as a strong contraction gripped the woman and she yelled her way through it. Jennie smiled at Caralyn and showed her where to put all their supplies.

"I am excited for this," Jennie said in a whisper, her cheeks aglow. "I love working with Brenna."

"Have you been at many births?" Caralyn asked her, hoping her answer would be aye.

"Aye, I spent time in Lothian with her. When she married Quade and moved away, we had no healer. My mother and grandpapa were both healers, so I wanted to try. I have delivered a couple, but I am still new, so thank you for coming."

Caralyn experienced a moment of panic, then she nodded to Jennie. Though she couldn't summon the right words, she knew exactly what to do. She had to believe in herself, just as everyone had been trying to tell her.

Taking a deep breath, she placed her hand on Nessa's knee and took a look to see how far along she was. Offering words of encouragement, she managed to get Nessa through the next contraction.

"Are you having frequent contractions?" she asked once the spell had passed.

"Aye, every minute or so. I am no' getting any breaks, and if I remember, that's what it was like right before I delivered my last." Nessa leaned back and took a couple of deep breaths before she surged forward. "Och, here we go, lasses. I have to push."

"Are your bairns lasses or lads?" she asked to distract Nessa from the pain.

"Two lassies. Gavin so wants a lad." The answer was delivered in between grunts.

Nessa strained and pushed for several minutes as Jennie and Caralyn watched the bairn's head get closer to the end. They gave Nessa many words of encouragement, holding her hand when she needed it.

Another strong contraction forced her to push, and Jennie shouted, "I can see the bairn's hair. Keep pushing, Nessa. The bairn is almost here." Caralyn helped her lead Nessa through the rest of her labor, the two of them encouraging her until she gave a last push and the head and shoulders slipped together into Caralyn's waiting hands. She took a deep breath, tugged on the baby enough to get a good hold on it, then did as Brenna had instructed and put her finger in the bairn's mouth to clean out all the mucus. The babe slid completely out with the next push and Jennie grabbed his feet, holding him up for a moment to make the cord taut. The wean squealed a loud roar to let everyone know he had arrived.

"A lad," Caralyn said. "He's a beautiful laddie."

Gavin came rushing in the door and stopped cold. "A lad? Did you say a lad? Do we have a son, Nessa?"

Caralyn nodded and held him up for Gavin to see. "Aye, you have a strapping lad." The bairn continued to bellow his dissatisfaction as Caralyn wrapped him in a plaid and Jennie tied string around the cord. She cleaned him up and set him into his mother's arms. Nessa started to cry and Gavin pushed his way past the maids to kiss his wife. "I am so happy to have a wee laddie," he whispered. Gavin couldn't take his eyes off his son and his wife.

Caralyn started to clean, feeling as if she were intruding on a private moment. The last part of the birth came through not long after, and she and Jennie were working together to help Nessa when the door banged open.

Brenna came charging in. "Everything is progressing?" She smiled when she saw the wean in his mother's arms, her eyes lighting up. "Well done, Caralyn and Jennie. Here, let me finish up." Brenna hugged Caralyn and took over.

Standing back, Caralyn tried to process everything that had just happened as Jennie filled Brenna in as the two of them washed Nessa.

Caralyn's hands started to shake as she realized what she had just done.

She washed them, hoping the trembling would stop, but it didn't. She had just delivered a bairn into the world. And she had done it well. Tears slid down her cheeks and her hands shook. Brenna glanced over her shoulder and, noticing Caralyn was upset, hugged her from behind. She turned her toward the door and said, "Go. You did a great job, but 'tis stressful. Take a step outside."

Caralyn walked out the door and saw Robbie standing outside leaning against a tree.

She threw herself into his arms and sobbed.

And again, as always, he was there for her.

***

Two days later, Robbie was in the lists early one morn when Alex came flying out to find him. Robbie took one look at his brother's face, and his gut clenched. Though he was unsure of what was wrong, he knew something was amiss. Alex pointed to the keep and said, "Now."

Robbie hopped on his horse and flew across the bridge and through the courtyard, not stopping until he was at the front steps of the keep. When he flew in the doorway, Celestina was waiting for him inside.

"What is it?" he asked, panting as he tried to catch his

breath. He didn't like the look on her face.

"'Tis Gracie. You must get Caralyn. She needs to be here now." Celestina pointed to the corner of the hall, where Gracie was surrounded by a number of people.

Robbie took one look at Gracie and tore out the door, then jumped on his horse and bolted toward the loch as fast as his horse could gallop. Everything had been going so well. Caralyn was actually coming out of her shell, finding a sense of purpose all her own.

But this? He had never intended for this to happen. Saints above, she would never forgive him. Why had he been so bull-headed? She probably would have come around on her own, given enough time. Hellfire, why had he insisted on getting his way?

CHAPTER FORTY

Caralyn heard the pounding of a horse's hooves across the meadow, but it was nowhere near midday meal. When she stepped outside to see who was coming, Robbie was already there, panting atop his horse. He dismounted in a moment and held a hand out to her.

"You need to come to the keep. It's Gracie."

They were on their way before Caralyn could even wrap her head around his words. Saints above, not her sweet Gracie. She prayed all the while they rode.

"Caralyn, I'm so sorry. I hoped to show you your own value, but please understand, I would never have done this if I had thought it would hurt your bairns. Please forgive me."

"Robbie, what is wrong with her? Tell me what has happened!" She couldn't unclench her fists or stop her thoughts from going to the absolute worst places.

"I'm not sure if anyone knows. I saw Gracie lying on the floor in the corner, not moving but staring out as if in a trance. I came to get you right away. Alex pulled me from the lists."

They ran in through the front door and everyone stood back so they could reach the wee one. Caralyn's heart was in her throat when she saw her daughter lying on her side on the floor next to the dogs. She was breathing but not moving. Her eyes were open and staring straight ahead, her thumb was in her mouth.

Caralyn knelt down in front of her. "Gracie?" Naught. She blinked but didn't so much as twitch at the mention of her name.

Ashlyn sat crying next to Gracie. "Mama, she's just like

before but worse. She stopped talking yesterday. She wouldn't eat last night, and this morn, she walked over and lay down next to Growley. She has been like this ever since. Lily, Maddie, everyone has tried talking to her, and she just stares straight ahead. What are we going to do?"

Caralyn put her hands under Gracie's arms and lifted her up, resting the wee lassie's head over her shoulder. Tears ran down Caralyn's cheeks. She had failed her daughter. Gracie was like a rag doll, not moving at all on her own, still not looking at anything or anyone, not even her mother or her sister.

Robbie put a gentle hand on Caralyn's arm and led her over to the hearth. "Hold her and talk to her. The deal is off, Caralyn." His voice shook with anguish as he said it. "You belong with your daughters. I am so sorry for getting in the way."

Caralyn nodded as she hugged Gracie to her chest. She reached over and tugged Ashlyn in close so she could kiss her cheek. "I'm sorry, Ashlyn. I won't leave you again."

Robbie stood next to her before leaning over to give Gracie a kiss. "We love you, Gracie." He kissed Ashlyn on the cheek before turning to leave. "I'll be outside if you need anything. Mayhap it would be best if you were alone with your girls."

Once Caralyn was settled in a chair close to the fire, Maddie and Brenna rushed over. "I checked her, Caralyn," said Brenna, kneeling in front of her. "There is naught wrong with her physically. I think if you sit with her and promise her you'll stay, she'll come out of it. She missed you verra much when you were gone. The wean has had too much in her life for one so young. All three of you. With your love, I think she'll come back to herself. We'll keep everyone away, and if you need anything, just ask. We are here for you."

Caralyn glanced at both of them, tears still flooding her cheeks, and said, "Could you make me a good mother? Apparently, I can't seem to do things right no matter how I try."

Maddie placed her hand on her shoulder. "You *are* a good mother. You love your daughters more than anything, and that's the only thing necessary." Maddie kissed her cheek, and then wee Gracie's, and walked away with Brenna.

Caralyn held her daughter and rubbed her back. "Gracie, I'm so sorry. I promise never to leave you again. You'll go with me wherever I go. I love you and your sister more than anything." She kissed her daughter's forehead. "Malcolm is gone, he will never bother you again. I was with Robbie for just for a short time. I needed to know if I could live with him, if I really love him. I do…but just because I love Robbie, doesn't mean I'll stop loving you. I love you, Ashlyn, *and* Robbie. 'Tis not wrong to love people. You love Lily, don't you?" She stopped to peer into her eyes for any movement or recognition, but there was naught.

Ashlyn reached over and rubbed Gracie's hair. "Mama, is she any better?"

"Nay."

"Mama, we missed you. Are you coming back?"

"Aye. I will never leave my sweet lassies again. At least, not at night. I may have to do a chore or two, but I will always be with you at night. I promise." She gave Ashlyn a kiss on the forehead, then stood up. "Come, let's go to our chamber. I think Gracie and Mama need a rest."

A few hours later, Caralyn awoke in their chamber. Gracie was still in her arms, but something was different. "Gracie?" Naught. Her daughter's gaze was still vacant of recognition. However, two things had changed. Gracie's wee hand held a tight grip on Caralyn's gown, and she was sucking her thumb. Caralyn smiled and ran her hand through Gracie's hair. "You are safe wee one; Mama is here for you now. Come back to Mama. I miss you."

***

Robbie was sitting on the front step of the keep with his head in his hands when Brenna, Quade, Brodie, Celestina, and Tomas came out to join him.

He glanced up at his sister. "Is there any change?"

"Nay, Caralyn took her up to her chamber. 'Tis not your fault, Robbie."

"How can you say such a thing, Brenna? 'Tis all my fault. 'Twould never have happened if I hadn't made Caralyn live with me in the cottage."

"I thought she volunteered to live with you in the cottage,"

Brodie said.

"Och, 'tis complicated. I hoped my plan would show her that she had value. She couldn't see it living in the keep with everyone else. In her mind, she could never measure up. Clearly, 'twas a lousy plan. She'll never forgive me now, and looking at Gracie in that state breaks my heart." He cradled his head in his hands once again. "What a fool I am."

Celestina said, "Sounds like it worked perfectly to me."

Robbie picked his head up to stare at her. "What? How did this work? Her daughter is a mess."

Brenna spoke up. "Because her daughter retreated not long after she left. Caralyn has always seemed lost to me, as though she thinks she's not wanted. It didn't help that Gracie did so well here from the start. The wee one started talking when she wasn't with her and Gracie started laughing when she wasn't with her. 'Twas the lassie's reaction to feeling safe and free of that wretched man, but I can see how Caralyn wouldn't see it that way. She could easily have interpreted that as her daughters being better off without her. But now she is learning how much she matters to them."

Tomas came over and grasped Robbie's shoulder. "Let's hope Caralyn sees it that way, aye?"

***

Caralyn and Ashlyn sandwiched in on either side of Gracie. Though she was still not talking, she had picked up her head and was staring at her mother. Overjoyed by this improvement, Caralyn started to cry and kissed her on both cheeks. "I love you, sweet lass. Please come back to me. I'll never leave you again."

"Mama, why did you really leave us?"Ashlyn asked in a quiet voice.

Caralyn sighed, "'Tis hard to explain about big people things, but you know what a difficult time I've had with men. But I love Robbie Grant and I needed to see if there was some way it could work."

"But Mama, he really loves you. He isn't like any of the others."

"Ashlyn, I know that now, but I needed to learn it for myself. I should have trusted him, but I was confused. You were right when you asked me if I loved myself. That has been difficult for me because of Malcolm, but Robbie has helped me to see that I am a good person. He has asked me to marry him and I'm ready to accept. How would you feel with Captain Grant as your stepfather?"

Ashlyn grew wide-eyed. "Aye. Can we call him papa?"

"We'll have to ask him that question, but 'twould make you happy if we all lived with him in the cottage? I thought you would never want to leave the keep now that you have so many friends here."

"Nay, Mama. We want to live with you. We could come back to play. Aye, Gracie and I would be so happy if you married Captain Grant and we all lived together near the loch."

Gracie reached up a hand and patted Caralyn's face, still sucking her other thumb in a fury.

"I think your sister likes the idea, also." She kissed the palm of Gracie's wee hand and smiled. "I was afraid you wouldn't go with me."

"Why, Mama? We love you." Ashlyn leaned in closer to her mother and Gracie.

She knew she needed to explain it a little better. "Ashlyn, you and Gracie have been so happy here that I didn't think you would really miss me. You have so many others to play with, Gracie was talking before I even came here, and you have many other mothers—Celestina, Maddie, Brenna."

"Nay, we don't!" Ashlyn's voice grew loud and severe. "You are our mama, they are not. We love them, but they aren't you. You are our only mama. We need *you*."

Caralyn climbed out of bed with Gracie in her arms and said to Ashlyn. "Come, there's someone we have to talk to."

***

She marched down the staircase into the hall and looked for Robbie, finally finding him on the front steps, surrounded by his family and friends.

He took one look at Gracie and stood. "She is better?"

Caralyn said, "Aye, she isn't speaking yet, but she is moving and her gaze follows me. I won't let her out of my sight for a while. She needs me."

Robbie smiled and kissed Gracie's forehead. "Aye, she

does."

She glanced at the others and said, "Thank you all for your help, but I wondered if I might speak to Robbie alone."

"Of course," Brenna said. "Would you like us to take Ashlyn with us?"

When Caralyn shook her head, Ashlyn leaned into her and wrapped her arms around her waist. "Nay, Ashlyn needs me, too. Come to the garden with me?" she asked, her eyes on Robbie's. He nodded and stood, taking Ashlyn's other hand when she held it out to him. Together they walked to Brenna's garden, stopping when they reached the bench in the middle of it."

He turned to Caralyn. "What is it? Caralyn, you know how sorry I am..."

She held her hand up. "Don't be. Your intentions were good and I understand what you were trying to do for me—," she glanced at her girls, "—for *us*."

Caralyn cleared her throat and her gaze locked onto his again, those beautiful gray eyes of his going straight to her heart. She could feel the butterflies in her stomach jump to life at his nearness, could feel her need to draw him closer, to have him hold her, to support her and to love her as much as she loved him. "Robbie, is your offer of marriage still open?"

Robbie looked stunned, but he said, "Of course. You know I love you and your daughters. I would love naught more than the chance to love you all for a lifetime."

Caralyn smiled and squeezed her daughters' hands. "Then we accept. Naught would make me happier than to be your wife."

Shocked at first, his gaze searched hers as if he wasn't certain he understood her correctly.

She nodded her head and smiled. "I love you, Captain Robbie Grant. I think I always have. Do you remember the day you ignored your commander to go in search of two hungry lassies in the forest? You grabbed a piece of my heart that day. I just had a hard time accepting that you could love me as much as I love you."

His eyes widened and he smiled, his big, beautiful smile. He cupped her face and kissed her deeply. Ashlyn clapped her hands. "Aye, Gracie, we finally have a da."

When she pulled back from his kiss, Gracie patted Robbie's chest and said, "Lu you, Captain Robbie." Next she patted Caralyn and said, "I lu you, Mama."

They all joined together crying and laughing to welcome Gracie back from wherever she'd retreated. Then Ashlyn pointed to Caralyn's chest and said, "Now you love you, too."

EPILOGUE

A few months later

Caralyn sat in a chair by the hearth in the great hall, warmed by the flames crackling in the midst of a cold winter. She caught her breath and held it. Could it be? She glanced around at all the activity going on in the room. Fortunately, she was alone by the hearth; she didn't want anyone to see the expression on her face just yet. Robbie, Brodie, Tomas, and Alex sat at the table on the dais, laughing and arguing about some challenge in the lists. Maddie had taken Connor and Kyla up to bed, but Celestina was reading one of Maddie's picture books to the other children.

How her life had improved since she met her husband. She and Robbie had married quickly so Brenna and Quade could attend the ceremony before they headed home. She hadn't wanted anything fancy, just a simple ceremony, and it had been beautiful.

The day after their wedding, Alex had brought her into his solar along with Robbie, Brenna, Maddie, and Jennie. His idea had shocked Caralyn at the time—he wanted her to become the newest Grant healer. She could remember exactly how he put it: "Seems I better not ever be dependent on just one healer in the clan. Lassies have a tendency to disappear." He gave Brenna a pointed look and she chuckled.

Brenna hugged her after she agreed, and said, "I have complete faith in you, Caralyn. You will be a wonderful healer. You and Jennie work well together."

And she had not regretted her decision once. Since that day, she had delivered several bairns and learned how to stitch wounds, and better yet, how to relieve her tension by relaxing in her husband's arms.

Robbie had taught her the true meaning of love and opened a whole new world to her. Their lovemaking was sweet at times and intense at others. She and her husband enjoyed their private room in the cottage, and she never felt a stroke of guilt for any of the new tricks he had taught her.

Sighing, she reflected on how wonderful her life was— every moment, every day. Only one thing was missing—a bairn of their own. She loved her daughters, but how she had dreamed of another, a bairn to share with her husband so they could delight in watching something their love had created bloom in front of their eyes.

Frightened that she would be unable to carry again because of her age, she'd even pretended to have her courses a couple of times, not ready to tell Robbie the truth. She'd been so scared she was wrong or something would happen to prevent the bairn from coming.

There it was again! Aye, she was sure now. The tiniest of flutterings spread inside her belly, much like the wings of a wee butterfly. A bairn. She and Robbie were going to have their own babe.

Tears flowed down her cheeks as she cradled her belly in her hands. She wanted to yell to her husband, but she was too choked up to speak. Her breath hitched twice before she was able to force another calming breath.

She watched her husband from afar, and all the other wonderful members of her family. They were going to have a wean together.

Robbie stood, staring at her. He headed her way, a puzzled look on his face. She wanted to tell him, she was finally *ready* to tell him, but she just couldn't speak. If she did, she would blubber loud enough for Brenna and Quade to hear her all the way in Lothian.

"Sweeting?" He increased his pace. "Is something wrong? Why are you crying?"

She shook her head, then stared down at her belly as he knelt in front of her. Silence descended on the great hall as everyone turned to stare at her. She took his hand in hers and placed it over her belly, then nodded, cradling his face with her other hand.

Robbie quirked his brow. "A bairn? Is that what you're trying to tell me?"

She nodded and let out a gush of a sob, wrapping her arms around his neck.

Robbie let out a whoop and picked her up, swinging her in a circle. He kissed her lips and whispered, "I love you, Caralyn Grant."

Caralyn nodded and glanced over his shoulder as Maddie came down the stairs.

Alex, Brodie, and Loki all let out a Grant whoop, while the rest of the family charged over to wrap her in their embrace.

The girls were at their mother's side in an instant. Ashlyn peered up at Caralyn and asked, "A bairn, Mama? Is it really true?"

Nodding, Caralyn patted her belly, not able to get the words out.

Gracie leaned in and kissed her belly. "Lu you, wee bairn."

THE END

Dear Reader,

Thank you so much for reading *Journey to the Highlands*! I am so excited to have published this fourth novel in my Highlander Series. If this was your first Keira Montclair novel, I appreciate your willingness to try a new author. If not, thank you for returning to find out more about Clan Grant. Either way, I hope you enjoyed the read! I strive to deliver unique and emotional stories in each of my novels.

I love to hear from my readers and I also value your opinions. Please share your thoughts with me on Robbie and Caralyn's story. There are several ways you can let me know what you think:

1. **Write a review on Amazon or Goodreads:** Please consider leaving a review. They can really help an author, particularly one who is self-published as I am. I don't have a marketing department or an advertising team backing me. Any reviews are appreciated, and yes, I do read them all. If you didn't like the novel, then please offer constructive criticism so I can improve. Angry responses do not help me and I ignore them. You do not need to use your real name for Amazon, Barnes and Noble, or Goodreads. These reviews are also helpful for other readers.

2. **Send me an email at keiramontclair@gmail.com.** I promise to respond!

3. **Go to my Facebook page and 'like' me:** You will get updates on any new novels, book signings, and giveaways. Here is the link: **https://www.facebook.com/KeiraMontclair**

4. **Visit my website: www.keiramontclair.com:** Another way to contact me is through my website. Don't forget to sign up for my newsletter while you're there.

5. **Stop by my Pinterest page:**
http://www.pinterest.com/KeiraMontclair/

You'll see how I envision Caralyn, Robbie, Ashlyn, and Gracie.

Once again, thanks for reading! Now on to Logan and Gwyneth's story!

Keira Montclair

ABOUT THE AUTHOR

Keira Montclair is the pen name for an author that lives in Florida with her husband. An Amazon best-selling author, she brings you the second novel in her Clan Grant Series, Brenna and Quade's story. Also a Registered Nurse, Keira enjoys adding medical issues to her novels and loved writing the story of Brenna Grant as a healer.

Keira loves to hear from her readers. Stop by her website at www.keiramontclair.com to sign up for her newsletter. She also has a Facebook page at Keira Montclair, Author.

See her view of her characters and the settings for this novel at her Pinterest page-the *Healing a Highlander's Heart* board.

Feel free to contact her at keiramontclair@gmail.com. She promises to respond to all emails and comments on her web page.

48547908R00129

Made in the USA
Lexington, KY
16 August 2019